JERSEY CITY - HOBOKEN

Chill town Reckoning

A Community Overwhelmed With Violence

William E. Wilson

"Of all men's miseries the bitterest is this: to know so much and to have control over nothing."

----- Herodotus, Greek Historian -----

This is a story about one man's effort in righting a wrong and his willingness to go that extra mile in pursuit of justice no matter the consequences

Contents

Chilltown

No, no, no!

The stillness of the night, was shattered, as the blood curdling scream echoed through the empty streets with a deafening crescendo.

Abducted earlier, Darla Sue Underwood now alone, her hands and feet bound, blindfolded, and terrified not knowing what or why this was happening.

Wondering to herself, [*why?*]

The only thing she remembered was exiting the club with her date. As they were leaving, a lone car pulled alongside the curb, and stopped. Three men dressed all in black jumped out, and two of the men grabbed her friend from behind, placed a hood over his head and immediately shoved him into the rear seat of the car. The third man grabbed Darla Sue, and quickly placing a hood over her head and immediately shoved her into the passenger seat where she sat on the lap of one of the abductors. It happened so fast it was hard wrapped her head around what just happened.

Not knowing the circumstance of the abduction realizing only moments later this was no joke, it was real. She and her date had been kidnapped. [*But* why?]

Driven around the city, and eventually stopping when she was quickly hustled out of the car. Darla Sue, was left standing alone on the sidewalk not knowing where or what to expect next. She then heard the car door shut as the car speedily drove away. Standing alone there on the sidewalk, she stood shivering in the cool night trying to collect her thoughts.

Suddenly, hearing someone in the distance running toward her. Frightened and alone stood absolutely motionless, afraid if she moved, she might stumble and fall making matters worse. She remained immobile in place not knowing what to expect next.

As the individual came closer asked, "What happened to you lady?" At which point she felt reassured as the stranger reached out and removed the hood which covered her head.

She said, "My friend and I were abducted a short time ago as we exited the club, after having a late dinner. Then she asked the stranger for help in removing the ligature's which bound both her hands and feet. Once her hands and feet were freed, she felt out of danger. Still scared, nauseated and weak from the ordeal, feeling she might collapse at any time. The stranger recognizing how unsteady on her feet she was, immediately reached out and took hold of her, and helped her to one of the stoops near-by. He sat her down on a broken step of the brownstone leading to the entrance, and once seated and regaining her composure; the stranger asked her, "Is there someone I can contact or come pick you up?"

Telling the stranger, "I'm new in town, and I don't know anyone well enough to call and pick me up. I really need to find a phone and call the police."

About that time one of the tenants of the brownstone walked out on the stoop to see what all the excitement was about. That's when Darla Sue looked up and asked, "Do you have access to a phone if so, would you call the police? I've been kidnapped."

The tenant rushed back inside where he phoned the police and reported the kidnapping. Not long after the police were notified, two police cars arrived on scene. One of the policemen began questioning Darla Sue about the alleged kidnapping, and afterwards took her downtown to get her statement concerning the incident.

At police headquarters Officer Roddy placed Darla Sue in one of the small cubical used for interviews. Officer Roddy once Darla Sue was seated asked her, "Would you like something to drink?"

"Water would be fine," she responded.

Officer Roddy left the cubical returning shortly with a cold bottle of water, placed it on the small table in front of her, then asked, "Is there anything else you need, if not, we needed to get started on your statement.

Time was of the essence.

Darla Sue told Officer Roddy she was ready to give him what little she remembered of the kidnapping while it was still fresh in her mind.

Officer Roddy sat down at the table across from Darla Sue, and asked her, "Is it okay with you if I tape the session?" "If it's necessary." She answered.

"It is." That's when Officer Roddy switched on the tape recorder.

This way if either of us forgets any part of the interview, we'll still have a record of the session to refer back to, if necessary, down the road. Officer Roddy then placed the small tape recorder in the middle of the table and began his questioning.

Could you please state your complete name and address for the record?

Darla Sue Underwood

4298 Park Street

Jersey City, New Jersey

"And would you state for the record the time and date and year of this inquiry?"

"Yes, (looking at her watch) it's 2:30 am, Saturday, August 7th, 1998." Thank you.

Now Miss Underwood, "Would you explain the extenuating circumstances which led up to this interview?"

Darla Sue began telling her recollection of what occurred earlier. "Around seven thirty last evening my friend Liam Drake came by my apartment and picked me up for a late dinner. We drove over to the

Phebe Reborn Nightclub over on Newark Ave. We had dinner a few drinks and danced. It was getting late and since I had to work the following day, I asked Liam to drive me home. We got up from our table and walked outside. As we began walking toward his car, a car pulled alongside the curb where we were. That's when three men jumped out of the car and hooded both of us. They dropped me off maybe twenty minutes later on the street where I was when you found me."

"Did you know or have any idea of who the kidnappers were or what their motives were for the abduction?"

"No, it was a complete surprise when they snatched us off the street. I'm not sure if Liam knew them or the reason for the abduction. But I'm sure, when you locate Liam, he will be able to fill you in; better that I can. I have no clue as to why they kidnapped us."

"Do you and this Liam work together? Or how is it you know this Liam Drake?"

"I was introduced to him by a co-worker where I work as a paralegal for the law firm of Williams and Brown." Yes, I've heard the name.

Okay, "In your own words, describe what you do specifically as a paralegal?"

"I preform duties the attorneys at the office don't have time to do or I'm qualified to assist. I mostly perform legal research, write draft pleadings, draw up contracts and leases anything considered a lawful court document. I basically help free up the lawyers to interview clients, and to make sure they have all the necessary information needed if and when they to go to court to defend his or her client to the best of their ability."

Thank you, Miss Underwood. Now, "Would you tell me after you were hooded if you remember anything that stands out in your mind about the men who kidnapped you and Mr. Liam Drake? Was there anything that you saw before the kidnapping that would be helpful in identifying them such as: were the men tall or short, what type of clothing were they wearing, do you remember a hair color, the language they spoke, the color of car, was it a two door or four doors?

Did any of the men exhibit any type of tics or accents either foreign, northern or say, southern draw?"

Yes, "One thing I remember was the person who slipped the hood over Liam's head, told him, don't be stupid, you know what you did and knew the price you'd pay if you screwed up. That someone by the name of Doc sent them and they were to bring him back to his boat."

"Go on."

They also told Liam, "Do as we say and your girlfriend here will be released unharmed. But if you play stupid then all bets are off." Liam at that point said he would cooperate and to release me.

"I see, and how long was it after that were let go?"

"Almost immediately. The driver was told by the one I was sitting on his lap to pull over to the curb. Opened the front passenger door and dropped me off. And after my release, I remember the one who had hooded me telling the driver as he closed the door, okay Sammy let's get the hell out of here." That's all I remember until you arrived.

"Okay Miss Underwood, we're finished here. If I need to get in contact with you in the future, I have your Name, address and phone number. We may need to talk again down the road so keep yourself available. You may be helpful in helping us tie a few loose ends together as we proceed with the investigation. You'll be hearing from me I'm sure, and thank you for your cooperation."

Chapter 2

Darla Sue was returned home later that morning in time to clean up, have a bite to eat, dress and go to work. On her way to work she could not stop thinking of her friend Liam, [*what was he was involved in to be literally whisked off the streets like that?*]

After leaving the police station, the information Darla Sue provided along with the two names she remembered, were helpful, giving the police a starting point to begin their investigation in earnest that morning.

When Detective Paulson arrived for work that morning noticed a file containing information about the kidnapping laying on his desk, and a note attached to the front, signed by Captain Cahill. He was to drop any and all projects he was working and devote his full attention to the kidnapping case of Liam Drake and his friend Darla Sue Underwood.

Detective Paulson immediately sat down at his desk and opened the file. As began reading its contents, it was incomplete not only in scope but detail. The file did provide him the two names and what Darla Sue told them in her statement. That was not much information to go on, but enough to help jump start the investigation.

After he finished reading the scant documents and Darla Sue's statement inside the file, he reached over and turned on the computer sitting on his desk. Soon the computer booted-up and he was now on line. He started by typing in the two names listed in the report, Doc and Sammy. It would take time to sort through several names that appearing on screen. It was a long shot but the only choice he had at the present.

Was Sammy the real name of the driver or an alias? As he began his search, several Sammy's appeared in the data base and showed most of the Sammy's had been arrested for domestic violence, trespassing, misdemeanors. Only two of the Sammy's were shown to have serve time in the big house, but served their time and been released. Only one had been rearrested and was housed at the county jail during the time of the kidnapping. That Sammy was immediately disregard as a suspect, the other Sammy's listed, showed only a couple Sammy's still resided in the community.

Detective Paulson started by making a copy of those Sammy's and their last known address. After running off several copies containing their names and addresses it was time, he and Detective Callahan (Detective Paulson partner) began the arduous and often difficult duty running down the Sammy's listed on the sheet.

As the day progressed, not making much headway; suddenly their luck changed when they happened upon Sammy "the man" Romano who lived in a flop house on the outskirts of the dock area in Hoboken. Once inside the flop house, they walked up to the second floor where Sammy lived, and stopped in front of his door. The two detectives looked at each other and Detective Paulson gave a nod to Detective Callahan to knock. While the two Detective's waited patiently after knocking on his door, when there was no response, ramped up his determination by pounded harder and louder on the door; telling whoever was inside, "Police, and open up."

Eventually Sammy "the man" Romano came to the door and opened it. That's when he came face to face with Detective's Paulson and Callahan, standing on either side of the door. Realizing immediately something bad was in the offing.

Detective Paulson stepped in front of the door where Sammy was standing and asked, "Are you Sammy Romano?"

Sammy answered, "Yea, I am. What going on?"

Detective Paulson without further ado asked him to get dressed and accompany them downtown to the police station.

Reluctantly, Sammy put on a shirt and shoes, and driven downtown, where he was quickly escorted through the long hallway toward the rear of the building. Reaching the back of the building, Sammy "the man" Romano was taken to a small cubicle set aside for interviewing, and left alone for a period of time. Later Detective Paulson and Detective Callahan returned to the cubicle where Sammy sat patiently waiting and thinking to himself, *[what the hell was going on, and why have I been brought in for questioning? Surely, they have not found out about the kidnapping already?]*

Detective's Callahan and Paulson after entering, introduced themselves to Sammy, but before starting the interview, Detective Callahan asked Sammy, "Would you like something cold to drink or a maybe a hot cup of coffee?"

Sammy answered, "Yea, a coke."

As Detective Callahan came back into the cubical, he handed Sammy a coke, then sat down alongside Detective Paulson. By now, Sammy had had a lot of time to think about the situation he found himself in and acting nervously as he sat squirming in the hard metal chair. Sweat was beginning to form on his forehead and slowly running down both sides of his face; still unsure as to why he had been brought downtown. But did not take the two detectives long to get to the gist of the matter at hand.

Detective Paulson found in his research earlier that Sammy "the man" Romano had connections with certain underworld figures in the past, and one in particular caught Detective Paulson's attention, Doc Neeson. Doc Neeson had been involved in many illegal activities in and around Hoboken and Jersey City for the past several years. Doc Neeson had had several run-ins with local law enforcement in the past because of his association with certain elected officials, council members, and county appointees, especially Jersey City concerning illegal activities.

Sammy "the man" Romano, a small-time con-man had lived and grown up in Hoboken. He began running with the wrong crowd at an early age, and since that time had accumulated an extensive juvey delinquent arrest record. Involved with everything from stealing cars for joy rides, to several misdemeanors and disorderly conduct charges while still a minor. He had been considered by those who knew him as a bonified juvenile delinquent. But those charges were small potatoes compared to the one he now found himself involved. Sammy had always been a follower, never a leader.

Subsequently, it was not long before the two senior detectives broke Sammy Romano down and had him singing like a songbird. He filled in a few blank spaces like times and places the kidnapping took place, but had no idea the reason behind the kidnapping. He was unaware who the other men in the car were and reason for the kidnapping. He had not been included in the loop. He had been hired to drive the car, nothing more. It was to protect the others from being implicated in case of an arrest later.

The inquiry continued for several hours at which time Sammy was given an ultimatum by Detective Paulson, "If you cooperate and turned state's evidence and finger those involved in the kidnapping, we will place you in protective custody; keeping you safe until after the trial." The two detectives then left the cubical for a short time giving Sammy time to mull over their offer.

After the two detectives walked out of the cubicle, Sammy, now beaten down and demoralized, rested his head on his folded arms on the table, where he thought long and hard about the proposition Detectives Paulson had run by him. Finally, after a lot of thought, decided it was the only way out of this latest mess he found himself. He was determined not to spent the next few years behind bars with those who would use him as their bitch, like while locked up in a state facility earlier on in his career. At least in a safe house he would be protected from any repercussions from Doc Neeson for the near future.

Doc Neeson was one of those who had eyes and ears in jail as well local police and security officers on his payroll. They protected his back and took care of certain problems that came up associated with Doc Neeson within the confines of the intuitions they worked.

It had been a good day for the detectives, but they still had lots of Ts to cross and I's to dot before those responsible were held liable and or accountable.

Chapter 3

Detective Paulson after returning to the interview room was going to have Sammy to describe the two other men in the car involved with the kidnappings. "Sammy, describe in your own words the other two men in the car with you that evening. We want a detailed account of what they were wearing, were they armed, nationalities, if either had a speech impediment, names, if possible, color of hair or if bald or balding, tattoos you may have observed, bearded, mustached, clean shaven, anything at all you remember. And if we were to bring in police artist, will you be able in helping create a rendering of those involved?"

"I think I can, but as you know it's been a while?"

Sammy gave as much detail of the two men as he could remember to the detectives and later a police artist came in the room and set up his easel at the end of the table next to Sammy. By now, Sammy had had time to think about the images of those involved. It was time to begin the difficult undertaking that of drawing those individuals with only vaguely remembrances of what the two individuals looked like.

Over the next several hours as Sammy described the best, he could what they looked like. Occasionally he would study the artist interpretation of what he had earlier described. Slowly, feature by feature, the image of the person began appearing on the artist's sketch pad, with notations of other distinguishing features such as tattoo's, some repugnant. One of the individuals had a shaved head with several tatts both on the top and sides of the head and a tear drop below the right eye indicating he had served time and was possibly a killer. Along with additional distasteful or unacceptable features notated. it had taken several hours to complete each composite drawings, and the artist was able drawing a general rendering and likeness of each individual who had taken part in the kidnapping. With the interpretation of both individual's likeness and features on paper, it was time to get and organize a search for the elusive abductors.

Once the artist's rendering of the sketches was completed, and the detectives finished questioning Sammy, several photo-copies of the two renderings were made. The photo-copies were quickly distributed among officers who made up the search team. Along with the interpretations, a recent photo of Liam Drake was included. Putting those sketches and photo out on the streets, maybe just maybe, the police would get lucky and locate Liam Drake along with the others before anything else happened.

Detective Paulson was now ready to remove Sammy from downtown police headquarters to one of the safe houses in the suburbs. Here he would remain until the offenders had been arrested, and ready to stand trial in criminal court. Sammy would not be safe in jail or out on bail until those associated with the kidnapping were apprehended and stood trial. If Doc Neeson or any one of his associates learned of Sammy's turning state evidence, his life as he knew it would be over.

Darla Sue returned to work the following day, and told her bosses what occurred the night before to her and her friend Liam Drake. They told her they would help in any way possible and help bring the culprits to justice, if they need them, on a pro-bono basis. That she and her friend would be entitled to full access of their services and not to worry. That she should continue working and those who instigated the infraction were arrested, tried and convicted.

As time passed, the police methodically gathered more and more evidence, most coming from CI's (confidential informant) or snitches (as sometimes referred too) on the street. The kidnappings as they learned had been ordered by Doc Neeson with ties amongst several of the local unscrupulous politicians and their hand-picked appointee's, under scrutiny already for their unethical and shady practices.

Liam Drake, a local reporter working for the local newspaper, looking into corruption and prohibited acts associated with illegal practices by certain city administrators, in return for money and personal gain. Because of their close proximity or relationship with contractors, the practice of kickbacks had been an ongoing issue as long as anyone could remember.

This practice of behavior of politicians and their cronies was nothing new, but Liam Drake, a reporter for the Jersey Journal had been covering the illicit practice of local politicians, and exposing those practices. Corruption seemed to be the norm for in authority and conducting the day-to-day operations throughout the city had been receiving kickbacks from developers and sub-contractors. They had become fair game when applying for new building permits etc., and other approvals by those in charge. Liam learned how far down the chain of command the practice ran while interviewing one of the disgruntled council members in his role as a member of that assembly. The council member had mentioned to Liam during his interview, "I was going to vote against one of the larger developments because I was displeased with certain politicians and council members who wanted the project approved only because they had skin in the development."

The irate and incensed councilmember, had been against not only the cost and location of a new school proposal, but questioned the need for an additional school as the number of students had been declining over the last few years, and the cost of building a new school was absolutely prohibitive. Several of the local politicians had previously invested heavily in the building site and not about to have it voted down, stopped, or moved to a different location.

Liam, learning of the situation, talked it over with his supervisor who saw a story that would be a killer headline if proven to be factual. He gave Liam the opportunity to take on the powers that be, and write a story of corrupt politicians running a city for their own personal gain; and while doing so, explain to the citizenry of the community what was going on behind their backs. The story, if told correctly, would expose corrupt elected city officials, and their role absconding with tax money controlled by them. How in the past they had placed large amounts of tax money aside to be used between known city elitist, certain city officials, managers, and several council members.

While city officials were heavily known to be involved in procuring certain high dollar projects, but occasionally things went awry. Doc Neeson, was a prime example of how things did not always go according to script.

Doc was hired by one of the wily city leaders to quell a disgruntled council members from interfering and upsetting their plans for build a new high school.

Liam decided to write about the new school and external forces associated with it. He began his latest editorial after an in-depth interview with the disgruntled council member.

After learning from one of his local CI's (confidential informant) of a secret meeting between this Doc Neeson and one of his associates at a local restaurant was overheard telling his cohort, "I needed your help convincing one of the local council members not to vote against an upcoming critical issue, which the majority of the council members have skin in the game, and in favor of adopting."

The following day, Liam's editorial revealed a scathing article of the secret meeting between the two crime figures, that certain council members had requested his assistance in convincing one of their own from voting no on a new project being considered. The unnamed council member wanted Doc Neeson to arrange a hit on the council member to convince them to vote in the affirmative on the upcoming project or face the consequences.

After the newspaper hit the street that morning, Doc Neeson, and what he and a certain council member had in mind; panic struck at the very core of the situation. The city administrator immediately called for the removal of the council member, who in turned called Doc Neeson and had him stop the hit.

Not long after the scathing article was released, the office-bearers who started the ball rolling on the school project, learned the scope of

Liam's editorial and ramifications they faced if they continued. What Liam uncovered relating to certain council members involvement in the school project went to the very core of corruption and deceit.

Doc Neeson after reading the article became enraged, and immediately put a hit out on Liam. He called one of his top associates in New York, and told him what he had in mind for the nosey newspaper editorial writer. He wanted this associate to pick up Liam and convinced him to discontinue writing the offensive stories about him and his involvement with the city.

Liam, as he was leaving work one evening was whisked off the sidewalk by force, then blindfolded and driven to a non-descript building on the east side of Hoboken to a small abandoned room and ruffed up. Prior to his release he was threatened with bodily harm and told, in no uncertain terms, "If you do not discontinue writing stories concerning Doc Nesson and his involvement with the city, your life will be in danger."

Still blindfolded, with his hands and feet bound, Liam, after hearing the ultimatum, was more determined than ever not to let this minor infraction dictate his future work trying to stop the abusive power within the city's work force.

First order of business after being set free, was to return to the newspaper and write the complete story as he recalled of the latest abduction and detention; and how he was roughed up, threatened and humiliated while in the custody of his abductors. And told to discontinue his criticism of certain city officials and council members or it would be lights out next time.

The story was of such importance it made the headlines for the next few days until it ran its course. Those named or believed involved with the kidnapping, quickly went underground and their locations undisclosed. Unable in reaching or contacting the known accuser, it became hard for Liam to find material to write about. With sketchy details arriving daily at the newspaper, most of the information was incomplete or inadequate. Not the type of information needed in writing an accurate editorial with conviction.

Police, meanwhile gathering evidence concerning Liam's kidnapping, obtaining bits and pieces on a daily basis. The information, sketchy at best, a couple of eyewitnesses found, but they were unable in the giving a true description of the individuals involved. Even with good intel, somehow those responsible for the kidnapping dropped out of sight and gone into isolation.

As the days and weeks dragged by, one of the suspects on their list was sighted and picked up on several charges from the past and had never showed up to face the charges was brought downtown. The police spent hours questioning DeWayne Sours.

Again, another road block, as he refused to relinquish any information of those possibly behind the abduction. After hours of interviewing Mr. Sours without success, placed him in a jail cell where he would be held until his bond hearing on his outstand warrants.

A day later as Mr. Sours attended his bond hearing, and heard the charges, and surprised the bond was set so high. The judge ordered his bond set at one hundred thousand dollars because the nature of the offenses, and considered a flight risk if released. After his appearance in court, DeWayne Sours was returned to his cell.

In the meantime, Liam contacted Darla Sue and arranged to meet her later that evening at her condo to find out if she had recalled any more details concerning their kidnapping that terrifying event after leaving the restaurant. They were just happy to be alive, and ready to move on. They planned on having dinner again the following evening and put this matter aside for the time being.

Detective's Paulson and Callahan continued beating the pavement trying to obtain as much information on the case as possible. The information coming in dribs, dabs and spirts. And, after several months of pounding the pavement had accumulated enough information to present to a judge and obtain a court order to search and seize vital information on several politicians listed in their affidavit, along with Doc Neeson's domicile. Since Doc Neeson lived on a boat moored along the waterfront in Hoboken, the two detectives decided to go there first.

Once police arrived on scene along the waterfront, located Doc Neeson boat named, "Catch Me". As they arrived, spotted Doc sitting on the aft deck reading the morning paper, and having breakfast with a large fresh brewed cup of coffee sitting in his hand. Hearing several car doors slamming shut, breaking the silence of the morning, Doc casually looked up and saw several men advancing toward his slip. He was immediately taken aback, wondering to himself, [*Who or what are they looking for? And why are they heading in my direction? It's too early to be playing cops and robbers?*]

It did not take the plain clothes officers long to reach Doc's boat which was tethered on one of the longer docks jetting out into the Hudson River.

As the two detectives and two other law enforcement officers approached Doc's boat, Detectives Paulson and Callahan removed their shields from inside their jacket pockets and flashed them toward Doc Neeson. Once he realized they were looking for him, he heard Detective Paulson ask permission to come aboard, (only as a courtesy had he ask permission to board).

Doc, quickly asked, "What's the reason for this early morning intrusion?" Detective Paulson did not mince words as he explained quickly to Doc Neeson, "It has to do with a kidnapping last month".

Doc, after hearing the reason told Detective Paulson emphatically,

"No, you cannot board my vessel without a search warrant."

At which point Detective Paulson reached into the left side of his jacket pocket, removing the search warrant, reaching over the railing of Doc's boat and handed it to him. Doc quickly read the contents and saw he had no choice in the matter, and had to let them come aboard.

The two detectives and two other law enforcement officers from the local FBI headquarters immediately boarded the vessel. Their mission this morning was to gather any and all evidence that may concern the kidnapping and or any illegal items uncovered during their search and seizure connecting Doc Neeson to illegal activities which could tie him to the kidnapping.

Spending most of the morning checking the vessel, "Catch Me", from stem to stern for anything relevant to the case, found several items relating to the case and removed all items which appeared to be germane to their case.

Finding several items of interest was definitely helpful in their pursuit of connecting Doc Neeson not only the kidnapping of Darla Sue Underwood and Liam Drake, but several items which showed tail-tail signs of kick-backs Doc had in the past received from city officials and their appointees during their tenure in office.

Returning to the police station it was time to start the grueling task arranging and piecing together those items and other information they had accumulated from other sources, giving them a time line and prove without a shadow of a doubt how this renegade regime locally was involved.

This was only the first day of piecing evidence together, but eventually turn out to be more complicated and detailed paper trail of Illegal activities of those holding public positions such as, school boards, and sub-contractors working for the city. Plus, underworld figures (like Doc Neeson) called upon occasionally to keep the illegal nooses around the necks of those who balked at paying their fair share of kickbacks. It was the beginning of a long and tedious process piecing the pieces of puzzle together in a clear and intelligible case.

Once the word hit the streets of an ongoing inquiry and investigation being conducted by the police and FBI. And any and all related evidence located and or seized from individuals tied to the recent crime wave. Those individuals not arrested but considered part of the larger picture, started coming forward, each trying to avoid having their names made public or their alleged association with the criminal elements inside city hall and throughout the local municipalities. It was not a pretty sight as those involved learned of the enormity of the situation in which they were involved. Those still active or had a part in the different schemes came spilling out of the woodwork trying to save what little face they still possessed.

Chapter 4

With help from the FBI and others law enforcement agencies, the investigation took up the next few months, with help from elected and appointed officials along with other individuals involved. It depended ultimately on how the pieces of the puzzle fit together. A monumental task to say the least, but someone had to take the bull by the horns and run with it. And that's exactly what Detective's Paulson and Callahan did.

They had proven themselves in the past handling these types of investigations with uncanny ability categorizing and organizing large amounts of evidence, while reading between the lines, and coming up with appropriate and correct assumptions. It was in their DNA and had always played a big part in the overall role and responsibility getting it right the first time.

As the days stretched into weeks, and the weeks into months the investigation had taken on a life of its own. Every piece of information confiscated from Doc's boat, "Catch Me", and bits and pieces of information gathered through local CIs, and other law enforcement agencies which turned into a wealth of information. It all fit together with each piece of the puzzle acquired from each organization like a glove vis-à-vis the felonious and unlawful elements plaguing the cities. They had discovered dishonesty and deceit running ramped at every turn. With all the information which had been accumulated by Detective's Paulson and Callahan and several other agencies, asked themselves, [Is it enough? Do we have enough evidence to charge certain individuals involved in corruption, and continuously committing wrongdoing, and other wrongful acts? It was time to finish with their conclusions and submit the paper work to the prosecuting attorney's office to consider charges against those listed. If prosecuting attorney's found reasonable juris prudence in the case (he or she) would continue to file an injunction with the court for further review. Once that process had been completed and approved, the case against those individuals named in the directive could proceed forward without delay.

Meanwhile, Liam kept the investigation active by continuing to writing of disorder by city officials and how crimes of this magnitude so often were mysteriously dropped or swept under the rug. There had been no arrest, no follow-ups or detention of any known individual involved with this latest illegal conduct by any city employee or their ragtag appointments.

Liam hoped by writing this latest editorial it would be enough to bring the main participants to the forefront, and they be arrested and eventually stand trial. Not another case of capture/release or slap on the wrist, but a full-fledged prosecution for those involved and charged with unauthorized/unlawful use of power. This time, those individuals appearing before the courts involved with crimes, would face the full extent of the long arm of the law and the legal system; and be held accountable for all their previous offences and unlawful use of their power, serving in whatever capacity and whatsoever the rules of that work place deemed appropriate and or unacceptable.

Once an injunction had been sworn too and signed in front of a notary or court clerk, it would then be filed with the court system, and after careful consideration, the judge at his or her pleasure, may issue a stop order on the individual in question. In this case, going to trial or adjudication were options in considering the nature of the crime.

Darla Sue and Liam Drake were both named in the suit brought by the prosecutors against Doc Neeson. Others were mentioned (but not by name) as being part of the kidnapping, the only other name listed in their inditement was, Sammy "the man" Romano, a willing participant in kidnapping and driver of the vehicle used in the abduction.

The prosecution was sure if and when Sammy "the man" Romano took the stand, he would turn state evidence against Doc Neeson and identify him as the person who initiated the kidnapping.

Doc Neeson, had a long and colorful police record dating back years. He began his life of crime as a small-time hoodlum, carjacking, petty theft. Later became a person with a reputation of being someone you could contact when needing a favor. He would hire either local thugs or occasionally outside help when someone required his services, eventually worked his way up the ladder and became highly regarded as "the go to guy." He was asked by one of the largest syndicates in New York City to work for them earlier in his career and had accepted without question.

Doc Neeson had worked with several minor elected officials requesting his services over the years. They were mainly local councilmen, city elected officials and appointees to assist in doing their dirty work. Doc's territory ran the gamut from Jersey City, Hoboken to New York City because of his effectiveness in getting things done when called upon.

Doc had always tried keeping a low profile until now. This time he had been careless when he hired Sammy Romano. Sammy was considered one of the best drivers around, but not the smartest rock in the pile.

After Sammy was arrested and hauled off to jail where he met Detective Paulson who after reading his rap sheet, informed him of the consequences if he were found guilty on the kidnapping charge, he could possibly spend the rest of his life in prison. When Sammy heard that, it was the most frightened he had ever been in his life. Detective Paulson after explain what could happen if he did not help in the investigation, turned and left him to think over his options. When Detectives Paulson and Callahan returned a short time later, that's when Sammy decided to take the offer and turn state evidence against Doc Neeson.

He later became the prime witness for the prosecution and with his testimony would blow the case wide open; turning Doc Neeson world upside down. It only takes one stupid mistake to ruin one's life and Doc had made that fatal mistake by hiring Sammy Romano as the driver in the kidnapping.

Several weeks later, visits by Liam and Darla Sue daily, watching as the jury selection was chosen. The judge, prosecutor and defense attorneys now satisfied with the selection, it was time for the judge to set the time and date for the trial. Once all the preliminaries were settled and out of the way, it was time for Judge Goodfellow to schedule a trial date. As the Judge Goodfellow sat on the bench, shuffling through a stack of papers then located what he was searching for, reread the paper and then looked up at the prosecutor and defense attorneys telling them, "I will set aside, Monday August 22, at 9:00 a.m. sharp to begin the trial. Until then, have a good weekend and I'll see all of you back here Monday morning.

Monday morning at 9:00 a.m. the Judge Goodfellow entered courtroom and before seating himself, the bailiff turned and asked everyone in attendance to rise and said, "The honorable Judge Henry Goodfellow presiding." After Judge Goodfellow sat down, the bailiff turned back toward those presence, and said "You may be seated now."

Judge Goodfellow took the opportunity to explained to those being present what he expected, and demanded in his court room, and would accept nothing less. After Judge Goodfellow had everyone's attention and on the same page, the bailiff declared "Court is now in session".

After the terms and conditions had been specified by the Honorable Judge Goodfellow, it was time the attorneys stepped up and gave their opening statements, and what they expected the jury to consider when rendering their verdict at the end of the trial. After hearing both the prosecuting and defense attorney opening statements, the judge adjourned the trial until the following day.

After the trial had been deferred by Judge Goodfellow and told it would convene on the following day, the courthouse became a beehive of activity behind the scenes. Reporters, going through the motions of getting their stories out to the newspaper, while attorneys were busy gathering their files together before heading back to the office for the long and arduous task of spending the evening getting ready for the following morning and first full day in court.

Darla Sue and Liam in the interim decided to walked across the street to a small restaurant near the courthouse for a late lunch before heading home. As they sat chit chatting about the morning's events, one of the attorneys (Kris Jolley) from the law firm Darla Sue worked came in and spotted Darla Sue and Liam. Jolly waved and Darla Sue motioned him over. He proceeded to the table, where he shook hands with Liam and asked, "Mind if he could join you?"

Liam said, "Please do."

Once seated, Kris Jolley turned to Darla Sue and told her, "I was impressed with the prosecution's opening statement and believed with the overabundance of evidence in the case it should be a slam dunk for the prosecutions side."

As they sat discussing the trial and what could be expect, Detective Paulson and Callahan walked in and noticed the three seated toward the back of the restaurant talking.

Without hesitation the two detectives walked back to where they were and ask, "Mind if we join you?"

"No."

Liam asked a waitress nearby, "Would you happen to have a couple extra chairs, if so, would you bring them over to the table, we have a couple more people joining our table."

Detective Paulson said to the waitress, "No, that's not necessary, there's a couple of empty chairs at that table," (pointing to a nearby empty table), and immediately walked over, picked up two of the chairs, carried them back to the table where Darla Sue, Liam and Kris Jolley were seated and sat down.

As they talked in generalities about the trial and the overwhelming evidence against those involved, when suddenly Doc Neeson entered. With a surprised look on his face, Liam quickly got up out of his chair, and suddenly realized Detective Callahan had taken hold of his arm and restraining him. Liam immediately lowering himself back into his chair as Detective Callahan slowly released the grip on his arm. Liam was angry at seeing the SOB who had him kidnapped and was ready to confront him.

Attorney Kris Jolley spoke in a low tone, telling both Darla Sue and Liam, "I understood your resentment, but I want you both to understand you need to avoid at all cost the urge to handle the situation you're in with kid gloves. If you happen to make one wrong blunder against the accused or any of the defense's witnesses, the case would more than likely be thrown out. So, I suggest to you, keep your composure and let's let the legal system work, okay?"

Hearing those words, it was hard for Liam to swallow, but promised he would not make waves at least until the trial was over, and only then in his editorial's.

A week into the trial, Sammy "the man" Romano was brought from the safe house where he had been housed the last few months, and into the courthouse. He had been led into the courthouse through a back entrance and immediately placed in a small holding room just outside the courtroom to wait until he was called to testify. Later on, that morning when time came for Sammy to testify; the court appointed officer was sent to bring Sammy into the courtroom.

Reaching the small holding room just outside the courtroom where Sammy had been place, but as the court appointed officer started to insert his key into the door where Sammy Romano was held, the door gently swung open exposing an empty room. Someone had removed Sammy from the holding room, but in haste left the door ajar and unlocked after removing Sammy.

The court appointed officer quickly went back inside the courtroom and approached the judge's bench. Leaned down and told Judge Goodfellow in a low voice, "The witness has been removed from the holding room and taken from the building."

Judge Goodfellow hearing what the court appointed officer found when he went back to the holding room was speechless. Judge Goodfellow did not know what to do or say to the overcrowded courtroom.

After a short pause, Judge Goodfellow leaned back in his chair, once he regained his facilities, slowly leaned forward and told the court, "There will be a thirty-minute recess." Then the judge stood, and quickly returned to his chambers along with the prosecutor and defense attorneys in tow. Reaching the judge's chambers, explained to the attorneys what occurred. The judge at that time decided to suspend court until there was a plausible explanation for Sammy Roman's disappearance.

After deciding what to do, Judge Goodfellow along with the defense and prosecuting attorneys returned back to the courtroom where Judge Goodfellow declared, "Court is now in recess until further notice." The judge before adjourning the proceedings, warned the jury not to talk to each other or anyone else about the case. Also gave both the prosecution and defense teams a stern warning not to give any statements to the news organizations.

Judge Goodfellow turned and stepped from the bench while jurors were escorted back to their hotel rooms to wait on word when court convened. The courthouse for the remainder of the day was in total chaos; completely sealed off as a thorough search of the entire building was carried out for the missing witness. As the day drew to a close, still no signs of what happened to Sammy Romano.

From all indications it had to be an inside job, but how could this happen in such a controlled environment? That troubling question was something to be addressed at a later date. The missing Sammy Romano was front and center on everyone's mind at present. Court would not continue until he was found, one way or other, hopefully alive. If Sammy Romano could not be located the case against Doc Neeson would be halted and a mistrial called.

Chapter 5

Several weeks later, the trial was branded a mistrial, at which time Doc Neeson was set freed and returned to his boat, "Catch Me," to muddle over the latest troubling situation he regarded as an unwelcomed interruption. This latest imposition found Doc Neeson to be disquieting, and intended to make whoever was responsible for placing him in this dilemma, pay and pay dearly for their action. After being released, Doc Neeson pick up where he left off, that of, taking care of business.

This time, requiring his nonconformist services with no unwelcomed judgment calls by those who were to carry out his request which now had far reaching significances. If those carrying out his orders made a bobble, mistake, or a careless error in judgment they would be dealt with in the harshest means possible.

As the months passed with no signs as to the disappearance of Sammy "the man" Romano; it become generally accepted by the police Sammy had been assassinated by those who removed him from his holding area at the courthouse. Without a body, and little hope of finding Sammy Romano, this case was over. No one, including the police believed Sammy Romano would be found alive. Not this long after the fact.

Liam continued writing his daily articles, attacking the character of local politicians, and appointees throughout Hudson County, New Jersey. The political hub of the city revolved around that "Good Old

Boy" mentality of scratch my back; I'll scratch yours. A big fat fraternity with unlimited power, running wild without supervision, rules or direction. As long as it continued unsupervised and without checks and balances, nothing would stop their illegal practices.

Liam, eventually made this his calling, that of uncovering illicit practices of the county's hierarchy and trying to put an end to the practices of bribery, and kickbacks that was running rampant. Liam continued his quest helping bring to justice those persons of interest, and ending their sphere of fraudulent and deceptive practices, that of making of money by shady or dishonest means. It was turning out to be a long hard battle between good and evil. But, perseverance and a channel or pipeline such as the paper, Liam believed he could eventually make a difference, come hell or high water.

Darla Sue helped Liam working through the law firm, gathering information brought to her attention concerning certain high-ranking city officials. Any and all information not considered client privilege material (only public information) passed it on to Liam. Not a lot of info, but enough to help Liam piece together a more accurate and detailed information that could be used in his articles or possibly in a court of law if it became necessary. Darla Sue had become an advocate of justice working with Liam, in his quest stemming the flow of illegal activity around Hoboken and Jersey City.

Any Information, relating to contractors, engineers, building inspectors and or purveyors was a top priority of Liam's during this time. There were many different skills, crafts and occupations associated with the building trade and almost impossible monitoring each and every kick-back and bribe going on underneath the table. But, if only a few of the main players could be identified and their unlawful practices of hush money curbed, the rest of the entities involved would fall like a house of cards.

Detectives Paulson and Detective Callahan continued their pursuit for Sammy "the man" Roman and those individuals believed to be associated with his disappearance. Meanwhile the deceit and dishonesty ran non-stop, hiding the truth in a way only Hudson County could do.

Dirty tricks, dirty dealings, and shady business ran deep inside the margins of each segment of the city, and even included the judicial system, police departments, city leaders, bankers, loan institutions, you name it, it was everywhere one looked.

Every stone Liam and the two detectives, Paulson and Callahan overturned or looked under, became a reminder at just how deep the corruption ran; it was mind boggling.

Several minor players were arrested occasionally and brought to the forefront, but none convicted. A slap on the wrist, released or placed on probation, then back to their life of corruption and wrong doing. So prolific and profitable was it, always outweighing the risk of being caught with your pants down or hands in the till.

As time passed, Darla Sue helped Liam as he continued work on the duplicitous way the city operated. Day by day, week by week, as they delved more deeply into the abyss, it became more apparent how widespread, bigger and how deep it ran into the fabric of the city.

Liam's articles become the most read article in the Jersey Journal. His articles appeared almost daily on the editorial page, but occasionally featured on the front page of the newspaper. Several of his scathing articles also appeared a few times in national newspapers like the New York Times or Chicago Tribune. In some circles, Liam had become somewhat of a celebrity as a home town journalist.

Doc Neeson, after being released, returned to his boat, "Catch Me," still moored to the long dock extending out into the Hudson River. Settled once again on his boat, picked up where he left off, but this time, his business began to falter, losing not only his local clout, but the momentum within the ranks of certain out of town organizations. With his hired henchmen, his bills and the many commitments he was expected to carry out, was time to rethink his course of action, and which he was truly bound or committed. This was not going to be easily to follow his new course of action. Doc Neeson had to be pursued and kept in the limelight 24/7, by Liam Johnson but Detectives Paulson and Callahan.

Since his incarceration, Doc Neeson found out he had nowhere to run or hide, and continuously shadowed with his every move. Life as Doc Neeson knew it, had been drastically altered. And somewhere along the line his phone had even been tapped. What could he do to overcome this travesty of injustice he was sensing?

By this time, Liam had become a force to reckon with; he became an unmatched justice fighter in the annals of Jersey City and Hoboken. This had a profound effect not only him but those in running the city.

As the city's upper echelon became more recognizable and scrutinized as they went about their daily activities; each now kept a much lower profile as they set about their professional and private lives. Not as openly or as willingly to conduct business in the same old way as before. Keeping out of limelight as much as possible, not rocking the boat as previously, and appearing below the radar as much as possible. They tried to avoid all propensity of doing things which attracted attention. It became a different world for a small number of elite city officials and their cohorts as Liam was seemingly running the show.

Liam, was like a bull in a China closet, reporting on every movement and hiccup concerning the most notable clusters of the hierarchy. Keeping in-check those individuals involved in duplicitous double-dealing around the city and surrounding suburbs. Liam had been a godsend for those who believed in fair and honest government and became a champion for their cause. But, no matter how much he exposed the enterprise of the municipality, there was still that underworld of activity which seemed to survive unscathed, but that faction was also keeping a low profile during this unusual transitional period.

Liam continued brow beating the illegal activities, as he and Darla Sue had become one during this short-term stopgap intervention. They met several times a week and often after work at one of the local restaurants to discuss what to do next. And when together like this recognizing how comfortable being together felt, even though things around them were quite volatile. There was this underlying current in which they had felt since being kidnapped. They were forced to be on guard constantly, while watching each other's back, before something else bad happen. This played an important part in their lives as they moved forward. Always something to think and worry about, and avoid if possible.

One evening after work, Liam was at home going over material he had collected from one of his informers when his phone rang. He answered, "Hello."

A voice at the other end of the line told him in no uncertain terms, "You needed to stop writing the articles bashing illegal practices around the city and go back to writing a column about normal, mundane, boring articles you normally wrote, if you want to continue writing," and hung up.

The call left him unsettled and unnerved once again. He immediately sat up straight before reversing the call. When he did get through, there was a voice message telling him the number was no longer in service, then a dial tone. This had been a wake-up call, he must be careful when alone or with Darla Sue, thinking, *[We both could wind-up dead in some dark alley if we are not careful.]*

Finding himself and Darla Sue in somewhat of a catch 22. he had to avoid at all cost the difficult circumstances he found himself in at present, because of mutually conflicting interest of his job and relationship with Darla Sue. His obligation to the newspaper and community was a top priority and was ethically and morally bound in following through with his obligations with the newspaper editorials. Not a situation he wanted for himself or Darla Sue. But that's the position he found himself, in which there was little hope of escaping the ramifications of his previous actions, that of achieving his aim. Vowing to stay the course and take a tougher stance against the offenders.

Chapter 6

After the call from the unidentified caller, Liam was more determined than ever in exposing the sleaze bags and exploitations going on in every level of city government. With time not on his side, Liam had to find a way to infiltrate the illegal activity inside city hall and shake out the dishonest management of employees who worked for the city.

It appeared from his findings, everyone from the mayor down including, the city manager, several city council members, attorneys, and even school officials were receiving kickbacks in one form or another. He learned many of the leaders having accountability representing the municipality, had dirty hands. He now found himself too deep in the bowls of inequality to turn back now; his life as he knew it hung in the balance until this folly or ludicrousness was nipped in the bud.

Traveling around the city on a daily bases, Liam met more and more people, who opened up to him and told him of incidents they had come across or chanced (upon) of fraud and abuse by those administrators plaguing the city. As Liam conversed more with strangers he often met on the street, they told the same stories of the bribery and kickbacks by the same officials he exposed every day in his editorials. This new information by strangers only confirmed the total amount of criminal activity or foul play was brought to his attention. And before long, those exposed by him in the articles were starting to worry. And those who run the city, were now beginning to run scared. It was just a matter of time until the city suffered a catastrophic downturn of its resources and cost its residents more in taxes and less services.

Doc Neeson, continued running his business at a reduced speed, as he tried to reclaim control. For him to stay out of the limelight was damn near impossible, as his name came up quite frequently among the anti-elitist.

Doc Neeson had been asked by a local building commissioner not long after his release to intervene in a menacing problem concerning one of the local electrical company's he was having an issue with. But somehow the incident went awry and backfired. Doc's partners in crime made a blunder and was arrested.

With the two partners in crime now safely locked up, Doc Neeson had himself was implicated in the fiasco and soon arrested. With all three off the streets and facing new charges; Liam breathed a sigh of relief. This was best news he had had since returning to work after the judge declared a mistrial earlier.

Doc Neeson, back to his old habits, but this time he slipped up and was caught red-handed coercing a local building contractor. This incident was the one that broke the camel's back.

Hopefully this time Doc Neeson, along with his two partners in crime, would be tried, but this time, hopefully convicted and serve jail time.

That compelled Liam committing to work harder in ridding the city's illegal businesses that was ruining an otherwise formidable municipality.

Liam, after hearing of Doc Neeson's latest apprehension, called Darla Sue immediately to find out if she had heard the latest news about the arrest of Doc Neeson? Answering her phone at the law office, she was surprised to hear Liam's voice. He seldom called her at work, but this was important. He wanted her to be among the first to know of the downfall of Doc Neeson. She was pleased to hear Doc Neeson had been caught with his hand in the cookie jar, and again faced prison time if convicted. If sent to prison, they would have no need to agonize or fret over him harming or hurting them ever again.

This was the vindication or redemption they hoped for since the kidnapping months before.

Liam told Darla Sue, "Doc Neeson's arrest calls for a celebration and dinner." They made arrangements to meet for dinner at Dino and Harrys Steakhouse later that evening after work.

Liam drove by and picked up Darla Sue at seven then it was off to the restaurant to have a leisure dinner and a small celebration. Liam had made the reservations earlier and glad he did, because after arriving, found a line of patrons waiting to be seated, the place was packed.

After a nice dinner and after dinner drinks, it was time to call it a night. On the drive back to Darla Sue's condo, she asked him, "Would you be interested in having a nightcap before going home?"

"Yes. That sounds great. I'm still upbeat about Doc Neeson's confinement, I'm really not ready to call it a night just yet." Great, Darla Sue responded.

"Now that that's settled, I'm not tired and it would give us a chance to get to know each other better. I hope the feeling is mutual?"

"I can tell you honestly, I've missed seeing you."

"Really, I had no idea."

Reaching Darla Sue's condo, Liam was immediately impressed at the condo in which she resided. He had heard of the condo where she lived but never gave it much thought. The condo was located near the waterfront in Hoboken and overlooked the river. As he was looking over the landscape from the condo balcony, he could see New York's skyline in the distance. It was an awesome site and impressive view from this location.

Soon, after arriving at the condo, she mixed a couple of cocktails and opened a bag of snacks. With Liam's help they carried the snacks and drinks out to the balcony where they placed the several items on a small bistro table. Liam could not take his eyes off the sights and sounds of the boat traffic, the lights of lower Manhattan flickering and dancing on still waters of the river, but eventually sat down at the bistro table next to Darla Sue. Liam told Darla Sue how much he enjoyed the view from her balcony and appreciated the opportunity to witness such a spectacular view. They were quite comfortable sitting there on the balcony, and talked until almost midnight.

Finally finished with their drinks and snacks, decided to call it a night. Both had to get up early for work. Liam pitched in helping Darla Sue clean off the bistro table and straighten up the balcony before heading back inside. Liam went back over and closed the sliding doors to the balcony then clean the dishes while Darla Sue dried and placed them back inside the cupboard.

After things had been cleaned and put away, told Darla Sue he had to be going and as he was leaving leaned in and gave her a peck on the cheek, telling her, "I certainly have enjoyed the evening and would like to do it again soon." At which she quickly concurred. Before leaving he
told Darla Sue, "I'll call once I arrive home."

"Yes, that's a good idea, don't want anything to spoil the evening, do we?" No.

As he walked over and opened the door, he turned to find Darla Sue had followed him. As he was heading toward the elevator, he heard Darla Sue's door behind him close.

Reaching the elevator Liam pressed the call button calling the elevator to the sixth floor for his ride down to garage level where he parked his car. All during the elevator ride to the garage level Liam reminisced about the evening and how much he had enjoyed Darla Sue's company. He then thought to himself, [*had this evening been the start of something he'd been waiting his whole life for? To be continued,*] he thought.

Chapter 7

As Liam returned to his car in the buildings parking garage suddenly realized someone else's presence lurking in the shadows. As he hastened his pace to reach his car, suddenly felt a sharp pain in his back. Not able in turning around at this point to see who it was; the perpetrator stabbed him several more times until he fell to the garage floor inches away from his car. Lying on the cold garage floor, bleeding profusely and finding it harder and harder to breath. He found himself alone, cold and no one to help, eventually passing out.

When he awoke several days later, found himself lying in a hospital bed at the Hoboken University Medical Center on Willow Ave. As he opened his eyes, and finally able in focusing his eyes, began looking around the room, but had no idea of why he there laying in a hospital bed? Trying to think back as to what happened earlier, but was unable in recalling. Whatever happened causing him to be hospitalized, was appreciative he was alive. With so much on his mind before the incident, this was not the way he intended what he started to end.

As he tried moving himself slowly over on his side, found he was not able in turning, as sharp pains radiated throughout his entire body anytime, he moved. Something with his back was causing a lot of discomfort, especially when trying to move himself. Thinking back, *[I remember leaving Darla Sue's condo, also remember taking the elevator down to the garage level,]* but for some reason could recall nothing else. His mind at that point became a total blank.

Not long after he awoke one of the floor nurses working the evening shift came into the room where he lay to change the bandages on his back side. As she was replacing the bandages and applying medicine on the stab wounds, he asked, "What happened and why am I in the hospital?"

The nurse could not tell him the extenuating circumstance causing his presence at the hospital, but did try and explain to him, "You were brought to the hospital a couple of days ago with multiple stab wounds in your upper and lower back. Your right lung has been damaged along with your spleen and liver during some type of altercation. Upon your arrival at the hospital, you were immediately rushed into the emergency room, then to surgery. There were several doctors who assisted with the surgery and was able to repair the damaged internal organs."

The nurse went on to explained, "You were lucky. When you arrived in surgery, the doctors said your chance for survival was zero to none. You lost several pints of blood which was replaced during the several hours you spent in surgery. You should consider yourself lucky to be alive. Your one lucky man."

After hearing the nurse's story, he could not imagine what happened after leaving Darla Sue's unit on his way to his car.

He told the nurse, "Would you kindly expressed my gratitude to the emergency staff and doctors who did the surgery and how grateful I am for their services."

"I'll pass your sentiments on to the emergency room staff and doctors on call that evening. I'm sure they'll appreciate it."

As she finished replacing the bandages, she told him, "Try not to move, it will only exacerbate the situation. Whether you know it or not, you still have a rough road ahead of you before being released. Also, you will be required to take several weeks of therapy but the excruciating pain that comes with the therapy sessions and months of healing will take its toll. You have a long way to go before you are one hundred percent again."

Lying flat on his stomach in the bed, he felt the pain radiating from his back after the nurse had given him a pain pill. Plus, while in the room the nurse noticed medication dripping from his drip line which was attached to an IV pole near the bed. Surely, he thought, *[Some of the fluid being administered through the IV lines was to help the pain along with* the *lifesaving bags of liquid.]*

As he lay thinking about his slim chance surviving the incident, his only thought was *["Who was it that did this to me and why?"]*

That night he was awakened several times as different nurses came into the room to check on him, and change the soiled bandages. For some reason the wounds he received would not stop hemorrhaging. If the wounds did not stop bleeding, he may have to go back in for more surgery and another blood transfusion.

The following morning after the shift change, a new nurse came in and checked his wounds. As she changed the dressings, told him, "The wounds are finally starting to stop draining and your blood has started to coagulate. That's a good thing, they are no longer a major problem." After she finished changing the dressings and left the room, Liam was alone once again. Left to ponder the reason for the brutal attack on him, and the only thing that came to mind was, he must have hit a nerve with one of his articles he had written. Why else would someone do this to him?

Later that morning after having the bandage changed, fed a liquid diet and the colostomy bag emptied. As he laid in bed Detective Paulson and Detective Callahan walked in.

They came to the hospital to see how he was doing, but also to ask him a few questions about the incident. And find out if he had recognized anyone after exiting the elevator or walking through the garage to his car. They were hoping to get a description of the perpetrator or perpetrators.

Detective Paulson greeted Liam as he and Detective Callahan gathered round the bed, and after a short period of time, they got to the main crux of their visit. Detective Paulson told Liam, "We've combed every inch of the garage where the incident happened with a fine-tooth comb and have come up empty handed." We would like to know, are you up to telling us your side of the story and add anything of substance to the altercation.

Liam, told what he remembered which was very little, and with nothing new to add to the occurrence; the two detectives told Liam, "We will keep on looking for a possible motive, but with so little to go on it's going to be hit and miss. If you think of anything at all, no matter how insignificant, contact us immediately." With that they left.

After his visit with Detective Paulson and Callahan, he suddenly found himself thinking of Darla Sue and wondering how she was doing? About that time, she appeared in the doorway. When he looked up and saw her, his whole demeanor changed. A smile appeared on his face as she continued over to the bed, reaching out and took hold of his hand. Her hand touching his was like a security blanket over him, and made him feel far less vulnerable.

She asked, "How are feeling?"

"Not as good as I felt when I left the condo." As he chuckled to himself.

I'm so sorry this happened, but at least you are alive. That's the most important thing. I got worried after you left when I did not get that phone call telling me you arrived home and was okay. So, I went down to the garage and that's when I discovered you lying on the floor near your car. I immediately called the police on my cell phone and explained to them, I found you laying on the garage floor, that it looked like you had been shot or stabbed and to send an ambulance A.S.A.P.

It was not long after that the police and ambulance were on scene. The paramedics took control and placed on you on a gurney and had you in the ambulance in a matter of minutes. I stayed around talking to Detective Paulson and Detective Callahan while they went through the motions looking for clues. I eventually returned to my unit and cried all night. I reluctantly went to work the following day, but could not stop thinking about what happened to you."

Later that morning I told my bosses, "I cannot continue working, I'm too distraught about what happened." They said they understood, and told me, "Take the rest of the day off, go home and try pulling myself together." I left almost immediately for home where I remained. I did call the hospital and checked on you periodically. I thought several times about visiting the hospital, but knew I would not be permitted access to see you because I was not immediate family. I knew when you recovered enough, they would transfer you out of ICU, and to your own room.

The second day, when I called, I was told, "Mr. Drake has been moved out of ICU into a private room." I asked if you were allowed visitors and was told yes, but only for a short time.

I immediately dressed and rushed over here, hoping you would be conscious and awake upon my arrival. I wanted to tell you how sorry I was this happened and if there was anything I could do for you prior to your release?

Liam told Darla Sue, "You're lucky, I don't have a dog or cat, there's really not much I need at this time. But I appreciate your offer and all you've done up until now. When I get out of here there will be things, I'm sure, I'll need assistance in doing, but will limit my demands.

Since you're familiar with what I'm up against concerning the corruption involving the city, "I'll will need all the expertise and legal help I can get."

"I will do what I can. I'm sure between the two of us and help from your newspaper, we'll be able to get through this together."

And as far as your concerns you have about the legal and moral aspect concerning the state of affairs of the city; I'm sure my office can supply you with legal information regarding any information you need concerning certain controls which hold the city captive. And as you are well aware, "The pen is mightier than the sword."

And I must say to you, "You have a mighty pen, so you must use it to the best of your ability in eliminating the graft and corruption going on in Hoboken and Jersey City."

Chapter 8

About that time, the nurse knocked softly on the door and told Darla Sue, "Your time is up and I must ask you to leave."

Reluctantly, Darla Sue took hold of Liam's hand once again and gently squeezed it, telling him she would visit him later that evening if he was up to it. He looked up at her and in a weak voice, said, "Noting would please me more, I look forward to your visit." And with that he closed his eyes as she turned to leave.

Leaving the hospital, Darla Sue drove through a fast-food drive-thru and ordered something to eat when she returned home. After eating her lunch made a call to the office, and was assured everything was running smooth, not to worry about coming in the following day. This gave her a breather and time to visit Liam without feeling guilty about missing work.

The following evening, Darla Sue drove to the hospital, and as she entered Liam's room, he looked more aware of his surroundings and what was going on. He appeared much more alert than on her last visit. She walked over to the bedside where she took hold of his hand and asked, "How are you feeling this evening? You're looking better."

He said, "I'm still hurting and very sore, but that comes with the territory," then a quick smile. That was the first sign of improvement she noticed during the two visits. She asked, "Is there anything you need that I get or have the nurse get for you?"

He replied, "Nothing at this time, they've taken care of all my needs so far. I'm happy you came; it makes my day."

"Thanks, glad I'm able in bring a bit of sunshine into your otherwise mundane evening," she said with a smile.

Oh, before I forget, "Detective Paulson and Detective Callahan came to visit me earlier, told me, "They were still working the case, but as of yet nothing concrete to report."

They have all eyes and ears open throughout the city looking for the perpetrator; told me, "Its only be a matter of time until something constructive turned up, opening the door leading them to the offender/ offenders."

Detective Paulson indicated, "Since Doc Neeson, and his two cronies were incarcerated, there's a new boss running the show, but his identity is not yet known. It was a matter of time until the new boss's true identity comes to the surface. Maybe by then your mystery case will break open and the players exposed." Hopefully that will shine a whole new light on the situation and give the police an extra shot of adrenaline on the case they've been working so hard on.

Detective Paulson told me, "When the identity of the new boss was known, he would inform you."

I'm looking forward to getting released soon so I can get back to work doing what I do best, which is investigating crime and corruption. Not laying around here day after day thinking about what I could be doing. The longer I lay cooped up in here, the more exploitation and bribery goes on the outside. The misuse of the city's money by corrupt officials will never cease as long as they are given a free rein to do what they are doing. I need to get well, and back to business, hunting down those dirty rouge scoundrels.

"Yes." Darla Sue said, "But you first have to get well, and as we both know that's going to take a while longer. I'm sure once you've recovered enough to be released, you'll back to work, pronto, and again exposing individuals who are hindering the city's growth. And the city itself, once those individuals are gone, the city will bounce back to the true standards of a metropolitan area like of Jersey City and Hoboken in no time flat.

Darla Sue told Liam, "I'm going to leave now and let you get some rest. I will drop by again tomorrow."

"I'm looking forward to it," Liam replied.

Darla Sue bent down and gave Liam a peck on the cheek, then told him, "I'll keep you informed of any new information I run across at the office which is instrumental in your pursuit of justice. I'll help you with whatever pertinent facts I find and information I can get my hands on that you are otherwise not privy too. In my position at the law firm, there are always legal documents floating around noteworthy of passing on to you for your assessment. It's just one more source of information that will help you get to the bottom of your systematic search for truth and justice." Ending her visit on that note, said good bye, turned and quietly walked out the door.

Several weeks and many rehabilitation sessions later, and daily visits by Darla Sue and the two detectives, the day came for his release arrived, and none too soon for him. He was sick and tired of the whole fiasco, that of being stabbed, the recovery period and all that rehab. It was time to get back to work, and continue his inquiries into the illicit and illegal affairs going on around the city he so profoundly admired and revered.

First thing Liam did after being released was go home where he removed that god-awful green hospital gown, jumped into the shower and took a long and deserving hot shower. After showering dried himself off, and shaved the heavy stubble of facial hair from his face, then changed into his work clothes.

Now that he had been released from the hospital, he thought of going to the newspaper office and read over several articles he had written and recently published to see if he could come up with a reasonable answer as to a motive why someone viciously attacked him. It was a long shot, but why would someone go to the trouble and try killing him? It was certainly not a robbery they had in mind, because he still had his wallet and keys.

Upon leaving the apartment, he headed straight down to the newspaper office where he was warmly greeted by his peers. They gave him a standing ovation as he entered the office which came as a total surprise to him. The staff treated him like some kind of returning hero. He knew he was no hero, but accepted their welcome with humility.

After the hoopla on his return, and the office settled down a bit, he was back familiar territory. It felt good being back. When he approached his desk, found mounds of paper work to review. Looking at all that paperwork he was hopeful somewhere in that pile were answers to the many unanswered questions which had eluded or dogged him in the past.

He pulled out the chair behind the desk, and sat down, where he brought up several copies of editorials on the computer he wanted to read to see if there was anything he could find connecting the article to the stabbing. After an hour or so, found nothing he considered important or tied the stabbing to.

Finished with the old editorials, began the daunting task reading the many documents amassed in front of him. As he began going through the letters, notes and documents, almost immediately commenced seeing a pattern emerge. As he scanned the pile of notes and documents, started jotting down some of the more interesting comments and observations. And when he finished for the day, had separated the mound of paperwork into three separate stacks. Individual stacks were separated by priority, urgency, and significantly less informative. He then assigned a numerical number to each category, depending on its substance and significance of value for later reference.

Among the pile of correspondence on his desk, he found two very interesting letters; one which grabbed his attention immediately. It was written anonymously by an individual claiming to have witnessed the stabbing in the garage that night. The nameless individual was willing to relate his story of the incident, but only from afar. He did not want to give up his name because he feared reprisals from those in power. He also indicated he did not want to divulge any information concerning his identity, his occupation, or where he lived. He was willing to talk to Liam, one-on-one.

The second letter was from one of the companies which had done business with the city for years. Forced by certain individuals working through the city called collectors. They collected weekly and monthly kick-backs on every job involving the cities controlling guidelines. They were willing to come forward and tell all. Tired of paying kick-back to a city which constantly inflated the cost of doing business in every aspect concerning the building trades. They were in a no-win situation. Fed up with the system, they were willing to testify against those individuals involved if and when arrested and brought to trial.

Liam was excited at what he saw and read. He was ready to talk with the company who could expose individuals involved in the illicit kickback scheme, not only in editorials but court. And with his (if called to testify) and other testimonies hopefully getting a conviction and sent to prison for a long time.

It had been a long and exhausting day for Liam, but with it now behind him, he had a greater perception of the situation at hand and stronger understanding in how to approach his concern finding and exposing those affiliates governing the city.

Before leaving the newspaper that evening, he thanked everyone for their concern while he was in the hospital, and all the flowers and getwell cards they sent. He left the office for home; and thought to himself, *[Its time I recast the commitment I've made to the people of Hoboken and adapt a different strategy from this point forward.]*

Chapter 9

Arriving home that evening, Liam contacted Darla Sue to see if she would be up to having a late dinner.

After two rings she answered her phone, "Hello."

"Yes, Darla Sue its Liam. Would you be interested in going to dinner this evening?"

She responded, "Yes, I have not eaten dinner yet, think that's a great idea. I assumed you would be exhausted since you've not worked the last few weeks and put in a full work day at the newspaper."

"Yes, I'm a bit tired, but feel like getting out and having dinner before turning in. That is of course if you are up to it?"

"Yes, I'm definitely up to it. I've missed our dinner dates and look forward to tonight. Nothing would stop me from being with you and having dinner."

"Great, now that's that settled, I be by to pick you up around seven thirty or quarter of eight if that's agreeable?"

"I'll be ready, see you when you get here."

Liam hung up the phone, then started walking toward the bedroom while removing his clothes. reaching the bathroom, removed the last piece of clothing (then raised the lid on the hamper,) tossing in the articles of clothing and closed the lid.

Now standing buck necked gazing into the full-length mirror on the wall, saw his reflection. He studied his reflection for a moment, thinking, [I'm not only tired but emaciated.] He could not believe his eyes as he stood staring at himself before reaching over and turning on the shower. He adjusted the water temperature and climb into the shower where he took a long deserving shower under the tepid water.

After finishing showering, stepped out and dried himself. Then stood in front of the medicine cabinet mirror looking at himself, and realized just how disheveled he looked. One thing that would help his appearance he thought to himself is, *[I really need to shave.]*

After shaving and brushing his teeth, returned to the bedroom and pulled opened the top dresser drawer where he kept his socks and boxer shorts. Then walked over to the closet and removed one of several freshly laundered shirts and a pair of dress slack. After dressing himself as casual as possible, it was time to pick up Darla Sue.

Leaving his apartment took the stairs down to the parking garage where his car was parked, hoping it would start. On the first turn of the key, it cranked right up. He let the engine warm up before putting it in reverse, and backing out of his assigned space and headed to Darla Sue's.

He found a parking space near the entrance to her building in the guest parking spaces, parked the car, exited got out, walked over to the front entrance where he dialed Darla Sue's unit from intercom system near the door. Darla Sue answered only after a second ring, immediately recognized the voice on the other end and quickly buzzed him in.

Reaching her unit which happened to be on the top floor, Darla Sue was standing at the door with a wide grin on her face, indicating to him, she was elated at seeing him, and quickly took him by the hand, and invited him in.

"Come in, we still have a few minutes before we have to leave. I want to give you some information I ran across concerning (Angelo) the new boss heading the syndicate in Hoboken and Jersey City. He's replaced Doc's Neeson and is running the show at the moment. He apparently was covertly hired by the mayor after Doc Neeson's conviction which you are well aware of and have often written about in the past. The city, is once again, heading into chaos. This Angelo is considered dangerous and has started out like gangbuster, committing the same crimes against contractors, local union affiliates and purveyors, same MO (modus operandi) as Doc Neeson. This Angelo does not pull his punches. He's much more ruthless than Doc Neeson ever thought of being.

"It's just a sign of the times," Liam said."

"I guess so," replied Darla Sue as she began telling Liam how she came across information in the dossier opened and laying on the table in her office.

"I ran Angelo's name in our data base at work and learned he's been in and out of jail beginning in his adolescents, and continued his crime spree into and throughout his adult life. He's merciless, remorseless, ruthless and uses every tactic available at his disposal. Has grown up working the system from the inside out. You'll need to watch your step with this one, staying as far away from him as you can, he's nothing but trouble, and when I say trouble, I mean trouble with a capital T."

Handing a copy of the dossier to Liam containing vital information on this Angelo she copied while Liam was in the hospital.

Liam accepted the dossier, and thanked her for her support, telling her how much he appreciated the assistance's she so selfishly provided.

After receiving the dossier, he helped with her shawl and out the door they went heading to Amanda's Restaurant over on Washington Street for a well-deserved dinner.

Arriving at Amanda's, they were greeted and immediately taken to their favorite table by maître d' Dominick. After being seated, Dominick turned to each and smiled. Then said, "Welcome back, your waiter will be with you shortly." It was going to be a night to remember, with a bottle of their favorite wine and one of their famous multi culture cuisines. The evening was meant for catching up on things that needed attention but inevitably included getting reacquainted. It had been a long time since they were able being together and somewhat intimate with one another.

Once the waiter arrived at their table, offered each a menu, then asked, "Would you care to start off with a drink before dinner?" Both agreed, a bottle of wine was in order. The waiter asked, "If I may suggest one of our finer wines to start, maybe a bottle of Cabernet Sauvignon."

"Yes," Liam told the waiter, "That's what we had in mind." Then, that's what I will bring to your table so you can get started.

A short time later, the waiter returned with a stand and bottle of Red Cabernet Sauvignon in the chiller with ice, placing the stand beside Liam. With one fluid motion retrieved one of the two wine glass (on the table) nearest Liam, pouring a small amount of the (red nectar of the gods) into the stemmed crystal glass. Placing the glass back on the table near Liam. Liam picked up the glass, raising it to his lips, took small taste, swishing it around in his mouth, he felt the soothing sweet taste of the two hybrid grapes, (a cross between cabernet franc (red grape) and sauvignon blanc (a white grape), (made from 100% cabernet sauvignon grapes) and blends.

As he sat swishing the wine around in his mouth it was pleasing to his palate. Nodding to the waiter his approval. The waiter then took the glass from him, finished filling it along with Darla Sue's glass. Before drinking, Liam made a toast, "May this night never end." Soon the waiter approached the table once again and asked, "Are you ready to order or do you need more time?"

They had looked over the menu and made their choices and told the waiter, "Yes, we've decided what we would like to order."

"Very well, what is your pleasure?" Giving him their order, the waiter made a small bow, nodded, then turned from the table heading in the direction of the restaurant's kitchen, while Liam and Darla Sue continued their conversation how their lives had changed since meeting. Both were honest in their feeling and looked forward to building their relationship to an even higher level.

Both agreed they were ready, looking across the table, smiled at each other with a different emotion and intensity. It seemed official. They indicated silently their stamp of approval and became committed to one another at that very moment. It had been a long time for both, not being dedicated to just one partner, but this time it felt right.

After dinner and the drive back to Darla Sue's, she was happier than she had been in a long time. Knowing there was someone again in her life that was kind, hardworking, and honest, a rarity these days. She had found Mr. Right and not letting this one slip through her hands.

Back at Darla Sue's condo, Liam shared a night cap with Darla Sue before leaving. As they sat on the couch talking about their future, there was a knock at the door. Darla Sue was not expecting anyone at this late hour and gave Liam a suspicious look. She got up from the couch to look through the door viewer to see who this might be. As she peered out the door viewer saw no one. Opened the door and look up and down the hallway but the hall way was empty.

Then out of the corner of her eye, looked down at the carpet in front of her unit and saw a small white envelope. Reaching down, she picked up the envelope, and closed the door. Taking a closer, looking at the envelope to see whom it was addressed, discovered no name or return address anywhere on the envelope, either front or back. After closing the door then locking it, returning to the couch, sat down next to Liam and with the mysterious letter in her shaking hand, looked over at Liam with distrust in her eyes as to whom it was from. As she slowly opened one of the corners of the envelope, a white powdery substance began falling out, immediately heightening their worst fears to the ingredient inside which appeared to be anthrax.

Darla Sue immediately discarded the letter quickly in a trash container under the end table nearest her, while Liam reached for the phone and promptly called police. He also told them to send an ambulance in case the white substance inside the envelope contains what they presumed to be anthrax and that they may have ingested some of the powder.

After the police and ambulance arrived, they immediately took charge of the potential volatile situation. Darla Sue showed the police what she found after opening her door. At this point she told police, "We were subjected to consequences beyond our control; it was now in your hands and others to sort out this latest life threating intrusion into our privacy and lives."

After police finished their investigation inside and outside Darla Sue's condo; Liam and Darla Sue were taken by ambulance to a local hospital as a precautionary measure and examined.

The letter, apparently a hoax and scare tactic had been used by a sick individual hoping to stop the bad publicity going around town of embezzlement, fraud and dishonesties used by local city officials and others in position of authority.

The white powdery substance inside the envelope was later identified only as finely ground white flour made to resemble anthrax. It was enough to scare the bejesus' out of both Darla Sue and Liam, a real eye opener that their lives were on the line. Later that night Darla Sue and Liam were released from the hospital and returned to the condo.

Liam, before leaving that evening, told her, "Once I leave, I want you to lock up and not do not, I repeat, do not open the door unless you are positive who's on the other side."

He then leans across the couch and embraced her, giving her a welldeserved kiss before departing. As he got up and leaving to go home, she told him, "I'm glad you were here when I opened that envelope earlier, I would not have known what to do and if it had been the real thing."

Liam replied, "I'm glad I was here too. Glad things turned out a well as they did. I have to admit, it frightened me." Then told Darla Sue goodnight, Liam exited the unit and made sure the door was securely closed before leaving.

Chapter 10

The following day Liam received a courtesy call from Detective Paulson concerning the suspicious envelope left in front of Darla Sue's apartment. Detective Paulson stated to Liam, "The lab results came back and confirmed what you assumed earlier, that the white substance in the envelope was harmless, that was good news. Also, after we checked the area around the front entrance to the unit for finger prints, shoe impressions, hair, and fiber not consistent with the carpet in the hallway, we came up empty handed. Whoever left that envelope was careful and had worn gloves and possible covers over their shoes? Detective Paulson went on to explain they had checked the entire hallway, the emergency stairs from the roof down to the first floor. Again, nothing linking anyone to who may have dropped off the envelope."

While Detective Paulson still had Liam on the phone, asked him a few general questions concerning the previous evening, that would tie the incident to someone they saw after arriving back at the condo.

Liam told him, "There's nothing I recall at the moment, but if I happen to remember something of interest, I will let you know."

Detective Paulson then said, "I want to thank you for your time and if I learn anything new, I'll call."

After talking with Detective Paulson, Liam revisited in his mind that evening spent with Darla Sue. He suddenly remembered seeing an individual as they left the condo in his car heading to the restaurant.

Closing his eyes, visualizing what he had seen and considered it relevant. A lone individual stood on the sidewalk near the outside parking used for guest. It was someone trying to look casual, but actually stood out like a sore thumb, come to think of it.

Liam could see vividly in his mind the person leaning against a mail drop box as they were leaving the underground garage that evening. As Liam was looking to exit the garage, he spotted an individual, and thought to himself, at the time, *[that person seems familiar? Maybe it was a coincident, but worthy of relating the incident to Detective Paulson anyway.]*

Heading to work, Liam decided to stopped at a donut shop along route and picked up a baker's dozen of donuts to share with office staffers during morning break. Upon leaving the donut shop parking lot, noticed in his rearview mirror a car pulls from the curb and appeared to be following him.

Since he was close to the newspaper office, it did not take long until he was pulling into his assigned space in the parking lot alongside the newspaper building. As he parked the car and turned off the engine, notice the car slowly drive by and the passenger starring intently at him as he exited his car with the box of donuts. As best as he could ascertain looking at the driver, it looked like the same person standing outside the condo leaning against the mail drop box and the same individual he saw as they left the restaurant that night.

Trying to get a good look at the license plate number as the car passed, was able only able to memorize only the first two digits of the New Jersey plate which he later jotted down on the lid of the donut box along with the make and color of the automobile before the car disappeared out of sight.

There was a chance Detective Paulson along with Detective Callahan could cross reference the information from their data base at police headquarters and find a match. This was of course, wishful thinking on his part, *[but possible]* he thought to himself.

Arriving at work, dropped the donuts off in the lounge area, immediately headed back to his desk where he dialed Detective Paulson, and relayed the description and information he had written down on the donut box.

Detective Paulson told Liam, "That's not much to go on but I will relay the information to the unit responsible for cross referencing such data. I'll give it to them and see what they can come find."

Several days later as things had settled down and back to some semblance of normalcy; Liam and Darla Sue were back to doing those things necessary in carrying out their daily activities.

Nothing strange or odd had happened lately to cause any type of anxiety or alarm.

Liam, was soon back out on the street meeting with his contacts to find out what the word on the street was concerning local the thugs.

Loui, who Liam phoned earlier asking him to meet with him at noon in one of the greasy spoon diners along the water front for coffee. As they sat drinking their coffee, Loui told him, "I heard this new boss Angelo put word out that the foreman working on the new project over on Clinton Street needed to be taught a lesson. Also heard the building commissioner in Jersey City apparently told his building inspector overseeing the project, "When you arrived at the new project site in

Hoboken, I want you to look up the foreman and collect payment."

I also heard, when the building inspector arrived on site and found the foreman, informing him of the payment he owed." The foreman when confronted by the building inspector told him in no uncertain terms, "I do not have your money and I'm going to notify the trade union association of the infractions used by the city building commissioner's office concerning such unfair practices." This did not go over to well with the building inspector who turned to the foreman and told him, "You're going to regret this decision".

I've heard nothing more, but sure something is going down and soon. I'll keep my eyes and ears open, and if I hear anything, I'll let you know. But, other than that one incident, things seem to be running rather smoothly here along the water front and around Hoboken.

Liam did a bit more probing before leaving the water front district by visiting a couple more places where his contacts usually hung out, but eventually left without any newer information.

He decided as he left the water front to drive by the Clinton Street project and have a talk with the site foreman. Arriving at the project, found the foreman talking with one of the independent contractors delivering a trailer load of steel rebar used for the new concrete flooring being poured on the next level of the building as they were speaking. Liam overheard the foreman tell the individual where to park his rig making it easier for the crane operator to offload the steel rebar from the truck. After the foreman finished talking with the driver, he turned to walk back to his office trailer parked on site.

Liam got the attention of the foreman before he entered the office trailer and asked if he had a moment to spare?

"What's it about? I'm awful busy at the moment as you can see."

"Yes, I can see. I'm a reporter with The Jersey Journal and would like to ask you a few questions."

"I'll be taking my lunch break in about a half hour; If you want to stick around until then, I'll have more time to talk."

"Great, that's my car over there, I'll wait and when you're ready let me know."

It took a bit longer for the foreman to wrap up his morning duties, but as he was leaving the construction site, looked over where Liam sat waiting patiently, and motioned for him he to join him in in his car. Liam jumped out of his car and into the foreman's car. Once inside the foreman's car, Liam noticed how harried he appeared. You could tell he had been overwhelmed with obligations and responsibilities' that morning, but that comes with the territory. After lunch Liam and the foreman returned to the job site where the foreman asked Liam inside his office to finish their conversation.

Entering the office there were tons of detailed drawings and paper work littering every inch of this tiny office; any surface available was piled high with papers. It would have taken a novice like himself a week to go through this mess before having any sense of order. This job required a certain type of person and this foreman certainly filled that niche.

Once seated, the foreman reminded Liam, "I have only a few more minutes so make let's make this quick, I have a lot to do this afternoon, sure you understand?"

Liam quickly explained the remainder of his concerns to the foreman, Anthony Iola, "I would like to interview you in length for an exclusive editorial on your take of the ongoing intimidation and violence practices construction companies such as yours face on a daily basis by local elected and their appointed representatives.

Anthony at first was cool to the idea, but the longer they talked and the more he thought about the idea, *[it could bring about a change in the way the city official and construction teams handled their individual business practices. Maybe just maybe if I explain the different aspects of working with the city managers, it could possibly bring about change and eliminate some of the terrorizing, brutalities often associated with organized crime which plagued building crews and independent subcontractors used by contractors.]*

Anthony told Liam, "Since I don't have a lot of time this afternoon how about we meet later this evening for dinner. That way we can have dinner and I can give you my take on the situation.

Liam responded by telling Anthony, "Great, we can meet after work this evening, say at Amanda's, and you can fill me in on what's going on?"

Chapter 11

Later that evening around six-thirty, Anthony and Liam arrived at Amanda's where Anthony was to give Liam the inside scoop on the improprieties of being duped into paying bribe monies to certain organized groups (which was nothing more than protection money, or bribes) just to stay in business and not hassled by those connected to the city.

Anthony began by telling Liam how he started working right out of high school in construction as a basic laborer. After rising quickly through the ranks, showing a potential aptitude, a special gift understanding the principals of construction and leadership. A year out of high school, he returned to study at a local college, and for four years after receiving a bachelor's degree in construction management, he never looked back. It became his life's passion.

But the job also came with a lot of headaches dealing with individuals and groups like city inspectors, managers, council members and others (known as outsiders) working under the radar with city officials, working on their behalf. It all boiled down to the same thing, kickbacks, payola, bribery?

Anthony explained several ways in which construction sites were harassed and or threatened by those different groups into paying kickbacks and told, "Without our help we can and will shut down your project until you comply. If you refused to grease our palm, we will find some foolish technicality and shut you down."

Shutting us down cost more in lost time and money while in the meantime having to spend more correcting the issue in question, and still forced to pay kickbacks. We are constantly harassed and stresses out by someone from the municipality or hired outsiders sent by those blackmailing up and to make sure we comply to their demands.

Liam asked Anthony straight up, "Would you be willing to give me a name or two I could contact about this impropriety? Names of individuals associated with bribing you and or your company?"

"Yes, I can give you a name of an individual whom I suspect is behind several incidents recently at the construction site."

His name has been mentioned several times to me and I believe it to be the person carrying out the hostile action and retribution at the work site. The difficulties one of their acts of violence against workers or destruction of property, not by not paying bribe money, sets us back weeks.

We've had several pallets of wallboard maliciously ruined by someone coming on site after everyone left the work site, and spraying some kind of chemical on the entire load of wallboard received the day before. The incident rendered the entire load of wallboard unusable, and took two weeks before receiving a second shipment, which put us behind schedule big time.

The week after that, a subcontractors' driver was harassed after he stopped his rig in front of the project on the street. Climbing out of his rig, was looking for someone to tell him where to drop off the new load of wallboard. The driver was approached by a street thug who threatened him and his family with bodily harm if the company he worked did not fork over payola.

I learned later who that person was running the illegal kickback scheme, it was none other than the person who replaced Doc Neeson after his conviction. His name, Angelo. I don't know his last name, but I've heard rumors he's behind the recent violence and disruptions at several local building sites.

This Angelo has been bragging how he runs a well-organized business and no one interferes with his practice, and if they try, he's ready to rein havoc down on them. He appears to be a very violent and uncivilized individual as I understand. I hope he's arrested sooner rather than later, and brought to justice, then prosecuted to the fullest extent of the law. That he will be removed from the streets before someone gets hurt badly. Other than his name and what I've told you, I really don't have much more information to pass on.

Anthony before leaving that evening, expressed to Liam how much he was helping the local contractors by exposing those responsible for all the upheaval in the community, and he should, continue writing about the unlawful activities they were confronted with on a daily basis, plus the catch 22 me and my company face on a regular basis. Hopefully this will be a thing of the past once this harassment is quelled.

Lam told Anthony, "I know how difficult the situations with local construction companies are regarding city inspectors and their hired outsiders."

"Yes, but you and your paper give us hope. I know the power of the press is far reaching and with your help, maybe just maybe we can stem the flow of injustice the city is raining down on us."

Anthony, as he stood up to shake Liam's hand, reiterated to him, "I hope our meeting has been productive, and if there is anything more, I learn in the future, I'll call and update you."

Liam, thanked Anthony for the interview and said, "I'll get back to you if I hear anything new about this Angel."

Liam paid the tab for dinner and together they walked out of Amanda's and headed off in separate directions.

Before going to bed that evening, Liam called Darla Sue, and made arrangements to meet for dinner the following evening.

The next evening Liam picked up Darla Sue and drove over to Court Street Restaurant and Bar. One of the older establishments in Hoboken where Liam made reservations earlier. As they entered, they were met by the maître de who escorted them to their table, and handed them each a menu. After being seated, it was not long until their waiter came over to the table, and introduced himself as Matteo.

Matteo asked," Would you care to order a cocktail from the bar?"

Liam looked at Darla Sue who nodded. Liam replied with an air of confidence, "Yes, we both will have a scotch. The lady, a scotch and soda tall, and for me, a scotch on the rocks." Great choices retorted Matteo.

After Matteo left the table, Liam looked gingerly at Darla Sue and inquired, "How did your day go? Busy as ever I'm assuming."

"Yes, as a matter of fact, I've had a very busy but productive day." The office is busy right now with an egregious murder case involving two young girls', both found beaten severely and left to die."

One was found alongside the docks near the river last year, the other was found only a day later near downtown in a deserted alley behind some large dumpsters.

I'm sure you've heard or read about both incidents? It was one of those cases you don't forget because of its, man's inhumanity to man syndrome.

The two young women were beaten so badly and brutalized it took a positive identification by someone who knew them to verify the bodies.

It so happened the parents of the first murdered victim came forward and informed police of their missing daughter the following day.

The parents gave a description of their missing daughter to police, and informed at the time of another a young woman discovered a day later. Both young women appeared around the same age, both Caucasian, brown hair, and both approximately five-foot six weighting roughly, one hundred and fifteen pounds.

After notifying the police of their daughter's disappearance were asked to drive over to the local morgue in Hoboken, that the two bodies found matched their daughter description had been taken there and neither had yet been identified. With that, they left the police station with heavy hearts, heading over to the local morgue, hoping by chance neither of the young women were their daughter. But if one was, it would be closure in one respect, but never a final closure.

Arriving at the morgue, the couple went inside and immediately led into the morgue's internal bowls. The bodies of both girls, one thought to be their daughter, lay stationary on a shiny steel table with a white sheet covering her body. A toe tag had been attached to the big toe of the right foot, with a name, "Jane Doe."

Both bodies had been moved from the refrigerated locker prior to their arrival.

As the couple stood at the end the cold steel tables waiting for the coroner to unveil the body, both hoping against hope it was not their daughter.

The coroner stood between the two steel tables and asked, "Are you ready to view the body?" Both answered simultaneously, "Yes."

The coroner reached over and with both hands-on top of the white sheet, slowly removed it exposing the girl's upper torso. The parents holding hands looked down at the at the young woman's mangled and mutilated body, and immediately recognized the body as their missing daughter. Along with clothing recovered at the scene she had been wearing at time of death, and the little pinky ring found at the scene confirmed by any shadow of doubt.

They immediately became distraught after identifying the remains and items worn by their daughter the last time, they saw her alive. Once a positive identification had been made, they were led back to the front entry door of the morgue, where the coroner shook their hands and thanked them for coming, and how sorry he was that they had to come to the mortuary to identify their daughter. After offering his condolences the parents were escorted outside, where they returned to their car and drove home.

A week later a suspect had been found and was being detained by police on possible murder charges. It was going to be a long and tedious process with only a limited amount of evidence so far, but the MO (modus operandi) was the same in both murders. It was a matter of tying the two dreadful deaths to this single individual.

Liam, suddenly remembering the two cases told Darla Sue, "Yes, now that you mentioned it, I do remember the story. I'd forgotten about it. I hope if he is the same deranged person who killed those two young women, he's found guilty, and put away for life or even better, faces the death sentence. He's one of those evil people among us who do not deserve to live."

Darla Sue told Liam, "Those two deaths will haunt those two families the rest of their lives. Never knowing if they could have prevented this tragedy. Probably not."

Matteo returned to the table with their drinks, asking if they were ready to order?

"No, not yet, give us a few more minutes to look over the menu," replied Liam.

"Not a problem, take your time." Responded Matteo.

As they sat looking over the menu trying to decide what to order. Liam suddenly heard a commotion in the front part of the restaurant. As he looked up, saw Anthony Iola arguing with the maître de. He appeared to be upset.

Liam excused himself, got up from the table, walked over to where the two were having a heated dispute. As Liam approached the maître De's station near the anterior of the restaurant, standing next to Anthony quietly asked, "What seems to be the matter, is there something I can do to help?"

Anthony turned to Liam and told him, "I made reservations for this evening and apparently it had not been entered on their reservation list."

At which point Liam asked Anthony, "Would you care to join me and my friend Miss Underwood at our table. We would enjoy your and your wife's company. We've just arrived ourselves and have not ordered, so please join us."

Anthony looked at the maître de and told him, "Since you don't seem to have the reservation I made for my wife and I, I'm accepting Mr. Drakes offer to dine with him and Miss Underwood."

The maître de smiled at Mr. Iola, turned and retrieved two more menus from the top of the podium, then ask them to follow him. The Maître de had no choice but escort the Iola's to Liam's table, where they were seated next to Miss Underwood, at which point Liam made the introductions.

Once everyone was seated, Matteo immediately returned to the table and inquired, "Are you joining Mr. Drake and Miss Underwood for dinner?

"Yes," Anthony said sharply, "We're joining Mr. Drakes and Miss Underwood."

Mateo asked Mr. Iola, "Would you and your wife care to order a cocktail from the bar before ordering?"

"Yes, my wife will have a Tequila Sunrise and I'll have a Vodka Gibson on the rocks." Said Anthony.

After the introductions and a bit of chit-chat, Liam learned from Anthony what the misunderstanding was about concerning his reservation. It had to do with the local politicians involved with more intimidation tactics. It happened before at other eating establishments he and his wife frequented. Another way the social fabric of the city and their partners in crime displayed their existences, pressuring by other means those individuals reluctant playing by their rules.

Darla Sue looked over at Anthony and told him, "You are doing the right thing, not backing down from what you believed in so adamantly. I'm sure with Liam's help, you two eventually will put a dent in the ongoing problem by placing a damper on the volatile statis quo that haunts you both. You and your contractors seem to be faced with an insurmountable burden or imposition at the hands of the city fathers and their hired hooligans. You two will never be able in eradicating totally the existing problem, but possibly abate or lessen the intensity eventually. It has to start somewhere, and who better to carry that weight to the end than you two?"

Darla Sue mentioned to Anthony, "I've mentioned to Liam in the past, I would help in any way I could; even asking the law firm where I work for their assistance on occasions. I know it will be a long, hard, and sometimes disappointing fight, but it had to start sometime, and there is no better time to start than now."

As Anthony and Liam sat mulling over what Darla Sue just vocalized, Anthony turned to Liam and said, "Okay that settles that. I'm in it for the long haul. If I have both your words in assisting me through this uphill battle with the city elite and their hired guns, I'm ready to jump in head first into this den of lions and try and make a difference?"

Darla Sue, Liam and Anthony all agreed they were in this for the long haul; and would do everything in their own realm of influence to derail this injustice placed on the contractors and subcontractors in the Hoboken and Jersey City.

With that said, they toasted to ending the unfairness of the city's unreasonable demands that had been running ramped and out of control for too long; hopefully eradicate the practice once and for all. It would take a lot of fortitude and dedication from everyone involved to make this happen, but were hell bent on trying.

Dinner arrived, as they continued discussing what to do next. They quickly saw the many pitfalls, dangers and downsides to this dilemma they had become involved in. It was not going to be a cake walk, but nothing in life worth fighting for was ever easy.

As they finished dinner and before leaving, Darla Sue asked Liam, "Can we meet for lunch tomorrow and try coming up with some rocksolid ideas how to proceed with this fact-finding mission we've committed ourselves to this evening and establish some sort of game plan?"

This was to be the biggest project Liam and Darla Sue had ever taken on, and needed all the help they could muster in finding a resolve to Anthony's and other contractors' difficulties with the city officials and their cronies. It was not for the faint of heart, and the impediments hindering future undertakings would seem unsurmountable at times. But, all three signed up for the long haul in order to correct this lack of fairness and injustice placed on the hard-working men and women of Hoboken and Jersey City.

Chapter 12

The next morning Liam walked into the newspaper building and was immediately confronted by the paper's editor-in-chief who asked him, "Do you have anything new concerning the exploitation by city building services against the construction sites?"

Liam responded by telling the editor, "Yes. I met yesterday with Mr. Antony Iola the foreman in charge of construction at the new building going up over on Clinton Street. He informed me he believes a lot of the illegal activities going on at the construction sites are being carried out by someone named Angelo. This Angelo has taken over after Doc Neeson was ousted.

Mr. Iola and I had dinner last evening, and he's decided to help me untangle this web of deceit by local officials and their hired local thugs. I should have something soon to publish on the matter. I'm going to start a series of articles concerning local leadership and their abuse of their position, and eventually (if possible) linking them with this Angelo. I should have something ready by tonight to publish in the morning paper.

That night before leaving the newspaper, Liam had written an article severely criticizing not only waste, fraud and abuse of power, but hinted at exploitation by certain administrators of Jersey City and inspectors heading several different departments. After finishing his article, Liam walked to the editor's office, and handed him his latest story for further scrutiny and approval. After reading over the scathing article, the editor decided to put it on the front page where it would bring immediate attention to the corrupt practices within local government by a few dishonest elected officials and their appointees. It would soon become the talk of the town by the afternoon.

Once the papers hit the streets, it was not long until the phones of the Jersey Journal began ringing off their hooks. It was like everyone in town had a story to tell about double dealing encountered when confronted by city fathers and code inspectors. Calls came in from new home construction, school roofing projects, even city projects such as, waste management plants, etc.…

Liam had opened up a whole new can of worms and was the conversation of the day in Hoboken and Jersey City. It would not end anytime soon; too many individuals had been duped by the city code inspectors and ready to put their two-cents worth in, now that they had their chance.

As Liam entered the Jersey Journal the next morning, his desk was bursting at the seams with memos and messages received from local citizens and others willing to get involved. Some of the communications received were not so kind for his vilifying, and libel story, but it came with the territory.

It came as a complete surprise to Liam that so many had been swindled, and tricked by the underhanded acts of the building inspectors and hired associates. A real eye opener to be sure. With the number of messages and memos received, Liam had plenty of material to work with on follow-up articles. Hopefully with so many willing to help with their own personal input The situation could conceivably lead to the top of the food chain and transformed into an attainable resolve of the problem that's been confronting the city for so long.

Only time would tell.

Liam had his work cut out as he began shuffling through the maze of messages which envelop his desk. As he started once again with the laborious task of reading and deciding which messages were worth following up on, and which to consider for future enquiry, and discarding or sitting aside certain informative notes and documents for future reference.

Liam sat aside those thought items he deemed to be worthy of a second look later. That stack had grown exponentially. A couple of hours later, after reading the bulk of messages, decided to take a break and have lunch. Once lunch was over, Liam returned to his desk where he started following up on some of the documents, letters, and notes by calling those whom he thought would give him firsthand information on their exploitation and abuse by certain corrupt city personnel. He learned early on as a reporter, follow up was as critical, and occasionally more important than some initial information. He was ready to get this show on the road.

His first call returning from lunch was to a gentleman who previously had contracted a local electrical company to update his original fuse panel box installed in his garage when the house was built. After the electrical company removed the old fuse panel and replaced by the new breaker box and the job completed. The city electrical inspector was notified to return, inspect the work and give the electrical company his approval. Instead of signing off on the job, the electrical inspector red flagged it. The electrical company (new to the area) was notified by the homeowner that the installation of the new service had been red flagged. When the electrical company came back to the job site, checked the inspection report and learned extra work was required before approval would be granted. This left the homeowner without electricity until the situation could be rectified by the electrical company.

It took three days before the repair was updated and approved. The owner was told by the electrical company there would be additional charges for removing existing wiring installed years earlier, and other infractions noted on the check list written by the city inspector. A small addendum at the bottom of the notice said, "Wiring throughout the house did not meet todays up dated electrical code."

Not only did it cost the homeowner for the extra work, but the electrical company was told by the city's electrical inspector they would be shut down on every job until they played ball with the city. Which the electrical company took to mean some sort of payment which everyone involved with contract work in the city knew meant only one thing, a kickback.

Not only was the homeowner out more money, but so was the electrical company who had contracted to do the job in the first place.

The electrical contractor was told in no uncertain terms: if they did not pay the additional fees, they would be black balled from conducting further work within the municipality until they coughed up the extra charges. The electric company had no recourse and reluctantly paid the extra fee to continue conducting business as usual within the city. They learned an expensive lesson early on; to do commercial business in Jersey City or Hoboken you had to grease the palms of city officials or inspectors before allowed to work in the city.

Subsequently, work requiring permits cost considerably more because of the obligatory higher fees charged by the city due to their unrecorded and underground black market in Chilltown.

Armed with this additional information from the outraged homeowner and several similar stories, Liam was able writing his latest editorial concerning the city's use of power. When the story hit the streets, the Jersey Journal was again swamped with calls from the city and organizations concerned with the newspaper's libel accusations. And of course, the city, wanting to know the names of those responsible for such slanderous accusations.

It was a challenge for Liam in sorting out the legal ramifications he subjected himself considering the number of different departments and toes he stepped on writing the story.

It was time he spoke with the law firm retained by the legal department at the newspaper; and feedback from Darla Sue and her view on this new circumstance he found himself entangled. He needed all the legal advice he could get as to what recourse he had dealing with this explosive upheaval caused by the latest editorial.

He had his work cut out for the next few months, not only the legal ramifications, but from the unscrupulous underworld business carried out within the city's criminal element.

He thought to himself, *[This is what I intended to do when I wrote the article. I needed to let the people know what type of corruption existed in the city, and try stopping it. Therefore, I must do what I can to finish what I've started.]*

With that thought in mind, Liam immediately contacted the newspaper law firm, Loman & Loman, to set up a time to meet with them to find out what he had gotten himself involved in. They were able in meeting him the following day at their office.

The following day he met with Tim Murphy an associate of Loman & Loman. He was asked to give a little background as to the situation leading up to this upheaval, he found himself involved. Liam started by explaining his current circumstance in which he found himself, and when he finished, Tim Murphy looked over at Liam and told him, "After hearing of your problem with the city, I suggest you let us handle the situation going forward. I can tell you are at the end of your rope. But remember we have your back as far as any lawsuits which are filed against you or the newspaper, all you need to do is sit steady in the boat, let us handle this. I ask only that you not cause more waves than you have already. You can still write your editorial, but only enough information to keep the story active and city inspectors on their toes, but citizenry informed.

You keep your editorials animated and lively as possible without stepping over the line until I've collected what evidence we need to crush any illegal activities by those responsible, in court if it comes to that.

After his meeting with Tim Murphy at Loman & Loman, Liam left Tim's office and returned to the newspaper. First thing after returning to his office, he placed a call to Darla Sue.

She told him, "I read your article in the paper yesterday. I was blown away by the way you exposed the city's irregularities as they go about their daily unground business. The only thing I can tell you is, you need to be careful now that you have revealed the underbelly of the city's most powerful. If there is anything I can do to help you, all you need do is ask. I will do what I can. Also, the law firm is at your disposal and will back you in any way possible."

Liam said, "I appreciate what you are doing for me, I owe you big time."

But I have one more question to ask of you, "If you could get some feedback from your firm's lawyers as to what avenue I should follow going forward, I would be forever grateful and even more indebted to you."

No problem. "I'll address that later this afternoon after they return from court, as to their opinion which direction you should pursue with your ongoing issue," Darla Sue responded.

It was turning out to be a difficult position for Liam no matter which direction he decided to go. But with help from the newspaper's law firm and the law firm Darla Sue work, he would have the support need in writing another day, and hopefully exit this catch-22 he was in and put the kibosh to those lacking self-discipline and or self-control in their tactics."

Liam felt good having those in the know watching, and backing him during this confused and chaotic period in his life. Liam finished his day at the newspaper, in an upbeat frame of mind. Knowing he had shaken up the establishment, and ready to continue his crusade no matter the consequences.

Chapter 13

After work that evening, Liam met up with Darla Sue at one of the local restaurants in Jersey City where they had dinner. He explained his situation at the office and the numerous messages received from the general public describing disbelief in the way the elected officials ran local government. He needed to figure out a way in putting more pressure without stepping toes on those individuals ripping-off of the hard-working contractors and violating their workers. It was not right for them to live in fear of reprisals by not abiding by the con games run by city officials.

After dinner Liam drove Darla Sue back to the condo, and after dropping her off, headed home for the evening. Arriving at his apartment, he found someone had tried gaining entry into his unit. He found the door frame and door slightly damaged, but was able in opening the door with his key. Once inside notified the police of the attempted break-in.

After police arrived and did what they could locating anything of substance connecting to the person who tried gaining entry into the apartment. But after an intense investigation of the crime scene, searching for clues, and looking for evidence in the hallway and stair well, found nothing of interest.

After police called it a night and had left the scene; Liam locked the door, ten took a hot shower, and went to bed. Waking up the following morning, he quickly got dressed and ready to head out the door for work when suddenly his phone rang. He answered it on the third ring to find It was Darla Sue calling.

He told her about an attempted break-in and that he had notified the police, but nothing was found. Liam told her, "I'm sure it has to do with the articles I've written and what happened last night will not be the last I hear from them."

After telling Darla Sue of the incident, it was time to head to work. Liam before hanging up said, "I'll talk to you later, then hung up the phone."

As he left the apartment, He ran into the manager of the apartment building in the hallway who stopped him, and told Liam, "I saw someone enter the apartment building earlier in the evening whom I did not recognize. It could have been the individual who tried breaking into your unit.

Lima immediately asked the manager, "Do you remember anything at all about the person? Like how tall, how heavy, was he thin, what type of clothing was he wearing, was he alone or with someone else, did he park a car in front, anything at all?"

The manager thinking back, told Liam, "All I remember is seeing a large scar on the left side of the individuals face along his cheek bone, he was not wearing a cap and noticed his head was clean shaven, and one thing struck me as odd was the tattoo on the very top of his head. It appeared like some kind of symbol; you know, like a German swastika. Other than what I've told you, I don't recall much else. As you know the hall ways at night are not well-lit so I was not able seeing clearly what he was wearing other than it appeared to be dark clothing. We don't need people like that running the streets and terrorizing the neighborhood."

The manager ended the conversation by telling Liam, "I'll have the door to your unit fixed by the time you return home tonight."

Liam thanked the Manager and proceeded outside to his car parked on the street. As he approached his car, noticed someone had tried breaking into his car through the driver's side door. The door had several small scratches around the door lock and handle. It looked as if someone tried jimmying the lock with some kind of device, but luckily for Liam, he was able opening the locked door with a minimum of effort before climbing into the car and driving off.

Arriving at work a little later this morning, Liam notify police and reported the attempted break-in of his car. Police, arriving at his work place later and did what they could locating clues like a finger print. Eventually they were able in locating a partial finger print on the driver's side mirror. If only they could match the partial print through the police's forensic headquarters maybe they could locate the individual and bring him in for questioning for both the earlier break-in attempt of his apartment and now the car.

Detective Paulson told him, "If we learn anything from the print, we'll get back to you." Liam thanked Detective Paulson, and the police department for their help.

As the police investigative group left the newspaper parking lot that morning, heading back to police headquarters to begin their search of the partial finger print lifted from the car's drivers side mirror, and attempted break-in into his unit. Maybe when they finished with the investigation it could tie the two attempted break-in together.

Liam, after a long night and a rather busy morning was able in sitting down at his desk where he began writing another scathing article about his latest run-ins with ruffians and troublemakers responsible for wreaking havoc and taking advantage of locals. This type of behavior was uncalled for and was at the top of Liam's shit list, and at the forefront in his pursuit of justice. More determined than ever putting an end to these atrocities, and exposing the responsible parties at the top.

He vowed to himself not to stop until those in power were brought to justice. The lawlessness of local city workforce and their henchmen had run its course. It was time to end this instability and distraction, and return the city back to its people. Where law and order could once again rein as a viable and capable working force, and without all the drama and violence.

Liam worked the rest of the day studying his notes and making numerous phone calls, verifying sources before completing his newest derisive article and turning it over to the editor-in-chief for his approval. After all was said and done that evening, Liam felt he had his bases covered with information supplied by his CI, Darla Sue, and material from the flood of documents, letters, notes and phone tips received at his office in the last few days. Sure, his editorial had stirred much interest among the populace and more amongst the city fathers.

After finishing his article that evening and presenting it to the editor, and as he leaving, told to have a good evening. Tired, hungry and in a state of great tension, walked out of the newspaper office.

On his way home, decided to lookup his street contact to see if he was aware of any new rumors as to who had been shadowing him the last few of days?

As he drove around the dock area looking for Loui, Liam spotted Loui sitting alone with his legs dangling off the empty dock smoking a cigarette.

Stopping the car beside one of the warehouses, got out of his car and approached Loui who had not heard Liam as he approached. Loui was mumbling to himself about one of his friends who was nearly killed by one of the local thugs for not giving them certain information on one of the delivery companies working at one of the local construction sites.

Liam sat down next to Loui and asked him, "Who was almost killed today?" Loui looked up and saw Liam. His expression was that of a wounded animal, who had just been through enormous a battle. The remorse shown in his face disclosed he was completely defeated and ready to end it all; as if life itself was no longer worth living.

Liam as he sat beside Loui trying to console him, Loui turned to Liam and was crying. Told Liam, "One of my best friends working on the project over on Clinton Street and inexplicably fallen from the fourth floor, landing onto a mass of steel beams being lifted by a crane to the floor above where he had been working. Somehow Kenny fell from the steel beams and landed several floors below on a pile of discarded wood scraps. I talked to one of the workers working on the sixth-floor waiting for a load of concrete told me, he happened to be looking down and saw Kenny leaning out from the building with arms stretched out trying to find something to grab hold of. And noticed at that instance someone's hand quickly disappearing back inside the building as Kenny began falling. I have a feeling someone pushed Kenny. His fall was no accident, someone definitely pushed him over the edge."

Loui learned later his friend was in serious condition at a local hospital and was not expected to survive the night. My friend Kenny Dugan broke his back, his left leg and right arm, plus had several major cuts and contusions covering his body. The doctor who aided in helping repair my friends broken and damaged body told his family, "If he lives through this, it'll be a miracle.

Rumors has it, the newbie Angelo, sent one of his henchmen to the site to put pressure on the foreman (Anthony Iola) and this was his way in getting his attention."

Apparently, the company Anthony Iola worked was behind in their dues owed a certain city inspector who was not a happy camper, not being paid his hush money and contacted Angelo to rectify the problem.

After the alleged accident, Anthony had been contacted and told in no uncertain terms, "This was just a precursor or wake-up call to things you can expect going forward, unless your company pays their debt. That type of accident will continue until your outstanding payments are paid in full."

A reminder just how crude and vicious these groups had become in carrying out their threats.

It was after hearing Loui's story of his friend's accident, that Liam asked, "Is there anything I can do to help you or your friend?"

"No, Loui replied. I've got to handle this my way. I have a friend who I will be meeting later today to see what we can do to get rid of this dirt bag who tried to killed my friend Kenny."

Liam reiterated to Loui, "Don't do anything that would jeopardize you or your friend or his family. Let the legal system do its job, and I'll do what I can to help resolve this ugly matter." "Okay," Liam aske Loui?

"I guess." replied Loui,

"But if I learn who the scum bag is, I may just have to teach him a lesson he'll not soon forget, then I'll contact you or the authorities."

I hope you contact me or the police before you do anything rash.

Liam told Loui, "Yeah you got-ta do what yeah got-ta do, but be careful. If there is anything I can do in the meantime contact me, you've got my number."

With this new information Liam learned from talking to Loui, he would start searching in earnest immediately for the lone individual who's possibly the same person that tried breaking into his unit and car earlier.

After leaving Loui sitting on the dock, got back in his car and drove to the police station where he asked the desk sergeant on duty, "Would it be possible to speak with either Detective Paulson or Detective Callahan?" The desk sergeant picked up the phone sitting on the corner of his desk and dialed Detective Paulson's extension. After several rings hung up and dialed Detective Callahan who picked up the phone after only a couple of rings. The desk sergeant informed Detective Callahan, "There is a Mr. Liam Drake here and would like to speak with you."

"Yes, send him to my office." Liam, was given directions to Detective Callahan's office which was upstairs on the second floor. Thanking the desk sergeant's, found the stairs, walked up to the second floor where he found the detective's door open to his office. Liam started to knock when he heard Detective Callahan's deep voice telling him to come in and have a seat.

After Liam was seated, Detective Callahan asked, "what can I help you with"

"I need your assistance."

"Okay, what is it you need, if I can help, I'd be more than happy to assist."

"I need you to help me locate a mystery man sent by Angelo into the neighborhood over on Clinton Street causing a lot of mayhem at the construction site, and possibly an attempted murderer."

Chapter 14

Detective Callahan was asked by Liam. "Is it possible to run just a description although very sketchy through your data system? I think I may have a lead on who was responsible for trying to break into my unit, and my car? Also, believe this may be the same person who was responsible for the attempted murder of a steel worker at the construction site over on Clinton Street yesterday. He may be the person allegedly responsible for pushing Kenny Dugan off the fourth floor?"

"Yes, that's something we can do. I'd be more than happy to run the description through our files and see if we can come up with someone fitting your description if one exists. Let me get someone in that department to come up and get your information and details you have."

Detective Paulson contacted data control and asked if he could send someone to his office and take a few notes to run through the data base. The data control officer told Detective Paulson, "Yes, I'll send one of my office staff up right away".

It was not long until one of the staff members from data control arrived in Detective Callahan's office, and introduced to Liam. Liam conveyed what information he'd received second hand from Loui that evening on the dock.

Liam also included the information he had previously questioned the building manager of the apartment complex he lived before heading to work that morning, and furnished a few more facts and details about a stranger he had seen earlier in the building.

Before the meeting finished, Liam was told by the staffer from data control unit, "This process will take a while." With bits and pieces of information collected from you, will be interred into our computer system which merges with millions of bits of information stored inside our data base, but other computers throughout the country. After commingling your data, and data stored in other computers around the country. And if enough data is found and corroborated, the profile verified, it will then be downloaded and sent to our office where it we will place it in a folder for pick up. In this case someone from our department will contact Detective Callahan, and he'll in turn contact you.

Liam thanked Detective Callahan and staffer, returning to his office and proceeded to write a report about the attempted murder incident over on Clinton Street. When he finished with the article, he walked over and presented it to the editor-in-chief. The editor-in-chief looked over Liam's latest article, pleased at what he read, told Liam, "I need to find room on the front page for your article. This is hot, should shake-up a lot of higher-ups in the city after reading it in tomorrow's Journal.

Liam left the editor-in-chief's office with a smile as big as Texas on his face. He was finally getting the recognition he so deservedly deserved. It was not every day that a journalist's article was featured on the front page. He could not wait to tell Darla Sue of this latest achievement. He knew with her help and others he would eventually expose the criminal element and deceit going on all over Jersey City and Hoboken communities.

Before leaving work, Liam phoned Darla Sue at her office to ask her if they could meet later that evening and talk about the next course of action should entail dealing with local corruption and exploitation.

She asked Liam, "Yes, why don't you come to the condo around seven, I'll cook dinner, and afterwards, we can go over the information you have and try validating your findings. That way I can take a few notes and relay the facts to certain individuals at the law firm and get a second opinion on the matter; an unbiased, impartial, and free of prejudice."

Liam communicated to Darla Sue, "Their assessment would be beneficial to my aims achieving success in this matter I'm involved. I'm looking forward to a pleasant evening with the smartest and best-looking woman in town. And by the way, I appreciate what you have in mind, see you at seven." With that, Liam hung up the phone and left the office.

Returning to his car, he could not help seeing the scratches below the door handle as he reached down to open the door, and shook his head. *[Why would anyone waste their time trying to gain entry into my car, he asked himself in disbelief?]* I never leave money, important papers, or articles of value worth stealing in my car.

His thought process continued, *[maybe they were trying to gain entry to rig the car to blow-up when I turned on the ignition, maybe damage the braking system, or install some type of tracking device?]* Were they that desperate in putting a stop to his nosing around into the underworld of corrupt activities going on all around the city? Well, who or whatever was behind the attempted break-in of his car and apartment, he was not going to cave-in, not now, not ever?

He again thought to himself, *[I'm in too deep to put this query aside and start over. I'm on a roll and nothing is going to stop me now, come hell or high water.]*

At dinner, he and Darla Sue had a long and honest discussion about what he was trying to accomplish, and how he was going about it. At which Darla Sue exhibited intense interest in every aspect of his explorations, and continuously asked questions about where and how he gathered his material. It was like she knew more that he thought and somehow more informed with certain aspects of the underworld activity, and more aware and convinced she was aware of important aspects of things goings-on around Hoboken, than he was aware of.

He asked her before calling it a night, "How is it that you know so much about the illegal activity around here?"

She explained to him, "Since I work with lawyers all day, I hear bits and pieces of information, and rumors from those I work with and I'm familiar with most cases they are working on. I know or have met some of those corrupt people you refer to during our conversations and you write in your editorials. They, (corrupt politicians and associates) constantly are showing up. Coming in and out of the office on a weekly basis, trying to beat some trumped up charge against them. Trying to have the case against them thrown out of court; They are always testing the waters to see if they can convince one of our attorneys to take over their case from another attorney. You'd be surprised at how much I know about corruption in the county from being around those types on a daily basis."

That's why I told you soon after meeting you, "If I could be of assistance, I would, and do what I could to help stem the tide of abuse and kickbacks by those uncouth individuals tearing the city apart."

Liam responded by telling Darla Sue, "I certainly appreciate what you are doing to help me. I need as much help as I can muster at this time. I'm up to my neck in this mess and it's going to take more than me to finish what I've started." Thank you for believing in me.

"That's why I offered to help, is get you through the maze of confusion and quantifiable data in your notes, and into some semblance of order. It gets confusing but with what I know and the information you've accumulated; we should be able straightening out this web of uncertainty you have into some comprehensive and cohesive story."

This is what I do for a living. I'll be able assisting you through certain aspects of this network of good old boys with minimum interference. Now let's see, "I'm assuming you have your notes handy?

"Yes."

"Okay. Give them to me and I'll look them over and give you my opinion as to which avenue you should take bringing those individuals down."

Liam went back out to his car where he retrieved his brief case, and returned to Darla Sue's unit. Back inside the condo, Liam opened the brief case and took out several notes he previously assembled and handed the notes to Darla Sue.

Sitting next to Liam on the couch, she opened the file and began studying the notes Liam had written. Immediately she recognized almost everyone mentioned in his notes.

Later she told Liam, "Now that I've read over your notes, I have a much better understanding of what the city inspectors are involved in and my recommendation of what you should include in your next editorial. You need write it in a way to get the biggest response from those involved. You need to identify each person individually not by name but reputation and description, their role in corrupt labor practices and fraud. But, make sure your information about each person you write about is correct, direct, straightforward and clear.

Before calling it a night, Liam thanked Darla Sue for her help and legal insight to his multifaceted problems. And explaining in terms of how to go about exposing those involved without causing more difficulty or complications. It was a complex encroachment into the city's management regarding unwelcomed and harmful occurrences by unscrupulous and corrupt city bureaucrats.

Darla Sue had given him insight in approaching his next article concerning bad behavior of a few which resonated throughout all construction sites in the city. If he wrote the editorial right, it would draw attention only to the principals that be. Maybe with gaining attention of the powers that be, their clout and influence within the city would slow down, and fraud and abuse by those with little or no morals or scruples left, and thought only of themselves and what they wanted or needed.

Liam thanked Darla Sue for her help as he left to go home to contemplate his next article. It was not to be an easy task, no matter what he wrote, or how it would be received. But the piece had to be written come hell or highwater. And no better time to start the article than tomorrow morning.

Chapter 15

The following morning, Liam fill with high spirits and self-confidence proceeded to work where he found himself thinking about what Darla Sue and he had discussed the prior evening. It all made sense to him now, and how he would approach his next editorial.

Arriving at work, Liam walked to his desk and would soon start putting his thoughts down on paper, but as he passed by the editor-incharge's cubical, he stopped briefly. He wanted to run his ideal by the editor-in-chief about the article he intended on writing, bounced his idea back and forth, and after several suggestions from the editor-in-chief, Liam brought up the ideal of involving local criminal activities, and how the criminal element had become such a complex matter over a long period of time locally. His superior wanted him to make sure he denoted without going to deeply into detail, those involved. Only that they be mentioned as suspect, in what appeared shady or dishonest arrangements involving several local servicers.

After his visit with the editor-in-chief, Liam left the editors desk and returned to his desk where he began writing a comprehensive and articulate article pertaining to those individuals behaving in such a dishonest and deceitful manor. The article was to be written in such a way, without accusing anyone directly as the one committing the wrongdoings. It was going to be the most difficult article he had ever tried composing. He was not directly accusing anyone specific, but indicating in a roundabout way who it was committing certain atrocities, but somehow implying circumstantially that a crime had been committed. Irrefutably who the alleged assailant was, but yet unnamed.

At the end of the work day, Liam finished his draft and reading it several times, making minor corrections, and when satisfied he had accomplished what he set out to do, was ready to present the article to the editor-in-chief for approval or rejection. Liam, walked briskly over to the editor-in-chiefs desk where he presented him with the final draft and told to wait while the he looked it over. Making sure there was no allegations, slanderous claims or incriminations against anyone by name only suspected.

After reading it thoroughly three times, making minute changes, told Liam, "I'm impressed with the way you went about describing the matter and the way you incorporated certain inuendo's within the article describing the guilty party without accusing anyone directly. *[It was definitely a Pulitzer Prize piece of writing,]* Liam thought to himself.

After all the scrutiny and analyzing, the editor told Liam, "This is the most comprehensive and detailed article you've written since starting to work here at the Jersey Journal. I want to be the first to congratulate you on how important this article will be to this community. And how you've applied yourself so conscientiously to your knowledge of the subject matter, plus the professionalism you've shown in your writing. It definitely comes through in this article." Good job.

Leaving the editor's desk, Liam left the newspaper building, totally pleased with himself for what he accomplished in writing this latest article. He could not wait to see it on the front page of the morning paper. He had had only one other article important enough to make the front page since he began writing for the opinion page. This article was going to be a banner headline, the coup de grace of his years of writing. He could not wait to inform Darla Sue of his latest accomplishment.

Once outside the newspaper building, Liam noticed a lone figure lurking on the opposite street corner watching him as he walked to the parking lot to his car. He did not recognize the individual that he could recalled. As he continued to his car parked on the side of the building, watched as the individual began walking across the street. The individual approached Liam just as he reached his car. Liam turned around before opening the door, and immediately confronted him, asking, "Who are you and what do you want?"

Excuse me but, I need to talk to you.

"I have first-hand information about a big score which is going down this evening or in the very near future. I had to warn you when and if it goes down, things around the city will come to a complete standstill."

This piqued Liam's interest, and invited the stranger to get in the car and he would drive over to a local restaurant, that he was interested in hearing more about this big score.

Upon reaching the restaurant, parked the car along the street and entering the establishment. Liam spotted a table located in the rear, near the back wall. They quickly walked back to the table and sat down. It was a section of the restaurant where they could talk without being interrupted or overheard; their own cozy little corner. The server arrived shortly and said, "Good evening gentlemen, would you like something to drink before ordering?"

Liam asked the stranger if he was thirsty, which he replied, "Yes, I'll have a cup of coffee black."

Liam replied, "Make that two cups of black coffee." The server left and walked back over to the shiny Braun coffee machine where she filled two cups with steaming hot coffee.

As the two sat at the table, the stranger began telling Liam about a conversation he overheard earlier in the day while visiting the mayor's office. He happened to be sitting just outside the mayor's office waiting to be seen; when he heard two rather loud voice inside the mayor's office. Whoever it was with the mayor was shouting about someone at the Jersey Journal writing articles on a daily basis involving the city's fraudulent handling of contracts, and intimidation of local contractors by certain city's employees. The longer I sat there the more they ranted and raved on about this journalist. I've been reading your articles lately about the fraud and mishandling of the city coffers by city officials and managers. After visiting with the mayor and discussing my grievances, I left the mayor's office, and thought I would find you and let you know you are under scrutiny and will be put on notice soon by certain groups of the city's hierarchy. It was you they were discussing, because before they stopped arguing, (one being the mayor) referred to you specifically by name.

Since I'm aware of your articles and reading how you lambasted how the city runs itself, if I were you, I would watch my back. Those in power around the city are fed up with your exposing their mismanagement and misuse of city funds. They're determined to stop this vendetta you have against them by including them in your editorials daily. You should be careful with whom you talk to, and in your travels, keep your eyes and ears open. They have moles throughout the city, they seem to know your whereabouts at all times. It's just a matter of time until they turn on you and teach you a lesson. I could not let this matter fester any longer, I felt it my obligation to tell you personally.

As they finished their third cup of coffee and before leaving, Liam thanked the stranger for the update. Once they got up ready to leave, shook hands and went their separate ways.

On the way back to his car, Liam once again feeling under pressure, kept a sharp lookout for any strange or threating activity. Reaching his car, looked around one more time making sure no one was hiding in the shadows observing him. He opened the door to the car and quickly climbed into the driver's seat, immediately locking the driver's side door before starting the car. He drove cautiously from the curb and when he was on the street and on his way home, constantly checked the rear view and side mirrors for signs of being followed.

Returning home, Liam parked his car on the street in front of the apartment building and made sure his car was locked and secured before continuing inside. Before he entered the apartment complex, he again checked his surroundings, making sure there were no surprises awaiting him. When things appeared to be secure, only then did he proceed inside. Once inside his apartment, first thing he did was call Detective Paulson. He was informed Detective Paulson had finished his shift and was no longer at the station.

Liam left a message with the desk sergeant to have Detective Paulson call him when he arrived at work the following morning; that it was very important. He left his name and phone number for Detective Paulson to call once he arrived to work.

Liam hung up the phone, and immediately dialed Darla Sue's number. Having just arrived home herself a short time before, had begun preparing dinner before relaxing for the evening.

Liam told her about the stranger he met earlier, and overhearing a heated discussion emanating from the mayor's office between the mayor and one of his cronies. It was about someone who worked at the Jersey Journal and writing articles about the fraud and misappropriations of city funds.

Darla Sue was amazed that someone off the street would make up such a tale. She told Liam, "It had to be true and he should take it seriously."

Liam agreed, but explained to Darla Sue, "I don't know how I'm going to go about quelling this latest threat if it is real. Should I try to learn who it is that's going to do me harm or continue writing the articles exposing more? I'm in a quandary as to what my next move should be."

Darla Sue stated to Liam, "Hopefully with Detective Polson's help, and your tenacity, I'm confident a sensible solution to this problem can be put to sleep with reasonable resolve."

Playing the hand, he'd been delt, Liam hope the three of them could come up with a workable strategy on correcting this matter, and he can continue writing his editorials on the misuse and mismanagement of city funds and collecting their personal kickbacks. Time was of the essence and not on his side. This matter had to be nipped in the bud soon as possible before it got completely out of hand.

Chapter 16

Greed, emanating from city administrators, along with many of the governing body controlled in amassing additional funds and kickbacks from contractors were up to their necks stealing funds set aside and used their offices to benefit from their positions. The city coffers, had become a broken piggy bank, with unlimited funds lying around for the taking.

Everyone who worked for the city seemed to have their hands in the cookie jar, and misusing city allocated credit cards and slush funds were used for supporting their lavish life styles which had become routine or expected. Also, someone in the city's aristocratically controlled society was incessantly on some trumped-up mission off on some convention trip using ill-gotten funds, credit cards, or paid by those who were in their debt. Traveling to far off places like Las Vegas, Biloxi Mississippi, on junkets for the weekend. It had become basically a perpetual vacation for several of the high-ups, especially that of city inspectors, and code enforcers, living the good life on the city's dime.

Sporadically, one would hear of consequences from a wife trying to slowing down certain extracurricular activities by their significant other by confronting them. The wives or companions often challenged the veracity of their partner and the sinister activity they were involved in. Occasionally one would meet head-on with their companion or wife who express in no uncertain terms, their pent-up frustrations, telling them, "Either you straighten up, walked the straight and narrow, or I'm going to expose you along with the rest of your group of the illegal activities and how devious and deceitful the assemblage at city hall had become."

That would work for a while, but the money was so obtainable and temptation so great, it was not long before they reverted back to their old habits and once again dipping into whatever fund remained available to abscond from.

On several occasions city fathers had elaborate fund raisers bestowing honor on those taking an early retirement, or departing after finding other fields of endeavors. Most fund raisers were disguised as a special achievement or off the wall awards ceremony trumped up by those in command, and invite several unsuspecting contractors and middlemen under the auspices pertaining to some huge social event. And as a captive audience told near the end of the ceremony, "Since there are those in attendance having been provided special services in the past by certain organizations or special interest group of the city, would be appreciative at the conclusion of the ceremony, you contribute to one of the worthy causes we champion. There are booths set up in the lobby, and we ask the when you leave you visit one of those booths. And that you donate a sizable contribution in helping support one or more of the causes near and dear to our community.

More often than not, funds raised by these get-togethers sponsored by the city were very profitable, and constantly tapped by those in charge of the event. Little if any of the money's collected was ever donated to the association or group linked to the fund.

Occasionally, when the mayor became involved with a larger fundraiser under the auspices of seeking financial support for a certain local institution or an enterprising new company's showing initiative and resourcefulness the mayor was pushing or felt strongly about.

The mayor would announce a special event, inviting the more affluent personalities in the community who donated to any party affiliates involved with whatever fund-raising event for the sole purpose of personal recognition as donating to a good or worthy cause.

Collecting thousands from the naïve groups gathered, and later allocating much of the ill-gotten funds to himself, and co-conspirators inside his private office behind the Gib Door at some later date. The Gib Door, a hidden room located inside the mayor's office with access only by him. The Gib door had been incorporated into the wall covered by pictures and awards. It had been the idea of the mayor at the time the building was constructed and created by the mayor, and totally indiscernible to all who entered the mayor's office.

But over time became the private chamber for the mayor to stash his ill-gotten funds. This practice had been duplicated many times since the first mayor occupied the office. Once the money had been distributed equally among those engaged in the conspiracy, the mayor immediately dismisses the assemblage in order for them to return to their respective offices where almost immediately they begin conjuring up their next deceptive event.

The mayor thought to himself as he divvied out the monies among his cohorts and himself; [*Ah, the mysteries of political power, its influences still live on and flourishes in the bowels of this town. Will the populace never learn?*]

With the city fathers and co-conspirators raping the community at will, made Liam's job more difficult in bringing to justice those involved. He, along with the help of Detective Polson and Darla Sue, was once again ready to roll up their sleeves and tackle what seemed to be an unsurmountable task of bring down those who stood to be accountable. With Detective Polson's CIs on the streets, Darla Sue's information at the law firm on individuals that was public information, and Liam's Moxy and determination, nothing was going to stop him, he had become a force to be reckoned with. His mission was not to be ignored buy those unscrupulous and crooked public officials.

After meeting with Detective Polson and Darla Sue, and amassing substantial material; had enough solid material to begin a daily editorial that would rock the community back on its heels. The newspaper itself backed him one hundred percent in this latest endeavor; of fully uncovering the deep-rooted crime consortium running wild within the bowels of the city.

His next several articles appeared in the opinion section of the Jersey Journal and had caused a flurry of anxiety, stress, panic, and fears among those involved in the underworld activity which violated every written city policy.

Those with the political clout questioned, *[how are we going to cope with this new intrusion into our life of deceit and corruption?]* Now that they had been exposed, it was time for them to answer the age-old question, stay and fight or get the hell out of Dodge. Were they going to counterattack their accusers by any means at their disposal, or run in the opposite direction fleeing the approaching bedlam which lay ahead?

Liam, his latest published articles stirred up such a hornets' nest locally, identifying the hoard of thieves, it was a matter of time until the undesirables and despicable came forward and try to clear their names trying to wash away the stain and stigma attached to them by any means necessary. The front-page articles set the community back on its heels. This had been a wake-up call bringing attention to the covert, secret, cronyism underworld which existed in most local government agencies. It was payback time. Not long after Liam's last article appeared, the phones began ringing off the wall at the Jersey Journal.

Like the old proverb says, "If you can't stand the heat, it's time to get out of the kitchen.". And they were not only coming out of the kitchen but the woodwork, plus every crack and crevice throughout city hall.

Chapter 17

Now, that the tables had been turned, city officials found themselves in term-oil, and participants in the wild corrupt system of government readied themselves for the battle of their lives. There was no turning back as all the safety nets were being dismantled and removed. It was time to contemplate being exposed as a thief and brought to justice; and losing everything they spent years of work honing their lifestyle into a fine work of dishonesty and deception; ripping off those very companies and workers that made their job possible. Those companies were at the very heart of their job they oversaw and worked with on a daily basis, and to run amuck at this juncture of their tenure was indefensible and inexcusable.

Inspectors, overseeing contractors, were to follow strict guidelines accordingly to the plans submitted to their office. Those plans were to ensure the project follow stringent guiding principles set forth in their plans. But the inspectors set aside all guidelines and turned a blind eye at times because of greed. Letting those contractors who paid them hush money slid on shoddy work, and those who refused to go along with the program, were dealt with by shutting downing the site or causing bodily harm to individuals working on site. When a contractor paid hush money or kickback it saved money in the long run, but set themselves up for further retributions from any and all inspectors in the foreseeable future.

If for any reason a contractor or foreman on the job site stopped paying their fair share, the inspector or inspectors working the job site, shut it down until retributions were paid.

After Liam exposed these arrangements, individuals with the most to lose began calling the companies owing them favors for assistance in this latest chaos.

As city officials and hired henchmen began circling the wagons; different groups of local, and state enforcement officers including the local FBI were alerted of the current situation in Jersey City and Hoboken, and were asked for their help in cleaning up the situation.

"It was only a matter of time before city officials and their appointed inspectors found themselves up a shit creek without a paddle," Liam told Darla Sue.

One by one individuals working for the city were summonsed to appear before the local magistrate or were physically rounded-up and brought downtown for questioning. If it was found-out they were involved, they were immediately served with a writ to appear before the magistrate of the courts. And after being released out on bail or by their own recognizance; the first thing the city's upper echelon did was contact Angelo.

Angelo, had become the man of the hour and had been called upon by several city officials out on bond asking him to quell the mounting problem they now faced. It had become an all-out fight between city officials and the city's protectors of justice.

Angelo, hearing of their plight, agreed to gather his small group of henchmen together and stop Liam from further disruption of city administrators. He told those who asked for his assistance, "I will do what has to be done suppressing this volatile state of affairs affecting all of city hall."

Now that that had been established, and Angelo now in charge of taking care of their problems, he had become their super hero, at least that's what they thought.

Liam, after capturing the attention of Angelo who by now had set his sights on Liam and his immediate removal, and in danger. Liam's life hung in the balance being hunted down and wiped-out by

Angelo and his thugs. He needed the assistance from the newspaper, local law enforcement, and FBI more than ever. And any group connected with the justice system throughout the entire state. When contacted most groups were ready and willing to assist with the massive undertaking which lay ahead.

Meanwhile several city workers in the know, quietly turned tail and asked for protection from the city prosecutors. Asking for clemency if they turn state evidence against those they worked for. Even though they were willing to provide evidence against the very agency they were now employed by. Those few employees volunteered to show their allegiance for justice, in betraying those responsible for the debacle. They asked for immunity, but not promised leniency, and were told later, "If you cooperate in this matter, things would go much easier for you going forward, but only if you testify against the establishment.

It was going to be a long and laborious task in rounding up all those responsible for the confusion, uncertainty and turmoil the city officials had created and brought upon themselves.

Liam was up to the challenge as he continued his relentless thrashing of the elected and appointed individuals. The lawlessness in which they took part and instrumental in the way city hall functioned. Activity around Hoboken and Jersey City were at a precipice. Things could not have been more chaotic. Interest inside the local community continued building from articles Liam wrote daily.

Those individuals named and involved in the local corrupt scheme, continued keeping a low profile or stayed out of sight completely. In other situations, some of the employees stopped showing up for work entirely and a couple actually left the state.

It was not long before Liam was being dogged by Angelo's henchmen day and night. No matter where he went, he was followed. Eventually Liam had been provided with an independent security service twentyfour seven by the newspaper. It became a dangerous time in his life, but he had made his bed, and accepted the consequences of his actions.

His extra-circular activities and his social life became nil; a fading memory of bygone days. Darla Sue and Liam conversed on the phone on a daily basis, but no socializing, or meetings in secret, and were not able in eating out during this turbulent and unsettling time. Liam felt alone for the first time in his life, and did not like the feeling.

Determined as he was to finish what he started, and hopefully at the end of this roller coaster ride, it would still include Darla Sue. She was the one he depended on to help him through this maze of madness. She had become his Rock of Gibraltar, his strongest advocate, his champion, and staunchest proponent of his work and at times his mentor. After this latest struggle was over, he hoped to settle down with Darla Sue, but there were still many bridges to cross and in seeing the light at the end of the tunnel, before that could become a reality.

After work one evening as he was being escorted home by one of the independent security drivers, suddenly out of the blue, several shots were fired into the automobile Liam was riding. One of the shots hit the security driver, and he had been wounded severely. One of the bullets fired from the car entered the left side of the vehicle and struck the security driver in the left temple, he later died at the hospital.

During this latest attempt at his life, Liam somehow was able to gain control of the car and made his way a short distance away to a local police annex. Liam after reaching the annex exited the car, with blood splatters on his clothes, hands and face from the fallen security driver, immediately ran inside the annex, disheveled and looking like a mad man surprising the desk sergeant on duty. He not only had blood stains covering most of his body, but his appearance was frightening. As the desk sergeant quickly rose from behind the desk and starting to draw his weapon, recognized Liam was not a threat only confused, and distraught, looked untidy and bloody. Liam, immediately captured the full attention of the desk sergeant. That's when Liam explained to the desk sergeant what had just occurred as he was being driven home.

Liam told the desk sergeant in a loud and demanding voice and no uncertain terms, "Call an ambulance there is an individual outside, inside a parked car who has been shot and severely wounded, he needs immediate attention, and losing large amounts of blood." The desk sergeant immediately picked up the phone on his desk and call for an ambulance.

About that time a couple uniformed officers walking from the back of the annex, when the desk sergeant said to them, "I want you two go outside and check out the car parked in front and do what you can for the individual who's been shot." When the two officers walked outside to look inside of the car, found the security driver laying on the front seat. They did what they could but was limited by knowledge and experience. They were able only keeping vigil and making the driver as comfortable as possible until the ambulance arrived.

Chapter 18

Detective Polson happened to be visiting the police annex, when he heard the commotion in the hallway while talking to another detective, happened to recognized Liam's voice. Immediately rushed into the hallway where he saw the desk sergeant holding Liam. He seemed to be unruly and appeared confused as he tried freeing himself from the desk sergeant's grip. Seeing he was splattered with blood covering him from head to toe, thought he had been attacked or shot.

Detective Paulson upon seeing Liam was taken aback, and rushed to his side asking him, "What the hell happened to you?" And before Liam had a chance to explain his latest run-in with a drive-by shooting; Detective Paulson grabbed hold of Liam's arm escorted him back to one of the empty offices. At this point Liam suddenly recognizing Detective Paulson began calming down. When Detective Paulson seeing Liam was no longer combative, let go of his arm, and took a good looked at Liam making sure he had not been injured during the hail of gunfire earlier.

Checking for any signs of injury and finding none, told Liam, "Sit down and tell me what happened. I want to hear in detail from start to finish."

Liam still shaken, looked up at Detective Paulson and began telling the detective what he could recall prior to the incident. "It happened so fast, but a lot of what occurred is still a blur. All I can tell you is we were about half way to my apartment, and while waiting on a red light, a car, black in color pulled up alongside, and began firing. I did not get a good look at the people inside the car, but believe there were at least three occupants inside the vehicle."

Detective Paulson then ask Liam, "Can you remember the type of car, were the occupants white, brown, black, anything, any hard facts that will help us in the investigation?"

"I believe at least two of the three occupants were white, one darker in color like Latino or Indo-Aryans (India). But I can't be for sure. Like I said, it happened so fast."

"Yes, I understand." Detective Paulson said. But can you remember anything else like the make, model or year of the car?"

Liam regrouped, and said, "Dark in color, maybe a dark blue or black, a two-door sedan if memory serves me correctly. I remember distinctly it had one of those continental kits on the back as it was driving away. That I remember well. I only remember that because I had always wanted a car with a continental kit, thought they were the coolest." "Yes, I concur," responded Detective Paulson.

"Are you aware of other distinguishable things about the car or occupants?"

Liam answered, "No, that's all that comes to mind. Wish I could be more specific, but sure you understand my surprise at the sudden attack."

"Yes, that's understandable. You have been a great help, but if you think of anything else, no matter how insignificant or minor, inform me as soon as possible."

"I will," replied Liam.

Detective called for one of the uniformed officers who happened to be inside the substation to drive Liam home.

Reaching home, the first thing Liam did was remove the bloody clothes he had been wearing, and threw them into the trash, then jumped into the shower. As he tried recalling what he saw once he noticed the car pull alongside and opened fire, it all become a hazy in his mind.

It was beyond his wildest imagination these things really happened, especially to someone like him. He thought, *[These occurrences happened to others, not writers.]* It was to be a struggle for him going forward, again having to look over his shoulder every time he out. This experience would change his life for the foreseeable future, and that he did not appreciate.

After washing the dried blood from his body and hair, Liam stepped from the shower, dried himself then draped the large towel around his body and walked over to the couch. Now seated on the couch, reached over to the end table and picked-up the phone then dialed Darla Sue. When the secretary at the law firm answered, "Good afternoon, you have reached the law office of Dunn and Walker; how may I direct your call?"

"Yes, my name is Liam Drake, I would like to speak with MS Darla Sue Underwood."

"Yes, please hold while I ring her office." It seemed like forever before Darla Sue finally picked up. Quickly realizing it was Liam on the other end and immediately felt the urgency in his voice, asked him, "What's wrong?"

"I'm calling because I need to talk to you after you get off work, if you're not busy this evening?"

"I don't have anything going on this evening, where do you want to meet?"

"At my place," Liam said

"Okay, what time?"

"Around seven if that's convenient?"

"Great, see you at seven."

"I will order in something to eat; I have a lot to tell you, expect a late evening."

Liam stressed strongly to Darla Sue before hanging up, "Please be careful." After hanging up Darla Sue wondered what happened that was so important Liam wanted to meet her at his place, and have food catered, that seemed a bit unusual even for Liam?

His demeaner she felt during their phone conversation had been highly unusual, and whatever it was Liam had on his mind had to be extremely important. This was only the second time she had been invited to his apartment, and at that time was after a scare from Angelo's group.

Liam, after talking to Darla Sue hung the phone up, stood up from up off the couch and returned to the bathroom where he dried his wet hair, shaved, then straightened up the bathroom. All the while thinking to himself, *[I've got to find out who did this act of cowardness against me and the security driver. If only I had been more in tuned to my surroundings, I may have been able to recognize those in the car who were responsible for such an unimaginable, and deplorable act.]*

Since this latest journey Liam had observed several different individuals as they followed him around town, keeping him under tight surveillance. He at least had a good idea who these individuals are, but not the slightest clue about the individuals who shot at him while being driven home that frightful evening.

They must have been from out of town, hired by Angelo, specifically to take him out then disappear. Thinking back while getting dressed, *[those were faces I do not recognize or recall seeing, ever.]* After he finished dressing, went back into the living room, again picking up the phone then called one of the local restaurants in the neighborhood and ordered carryout to be delivery around 7:30 that evening.

Chapter 19

Seven o'clock sharp the intercom inside his unit buzzed. Liam got up from the couch to answer and hearing Darla Sue's voice, immediately buzzed her in. As the door behind her was closing; she momentarily glanced out the corner of her eye and caught a glimpse of someone across the street who appeared to be watching her. She recognizes the individual and thought to herself, *[why was he there, why was he watching me? She turned from the door and entered the apartment building, still wondering why this individual was there observing her?]*

With the door now fully closed and locked, she continued down the hall way to the elevator. Riding the elevator up to floor Liam's unit was on, As the doors opened, she exited the elevator and walked down the hallway to Liam's apartment where she was met by Liam standing in the opened doorway. They briefly embraced before giving each other an air kisses on the cheek. After a brief pause, they looked at each other, then he invited her inside. Entering the apartment, Liam helped remove Darla Sue's wrap, and laid it on the empty chair near the entry door. Then escorted her over to the couch and asked if she would like a drink. "Yes, thank you, a glass of sherry if you have it." She replied politely.

After seated, she looked around observing Liam's well-appointed unit. This being only her second visit, was pleasantly impressed with new decorative items displayed around the living room since her last visit. It was not at all what she envisioned or had expected. For a bachelor such as Liam, he seemed to be more particular than most in the way he lived. This pleased her.

Liam, returned with a glass of sherry for her and a dry gin martini on the rocks for himself. Sitting the two drinks on the coffee table, sat down next to her on the couch and they talked for the next half hour in generalities. Suddenly the intercom buzzed.

He was not surprised when he heard the buzzer, assuming it was the restaurant delivery service. Getting up from the couch, Liam walked over and pushed talk on the box mounted on the wall and said, "Yes."

That's when he heard a voice say, "Delivery." Immediately he pressed the button unlocking the front door's electric locking mechanism, allowing the door to unlock. A couple of minutes go by when there was a tap or gentle knock at the front door. Again, Liam got up from the couch, walking back over to the door and when he opened the door; the first thing he saw was a large caliber gun pointed at him, and told, "Quietly turn around and get back inside."

Liam, let go of the door and turned back around and started walking to where Darla Sue was sitting on the couch and sat down beside her. The gunman quickly closed the door, still pointing the gun at Liam, when he suddenly saw Darla Sue. Immediately recognizing who the gunman was, she said, "Hello, don't I know you?"

The individual told Darla Sue in no uncertain terms, "Shut up and keep quiet," now pointing the weapon at both of them. Soon they heard someone else at the front door. As the second individual opened the unlocked door and entered, Darla Sue recognized the second individual also, but this time said nothing. Both individuals had been clients at one time or other at the law firm where she worked.

The second person entering, told the individual with the gun, "Go stand by the door, if you hear or see anyone in the hallway, let me know immediately." Right boss.

That when the second person approached Liam and told him, "I've been sent to convince you to halt your editorials against the city and certain sections associated with it. That it's in your best interest, if you refrain from such slanderous inuendoes in your articles. And if not, things will not bode well for you in the future."

Looking at Liam, asked him point blank, "Do I make myself clear?" Without further ado, immediately hurried out of the room along with his gun toting sidekick, closing the door; but not before sliding the delivery inside the apartment.

Darla Sue and Liam looked at each other with surprise and shock.

"What just happened," asked Darla Sue, with trepidation in her voice?"

"Guess I've been warned not to continue the series I've been writing. I must have stirred up a hornet's nest. Think I've hit those responsible where it hurts most. Things must be heating up down at city hall and those involved in their shady deals and kickbacks. I think they're worried about potential problems if I keep up the attack on them."

Liam, picked up his martini and took a drink, then asked Darla Sue, "Who were those two, you seemed to know them?"

"Yes, both have been previous clients at the law firm. Both have been in several time recently and both are bad news. The one holding the gun was Zenoah Ricci, known in criminal circles as, Hatchet Man. He was released only a short time ago from prison and currently on parole. He's been in the office within the past few weeks asking help from the firm about getting some kind of compensation from the state after being accused falsely of a crime he supposedly did not commit.

The second man is a mob hitman from New York, Jacopo Gallo, and goes by the street name of (Jonesy). He too has visited the office just this last week, trying to get someone to represent him on a felonious crime he'd been accused of in Hoboken. Both cases are non-starters, both were caught red handed, and authorities have solid cases against both.

Liam looked over at Darla Sue and asked, "What do you think I should do about informing the authorities of what happened tonight?"

"I think you need to inform Detective Polson, but if I were you, I would not consider pressing charges at this time. Maybe Detective Polson and Detective Callahan can keep both those thugs under surveillance until this latest turmoil you've caused blows over. Pressing charges at this time would only complicate matters and your life even more; it's not worth the time and effort bringing more confusion and carnage into the mix. The law is too slow, it takes forever filing charges, especially one this complicated and challenging.

With the means and support by those individuals named in a lawsuit are more likely than not able in delaying the charges indefinitely with the right lawyers. There's too much money backing them. They'll keep buying time for themselves or until they're caught doing something else or be neutralized in the meantime.

After talking at length about the incident, and other matters of importance which came up during their evaluation of the situation Liam found himself, called it a night.

Ending on that note, Liam told Darla Sue he would feel better if he escorted her home. Without objections she agreed.

Reaching Darla Sue's condo, Liam walked her to the front entrance and followed her inside, where he gave her a huge hug before calling the elevator.

Liam told her, "If you have any problems, any problems at all, call me." At which she acknowledged. She turned facing the elevator and pushed the call button. The elevator doors opened immediately. She entered, turned around as the doors were closing; Liam quickly told her good night, turned and headed back to the front entrance of the building and to his car parked along the curbing directly in front of the condo.

The following day Liam called Detective Paulson, and briefed him about the prior evening and what happened. Detective Paulson said, "I'll put a couple of my best undercover men on the two individuals you've identified as the perpetrators, and if they even as much spit on the sidewalk, I'll have them arrested, and not to worry. I have yours and Darla Sue's back." Liam thanked Detective Paulson. Hung up the phone and left his apartment heading off to work.

That morning he wrote another contemptuous article about crime and corruption carried out by certain inspectors and unscrupulous individuals.

Again, the article Liam wrote sent shock waves through the community. The phones at the newspaper rang off the hook once again, with calls asking why this type of activity was allowed and continue to proliferate? Questions, lots of questions, but no answers.

That afternoon the foreman at the building site over on Clinton Street called the Jersey Journal and asked to speak with Liam. When Liam picked up the phone, Anthony Iola quickly explained to him, "I've heard through the grapevine, one of my construction crews was threatened earlier and has not shown up at the work site this morning. I'm worried more delays are in the offing if you do not ease up on your editorials.

Liam explained the best he could to Anthony Iola, "The only way we are going to stop this type of abuse happening to you and others in the building trades is by putting more pressure on those involved. I know it's not a good time for you and your workers, purveyors and such, but hang in there a little while longer with me. Thanks for calling, I'll have Detective Paulson look into it. If I find out anything, I'll call you back." Then hung up the phone.

After the phone conversation with Anthony Iola, and learning the situation Anthony found himself tangled in, Liam immediately called Detective Paulson.

After Liam talked to Detective Paulson, Detective Paulson called the local sheriff and FBI informing them of the explosive situation on Clinton Street, and requesting help in squashing the unrest before it escalated into a more volatile situation.

After several local law enforcement agencies had been informed as to the situation intensifying in and around Hoboken, immediately began circling their wagons. It was not long before a skirmish broke out near the building site among a small mob of thugs and workers. Luckily for Anthony Iola, law enforcement arrived on scene in time to intervene before anyone was seriously hurt.

Several mob affiliates were arrested that afternoon for trespassing and hauled off to jail only to be bonded out a short time later, released and back on the streets within hours.

Later that night, several individuals (presumably one of those individuals who had been arrested earlier), were sighted in and around the building site wreaking havoc on machinery and materials around the construction location. Someone living nearby reported hearing and seeing the mayhem to the local police. After police arrived, and saw the destruction and damage, immediately informed Anthony Iola.

But, by then those responsible for the damage to the building materials and machinery had fled the scene prior to the arrival of local police. Finding no one on site, police had no idea who the perpetrators were. Hopefully with the help of canvasing of the neighborhood and collecting information and what evidence they find will eventually learn who was responsible, and face justice.

However, this type of investigation takes time, but sooner or later those responsible would be brought to justice. It's just a matter of time.

In the meantime, Liam kept writing his editorials and kept the pressure on those inside city hall involved in their fraudulent and deceitful activities. Liam had become a thorn in their side and was under the microscope by a small number of despicable, and contemptible city workers plus local mob bosses such as Angelo. It had become a matter of impartiality or fairness with Liam, and he would not stop until those persons causing such disorder and chaos were brought to justice. It was game on.

Chapter 20

As time passed, the episodes of criminal behavior sanctioned by local city employees and mob bosses continued, but at a slower pace. Detective Paulson and Detective Callahan pursued each incident with forcefulness and vigor. Like Liam, neither Detective Paulson nor Detective Callahan was easing up or slowing down with their investigation. Both detectives were determined to find and charge those responsible for corrupt labor practices and put them away.

Detective Paulson one morning had been notified of the arrest of Jacopo Gallo (Jonesy's), who was picked up off the street for a minor infraction. Jonesy was already under the microscope at the time and believed to be responsible for part or all of the destruction at the site over on Clinton.

With Jonesy now in custody, it was time for Detective Paulson and Detective Callahan to take a close look at his rap sheet. As they looked it over, could not believe their eyes or luck. Jonesy's rap sheet listed several outstanding warrants for not only minor but major violations. His arrest was icing on the cake.

Detective Paulson sent one of the uniformed officers to Jonesy's isolation cell, and brought him to one of the interrogation rooms inside the building to ponder new charges. Jonesy, was left alone for a considerable length of time to reflect back on the new charges were being filed against him.

Once Detective Paulson and Detective Callahan finished reading over Jonesy's rap sheet, had a much clearer understanding of the many previously charges against him and what it meant if Jonesy would cooperate by helping them with get to the bottom of multifaceted problems the city and police force faced.

An hour later, the two detectives arrived at the small room where Jonesy was sitting. As they entered the interrogation room, Jonesy was sitting in a chair with his head resting on top of his arms on top of the table pondering his fate. Once Jonesy heard the detectives entering, instantly jerked his head up. Detective Paulson and Detective Callahan continued over to where Jonesy sat handcuffed to the floor by a long chain. He looked ill at ease as he suspiciously watched the two detectives enter.

With several files in hand and coffee in tow, the detectives walked over to the table and sitting their coffee, along with their files on the table and sat down. Immediately opened a couple of the files briefly, taking one last look before starting their interview.

Jonesy, now with beads of perspiration starting to pop out of his wrinkled forehead, gave the impression he was at his wits end at being subjected to such annoyance.

Detective Callahan looked over at Jonesy and asked him, "Do you know why you are here?"

Jonesy replied, "No, but I'm sure you are going to enlighten me sooner or later."

That's when Detective Paulson looked up at Jonesy and informed him of his rights, then asked, "Do you understand those rights I've just told you?"

"Yeah, but don't know what I've done to deserve this harassment."

Well, Detective Callahan said, "Be patient; you will be enlightened I'm sure by the time we're done."

Detective Paulson and Detective Callahan had numerous questions for Jonesy, not only about him and his group visiting the construction site over on Clinton Street where they had previously caused considerable damage, but the numerous outstanding warrants found in his personal file.

Detective Paulson was first to speak. Looking Jonesy straight in the eye, Detective Paulson told him in no uncertain terms, "You know we've been looking for you and your cohorts concerning the havoc and destruction you caused on at the construction site on Clinton. If you don't want to be held singularly responsible for all the chaos and damage, you can help yourself by divulging the name or names behind the scenes orchestrating the mayhem. If you help us expose those you work for, you can expect some type of leniency by the court. I'm only going to give you that proposition one time and one time only. If you cooperate, I'll personally speak to the judge; if not, you're on your own. Have I made myself clear?"

Jonesy kept looking over at Detective Paulson and Detective Callahan as he carefully considered the proposal Detective Paulson offered, and possible ramifications of his situation if he did not take Detective Paulson's offer. After a period of time contemplating his dire situation at present, Jonesy finally agreed to Detective Paulson's proposition.

If he delivered the names, dates, and places as promised, Detective Paulson and Detective Callahan knew the information provided by Jonesy would help in breaking several incomplete and unsolved cases wide open. Those responsible for the mayhem and havoc throughout the city, could at last be rounded up, charged, and if found guilty, put away for a long, long time. But it depended on Jonesy and whether he was able to delivered.

They recorded the information provided by Jonesy and also entered into the police data base, to be available to anyone needing information, especially those with connections to the case. It was time to get this show on the road once again.

Detective Paulson and Detective Callahan wasted no time launching a new and expanded investigation of those names Jonesy provided. It had been a treasure trove of names and certain critical evidence unknown previously against top city officials, as well as certain individuals, groups or organizations dealing in crime, whose job it was to carry out the objectives requested by certain city administrators and building inspectors. This work by outside groups kept the city officials out of the lime light, but Jonesy had brought all that to the forefront. With his identifying names, dates and places cleared up a lot of unknowns and confusion. And directly leading them to the chain of command of several different groups and organizations.

After Liam had been informed about Detective Paulson and Callahan's investigation of Jonesy, he immediately drove down to the local police station to learn what he could about this latest informal inquiry of Jonesy.

Arriving at the police station, Liam parked his car in the parking facility and hastily proceeded inside. Approaching the desk sergeants' desk, asked, "Would it be possible to speak with Detective Paulson?"

The desk sergeant called Detective Paulson and informed him, "A reporter from the Jersey Journal, a Mr. Liam Drake was there and wished to speak with him." Detective Paulson told the desk sergeant, "Yes, send him in."

The desk sergeant informed Liam that Detective Paulson would see him. Liam immediately turned toward the hallway leading back to Detective Paulson's office.

Reaching Detective Paulson's office, Liam knocked on the closed door and was told, "Come in." Liam entered and was greeted by Detective Paulson and told to take a seat.

He found both Detectives Paulson and Callahan busily reading over several files.

Liam found a chair nearby and sat down. Detective Paulson asked, "What can we do for you today?"

Liam, replied, "I'm here to find out what Jacopo Gallo (Jonesy) told you during your questioning of him and his association with the underworld organizations."

Detective Paulson looked at Liam and raised a quizzical eyebrow. "Jonesy? Whatever makes you think we talked to Jonesy?"

Liam replied, "I just heard by way of the grapevine about an hour ago that you interrogated this Jonesy; I need whatever information I can get and include it in my next article."

Detective Paulson looked at Liam placatingly and remarked, "Okay, we did talk to Jonesy. You know full well we cannot divulge the results of an ongoing investigation.

However, because of your interest and assistance with this case, can only promise you, when we can an exclusive before we go public."

Liam started to object, but Detective Paulson raised his hand and said, "That's all I can do for you at this point."

Liam was having a hard time controlling his emotions, but had no choice, but accept the offer of an exclusive later.

Liam then asked, "Can I use the information I heard earlier in my next editorial?"

Detective Paulson told Liam, "No. I prefer you wait until we have more creditable information, as I just said, you will be the first to know. Give us a few days to check out our information and we'll get back with you. In the mean time I can tell you, "You can use the information about his arrest and about all the outstanding warrants, but nothing else. Do I make myself clear?"

"Perfectly," Liam responded.

Liam left Detective's Paulson's office knowing Jonesy had been arrested and those he works for would soon be in custody along with others from the city's upper echelon within the city's employment. It was a start; Liam would have to wait to see what develops going forward. But, with limited information from the two detectives, he had to sit steady in the boat until more information developments in this case came his way.

Back at his office, he began his next day's editorial writing about Jacopo Gallo, known as "Jonesy" arrested on a minor offense.

After the arrest of Jonesy, Liam thought, *[Detectives Paulson and Callahan would be delving into his arrest record and more than not, find more outstanding warrants.]* Currently Jonesy was being held without bail in jail, awaiting formal charges of more wrongdoings and possible indictments for conspiracy. With his arrest, hopefully there should be less crime around construction sites, at least for the moment.

He had been instrumental in causing destruction and disorder on several sites in the past and yet to be held accountable. Maybe with his latest apprehension, Mr. Jacopo Gallo (Jonesy,) will finally be brought to justice and the mayhem he has been involved will cease.

After writing the editorial and submitting it to the editor for his approval, the editor-in-chief made a couple corrections; then told him, "It's good to go." It was going to be published in the next day Jersey Journal, again on the lower left-hand column of the front page.

Returning to his office, he dialed Darla Sue to give her an update on his latest visit with Detective Paulson and Callahan. After answering her phone, Liam told her about this Jonesy's arrest, and she too became delighted at hearing Liam's good news. It meant they could again move freely around town without having to look over their shoulders constantly to see if anyone was following.

With Jonesy's incarceration, Liam was still hesitant in taking Darla Sue out to dinner. It was possible someone had already replaced Jonesy and already following Liam. But that was the least of his worries as he continued putting the pressure on city administrators and local sleaze bags with his scathing articles. Liam could only play it by ear if deciding to go out to dinner or other venue.

Chapter 21

Several days had passed as Liam kept pressure with his editorials concerning the city's involvement with fraudulent double dealings and or trickery relating to the way they conducted business.

Time was money to those working in the permitting departments. It was in their best interest to keep the pressure on companies who refused to comply to their demands, found themselves shut down for the smallest infraction. If nonpayment remained an issue the companies or sub-contractors received a wakeup call by some notorious brute hired to go to the site and rough up workers or destroy construction property. Which cost the companies more time and money, but also displeased employees. More often than not a company or sub-contractor simply complied.

Detectives Paulson and Callahan, working feverishly behind the scenes, were able in getting a handle on each situation encountered quickly. They began visiting the last known addresses of individuals and hangouts they were known to frequent. Methodically, one by one rounded up the individuals listed in their files and presumably responsible for carrying out unrest and hampering construction in and around the Jersey City and Hoboken metropolitan areas. As individuals were removed from the streets, it was not long before things started returning to some semblance of order.

As persons of interest were arrested and booked, it was Detective Paulson and Callahan job also to interrogate those in custody. It was not long until varied stories began developing and showed just how large the problem really was. It was diverse, larger and wider spread than anyone previously imagined. It encompassed a variety of parties raping and pillaging construction companies and sub-contractors with what seemed to be absolute immunity.

Everyone in authority throughout the city's administration seemed to have their hands in the till, taking advantage of the lucrative circumstance they found themselves.

Construction companies', sub-contractors and their employees continued working and carrying out their daily responsibilities, but were no match for the ruthless inspectors and individuals assigned to monitor them. If companies or sub-contractors, on the job did not conform to certain demands, the project was written up, forced to comply, or closed down.

The violence and intimidation for political gains at most of the sites had to come to a screeching halt, as those responsible for the unrest were removed from the streets. Liam, Darla Sue, and Detectives Paulson and Callahan, made it their mission to put an end to the illegal activities post haste by any means necessary, but within the law.

Once the word was out, an all-out effort to bring those responsible for the injustice, and illegal activities be stopped almost immediately. Hoboken and Jersey City became isolated cases as damage to construction sites and intimidation stopped.

Everything around the construction sites returned to normal quickly, as troublemakers were picked up, detained or headed out of town. Those individuals rounded up were brought to police headquarters where they were read their Maranda rights, booked on whatever charges they could link them with, then placed in jail while others cooperated and promised some sort of leniency. Those promised leniency sang like song birds.

As the list against those with authority grew, so did the charges. Not only were inspectors and service personnel of waste management companies, and contractors suspected of engaging in illegal activities, they were thought to be co-conspirators working in conjunction with city officials and inspectors. It was just one big happy family of thieves.

Once Detectives Paulson and Callahan finished their investigation, interrogations and research, was able in handing their results over to the city prosecutor's office. Once that was accomplished, all they could do was sit back and wait until the prosecuting attorneys filed the motions with the court.

Meanwhile, Liam kept the editorials coming and the pressure on those groups responsible.

With Darla Sue's help, information associated with persons of interest who were clients of the law office was being extracted as Information was amassed by Darla Sue from many articles previously written or of a contingent nature, but nothing considered privileged information was removed or used. Public information kept at the law firm was used for reference to someone or of interest. With the help of the two detectives, Liam, and Darla Sue working in tandem, had pinned their hopes towards achieving the same end results as they fostered greater collaboration from their combined efforts.

The journey they were on provided an understanding of the obstacles each faced daily. But, even with all the information at their disposable, they were still a long way from the finish line. It was not over by any stretch of one's imagination. But everyone involved was breathing a little easier once certain obstacles were removed and the wheels of the justice system began its long arduous journey.

Chapter 22

Since prosecutors now had possession of the information Detectives Paulson and Callahan submitted. It became their job to assemble the information into a cohesive way by connecting different aspects of the information linking them together in a way as to make the data definitive, and dotting all the I's and crossing all the Ts in a systematic manner before presenting the case to the court. This was not an easy task since numerous city personnel were involved, from the local mayor, his appointed city officials, individuals hired for top management, and inspectors. This was going to be the trial of all trials in Jersey City and Hoboken if and when it went to trial. It would attract national attention eventually and prosecutors had to get it right before proceeding.

Detectives Paulson and Callahan now turned their attention to the backlog of paperwork on unresolved cases which had accumulated while focused on the corrupt labor practices of the city fathers. The caseload they faced was more daunting than ever. But with their undivided attention to the massive amount of paperwork to be addressed, they should be able to clear it in a timely manner. Then, they could return to their daily routine of interviewing individuals brought in and or arrested with vital information concerning certain state of affairs only they knew or possessed.

Meanwhile, Liam and Darla Sue continued working their respective jobs. They to faced a backlog of paperwork, awaiting them. But was nothing compared to the amount of work previously handled. Having extra time on their hands, they could now concentrate on the aspects of their lives.

Once again, they began meeting a couple times a week after work for dinner. They still were not comfortable in public, but unwilling to become prisoners in their own homes. Both looked forward to the day they could move around town and not feel as if they had a target painted on their backs or look over their shoulders to see if they were being shadowed.

Liam anxiously awaiting to be up dated about when the court and attorneys were to begin jury selection. He knew until then he was still in a lot of danger from retribution by those he helped expose.

The longer it took selecting a jury and getting court proceedings underway, the longer Liam's and Darla Sue's lives remain in peril. Once the trial began, with any luck, it would take attention from them and place it on the accused, making them the main focus.

A month later, a trial date had been set, and the pressure on Liam and Darla Sue was lessened. They celebrated the occasion by going to one of their favorite haunts for an early dinner.

The first day of trial Liam sat in the courtroom along with Detective Paulson and Callahan and several council members from city hall. You could feel the tension inside the courtroom as Judge Henry Goodfellow arrived to begin proceedings.

After Judge Goodfellow was seated, he explained to not only the jury, but those in attendance. "I will not put up with any shenanigans from either the attorneys or those in the audience. It's my courtroom and I intend to run it accordingly."

The attorneys were warned separately. "I will not tolerate any devious maneuvering by either defense or prosecution attorneys during the trial, understood?"

After his announcement, it seemed everyone understood his message loud and clear.

Judge Goodfellow was known as a fair but a no-nonsense judge and did not permit irrational or underhanded conduct in his courtroom by either attorney.

The jury pool was led into the courtroom soon after his opening remarks and took their seats. The first order of business was for the judge to explain the process of selecting a jury and alternates. The process he referred to *voir dire*.

After updating the jury pool, and how the trial was to be conducted and what he expected, the judge asked point blank, "Do you understand you are here to determine the innocence or guilt of the parties brought before this court, and your verdicts will determine the fate of each accused and outcome of this trial." Then the judge explained what he expected of the jury during the trial.

Once the jury had been selected, the judge turned his attention to the prosecuting attorney, and asked, "Are you ready to proceed with your opening statement?"

The prosecutor answered, "Yes, we are your honor."

"Please approach the podium," said the judge.

"Yes, your honor."

The prosecuting attorney, Max Radcliff, stood and approached the podium, as he did, a muted sound could be heard reverberating from the gallery.

Judge Goodfellow quickly picked up his gavel, banging it on the round disk sitting on his desk and declared, "I will not tolerate this type of behavior in my courtroom. The next time I hear such an outburst, I will clear the gallery, do I make myself clear? Continue with your opening statement, Attorney Radcliff."

Max Radcliff continued to make his way up to the podium. Upon reaching the small podium, placing his notes atop the pedestal, looking over at the jury then at his notes, he began with his opening remarks, "Members of the jury, I am here to give you the alarming and chilling background of criminal activity and behavior not only of your elected officials who now are on trial for a multitude of charges of violence and fraudulent practices encouraged through their inappropriate actions while in office. Not only using their position for self-gratification, but for their own selfish financial gain. It has become a governmental debacle that needs halted before it becomes a physical assault on the community and you the people.

Hopefully by the time I'm finish with my assessment of the situation before the city, I hope to have given you an in-depth and accurate understanding as to what a difficult and comprehensive understanding of what we are up against by the accused and their involvement."

As prosecutor Radcliff approached the end of his opening remarks, told the jury, "You the jury must do you part by devoting your full attention listening to both the prosecutors and defense's arguments. And especially the testimony of each witness. Giving both sides equal opportunity as they present their case and not to draw any opinions, assumptions or conclusions of guilt or innocents until you've heard the relevant facts and complete circumstances surrounding this case. Thank you." Mr. Radcliff closed his file and proceeded back to the prosecutors table and sat down.

Thanking Mr. Radcliff, the judge looked over at the defense table and asked Attorney Daniel Brubaker, "Is the defense ready to present their opening remarks?"

"Yes, your honor." The judge told Attorney Daniel Brubaker, "You may proceed."

Mr. Brubaker rose from his chair slowly walked over to the podium as he continually scanned his notes. Upon reaching the podium, carefully laid his notes down on the podium, then turned his full attention to the jury. "I'm here to convince you [the jury] the innocence of my clients on trumped-up charges brought against them by the prosecutor office. It is my obligation and civic duty in bringing out the truth and innocence's of my clients, who've been accused of utterly odious crimes against the city. I want to thank you for your attention and obligations in this case and allowing me to present to you [the jury], the real truth in this case." Thank you.

He delivers a breathless and effortless spiel, promoting the innocence of his clients for the next hour. Intended as a means of influencing the jury in finding his client innocent of all charges.

Attorney Brubaker was especially eloquent and skilled orator, as the prosecution quickly learned. By the time he finished his opening remarks, the jury was memorized by his articulate and persuasive way he presented his remarks. Returning to the defense table, attorney Brubaker sat down and rejoined his staff.

Judge Goodfellow, after listening to both attorneys opening statements, told the jury and attorneys, "I'll be pausing this morning session as we adjourn now for lunch.

With opening statements out of the way, trial had officially begun. It was going to be a long and trying time not only for the jury, but everyone involved with the trial.

After lunch, the judge returned from his chambers, once again taking his seat behind the bench and begin the afternoon session by looking over at the attorneys, asking each, "Is there anything either side would like to enlighten us on before we begin the afternoon proceedings?" Both sides responded by answering no.

The judge replied, "Then I guess we are ready for the next phase of the trial, that of direct examination?"

Both sides remained standing and answered in the affirmative. With that, Judge Goodfellow told attorney Radcliff, "You may begin by calling your first witness."

Attorney Radcliff voiced, "Thank you your honor. I wish to call my first witness, Mr. Anthony Iola."

Mr. Anthony Iola was brought into the court room and escorted through the court room to the witness box, where he was told to raise his right hand and repeat, "I solemnly swear to tell the truth the whole truth and nothing but the truth so help me God. After being sworn in, at the same time Attorney Radcliff was approaching the podium looked up at the judge and then Mr. Anthony Iola.

The judge looked over at Mr. Iola, and told him "You may be seated." With that, the trial was officially underway.

Attorney Radcliff, facing his first witness started by saying, "Good afternoon Mr. Iola."

Mr. Iola answering, "Good afternoon, sir."

Anthony Iola as he sat in the witness's box appeared nervous as he waited for the volley of questions he was about to be asked.

Attorney Radcliff began his questioning of Mr. Iola by asking him several relevant questions about certain matters only he knew and was relevant to the case.

Then asked by Attorney Ratcliff, "Would you please explained to the court the ongoing disruptions at the job site you've work during the past several months?"

Anthony Iola began by giving a vivid description of strong-arm tactics and harassment he and other employees encountered on a daily and weekly bases at the job site. The company Mr. Iola worked for had been threatened several times not only by city inspectors and their hired outsiders forcing unfair, deceptive and abusive acts and practices which Mr. Iola could described only as, out and out blackmail. Causing his company significant financial obligations, they were forced into paying. Along with several workers who had been injured because of noncompliance in certain incidents. The very sole foundation of the legal, social and ethical principles of entitlements they were owed by city overseers had been undermined by their greed for power and wealth.

After several hours of testimony, Mr. Radcliff told the judge, "I have no further questions for Mr. Iola your honor."

Since it was late afternoon, Judge Goodfellow looked over at Mr. Iola and said, "You may step down."

The judge asked both the attorneys, "Do you have any other significance or vital information relevant to this case that the court should be aware or informed of before I adjourn court for the day?"

Neither the defense nor prosecuting attorneys informed the judge they had nothing new to add at this time, court was adjourned until the following day at 9:00 am.

The next morning as court resumed, judge Goodfellow asked defense Attorney Brubeck "Is the defense ready to begin their cross examination of Mr. Iola?

"Yes, your honor the defense is ready."

"Mr. Iola would you take the stand, you've already been sworn in. Mr. Iola once again took the witness stand.

After Mr. Iola was seated, the judge again turned his attention to defense attorney Brubaker, "You may begin your cross exanimation of the witness?"

Attorney Brubaker answered with a notable and impressive, "Yes, thank you your honor."

Attorney Brubaker approached the witness stand and as he did, quickly looked in the direction of the jury with an immense smile as if to say, "I acknowledged your presence." Attorney Brubaker was a crafty orator and impressively smooth-talking attorney. Had been hired by some of the wealthiest clients in the country accused of some of the most serious and heinous crimes against their fellow man. Many charged with murder, extortion, kidnapping, any and all types of grave crimes against humanity?

And those accused of the same types of crimes locally, spared no expense in hiring the best defense money could buy.

Once Attorney Brubaker reached the witness stand, he immediately turned his attention to Mr. Iola and said, "Good morning Mr. Iola." Anthony Iola nodded his head, but did not return the salutation.

This was the beginning of a battle between a formidable adversary, and novice opponent. Once the volley of questions began, the skirmish continued all morning until the judge decided to stop the exchange and called time out for lunch.

With neither party giving an inch, the exchange hinged on one unanswered question, "Who in city hall was the ranking culprit controlling the biggest share of the violence and mayhem throughout the metropolitan area?"

This was the question Anthony Iola's attorney was waiting on, but Attorney Radcliff was too smart to open up pandoras box. He knew if he exposed his client at this early date the prosecuting attorney would be able breaking the case wide open, leaving only the minor players, the outside hired thugs and city building inspectors alone to drown in their own clumsy and inept incompetency. Attorney Brubeck was not about to jeopardize his reputation by losing this case on some avoidable slip of the tongue or minor technicality. The case was too important and still far from over to expose this silent client who hired him and had giving financial support to this charade.

Anthony Iola, Darla Sue, Detectives Paulson and Callahan all knew who this mystery person behind this sham was, but his identity could not be brought into evidence unless released by the defense team since it had not been included in Attorney Brubaker's original court brief.

That was not happening unless Attorney Brubaker was backed into a corner where he became duly bound and legally obliged in releasing his client's name. Attorney Brubaker had to be careful not to overstep his bounds or veer off course this early in the game. The case was too high profile an event to change direction suddenly in mid-stream. After vacillating a few moments in front of Anthony Iola, wondering what to do next, contemplating on how to get back on track, but this wavering was not something he was accustom to, and was taking its toll on the infamous Attorney Brubeck. But soon after, Attorney Brubeck regrouped and used his self-discipline to control his ability in overcoming the temptation of the moment. He was not about to give up his ace in the hole not now not ever. He had too strong a willpower and self-control to give away his hole card so early in the trial.

The judge hearing several hours of Anthony Iola's testimony decided to shelve court proceedings until the following day. It had been a long day for everyone involved, especially the jury.

The judge informed the jury, attorneys and gallery, "I'm going to stop court proceedings at this time, it's been a long day for the jury, and Mr. Iola. Court will convene again at 9:00 a.m. sharp tomorrow morning. Everyone, have a good evening." At this time the judge rose from his seat and left the court room.

Once the court room was cleared, Anthony Iola approached his attorney and asked, "How much longer do I have to be on the witness stand?"

Attorney Radcliff said, "When the defense attorney finishes his questioning of you and is satisfied, he has done all he could do to cloud the issue and confound the jury. Only then will you be allowed to step down. It could take a few minutes or hours tomorrow, depending on if the defense is gratified, they've made their point. The defense attorney will stop when he feels he has done all the damage he could to you and your testimony."

The following morning Anthony Iola once again took the stand. When Attorney Brubaker approached the witness stand, he told Judge Goodfellow, "I have only a couple of questions I wish to ask the witness at this time. It concerns a couple of issues with the witness's testimony yesterday afternoon which I've vacillated over after hearing his damming assertion of my client.

After presenting the questions to Anthony, and received an answer to each of his question, Attorney Brubaker told the judge, "I have no further questions for the witness your honor at this time. The judge looked over at Anthony and said, "The witness is excused, but do not leave town, you may be asked to return and testify at a later date.

Chapter 23

As the trial continued, for the next couple of weeks, it was going smoothly for the prosecution, when suddenly it hit a snag. Angelo, the mob boss who followed Doc as the go-to person in charge, had been scheduled to testify for the prosecution, was informed earlier, had been found murdered the day before he was to make his appearance to testify in court.

The prosecuting Attorney Radcliff, asked the judge for a delay in the proceedings in order for him to prepare additional witnesses because of losing one his main witnesses.

The judge took it under advisement and permit a continuance in the trial granting additional time to the prosecution. This had been a severe blow for the Attorney Radcliff, but circumstances such as this happens but not often.

Angelo's death threw the prosecution's case into chaos as well as the legality of the system by Attorney Radcliff's inability in presenting his client's evidence and legal argument to the court. Especially a highprofile case as this.

When unavoidable situations like this emerged, meant only one thing, Attorneys such as Max Radcliff and his staff had to regroup quickly, circling their wagons in order to locate others in filling the void left vacant by Angelo. This would not be easy since some of those accused or suspected had left town or gone underground.

Angelo, assured Attorney Radcliff he would cooperate fully if granted complete immunity from prosecution. He was the only one with first-hand knowledge of how the city's politicians worked with the likes of him, and how the city's higher-ups ran their con or rip-off tactics against contractors working within the boundaries of city requirements.

Angelo, had been their secret bomb shell, their ace in the hole. With such a huge voided now in Attorney's Radcliff's case, it was essential he and his team locate someone as well-versed or informed as Angelo in these matters. Angelo had been the pivotal factor in Attorney's Radcliff's case. Since Angelo was no longer available; the outcome of the case was now in peril. The prosecution had to start from scratch in finding a credible witness willing to sell his soul for total absolution by testifying against the defense. A tall order in any sense of the word.

Attorney Radcliff, would be given ample time by the Judge Goodfellow, un reorganizing his priorities and locate a new reliable witness. Anyone Attorney Radcliff found at this late date wondered to himself, *[Would they be as reliable or stalwartly as Angelo?]* Attorney Radcliff had no choice, since coming under such pressure be able in finding a credible and reliable witness like Angelo? One who could validate all the evidence or pertinent actualities in the case. It was a long shot, but with Angelo out of the picture, Attorney Radcliff had no other choice if the prosecution was to stay the course in the case.

After the judge recessed court for an unspecified period of time; Attorney Radcliff's first agenda was quickly consolidated his team into pairs, and going through the names and addresses of those acknowledged to have had some part or ties to the case in question. If they were able in locating an individual who had admissible information, that person would be summoned immediately to the prosecutor's office where he or she would be interviewed. If the person seemed knowledgeable enough about the status quo, they would be asked to give a sworn statement which would then be inserted in the brief or record on file and copies given to the judge and defense attorneys to read through and establish its merit. At which time the defense could do their own research of the individual. If the new witness passed the smell test and was accepted by all interested parties; then and only then would he or she be allowed to take the stand and testify.

After a few days searching and digging around to find a new star witness, they happened up on a most unlikely person by the name of Al Dillinger, [better known as Digger].

Al Dillinger had grown up in Hoboken and had a reputation as a person who knew everything going on in the community. He had his own confidential informants, same as police, the newspaper and those degenerates in city hall. Digger used his information from his CI's and others running his day-to-day business of racketeering, gambling, loansharking and extortion. He was a no-nonsense self-made man who kept a close watch on those who could or would cause him trouble. He happened to be on the prosecutors short list as a possible witness since he had ties with the local criminal element, police and city hall.

The prosecutor's office had recently been notified by one of the local bank's presidents of illegal activities by one of its bank managers, a Mr. Thomas Freeman. Mr. Freeman had been quietly removing money from the bank for his own personal use for some time. The bank president indicated Mr. Freeman had at least two other possible individuals involved in the thief. One, a local councilman, Mr. Raymond Lockhart, and Al Dillinger. Both somehow were involved in the manager's fraudulent scheme. The bank president was asking the prosecutor's office to have the three arrested. Mr. Freeman for embezzlement and the two outsiders prosecuted for receiving stolen property.

The bank president was informed by the prosecutor's office, "Lets hold off until evidence on the bank manager Mr. Freeman, Mr. Dillinger, and council member Lockhart in the embezzlement claim was verified. Once that's accomplished, we can proceed with a writ ordering all three to attend a separate formal hearing."

It took the prosecutor's office the better part of two weeks to complete their investigation and when finished, drew up the necessary papers and presented their finding to a local judge for his approval. Once accepted by the judge, we will be ready to serve papers on your Mr. Freeman, this Mr. Dillinger, and city council member Mr. Raymond Lockhart.

When the process server received the papers and served them on Mr. Freeman, Mr. Dillinger and council member Lockhart. The papers served to the three requested their presence at the prosecutor's office for an informal investigation on embezzlement and extortion.

At first, all three were hesitant before each contacted their lawyers to discuss the letters they received. Each with the consent of their lawyers made an appointment to visit the prosecutor's office to learn what this was all about.

Mr. Freeman had a sneaky suspicion, but not one hundred percent sure it concerned his stealing from the bank. Mr. Freeman and his lawyer were the first to be questioned by the prosecutor, Mr. Radcliff. He, at the time informed Mr. Freeman and his lawyer of the charges filed against him by the bank. Mr. Freeman immediately asked the prosecutor, "Could
I have more time to confer with my lawyer, Mr. Newsome."

"Yes, take as long as you like."

Half hour later Mr. Newsome informed Attorney Radcliff of his clients claim of not doing the things he'd being accused of.

"Okay, I will file a formal charge and will see you both in court."

Next to visit the prosecutor's office, was Mr. Dillinger. along with his lawyer Frank Malone. They were informed that Mr. Dillinger [Digger] had been under suspicion for some time concerning an extortion plot, receiving money's [without proof] along with a certain councilman sitting on the local board. It was a well-known fact around the prosecutor's office, that Digger as well as the councilman had been receiving moneys from a local bank manager by the name of Mr. Freeman who'd been stealing from the bank coffers for several months.

Not knowing to what extent, the charges, the prosecutor's office had on him. It was incumbent for Digger along with his lawyer to visit the prosecutor's office, and learn the full extent of the charges. Digger had been in this situation before and knew it best to comply with the request as opposed to running from it. It would only complicate matters if he did not appear in a timely manner with his lawyer, Frank Malone. Digger ask his lawyer Frank Malone to call and schedule an appointment to get to the crux of the matter quickly as possible.

Arriving at city hall a few days later, Digger and his lawyer Frank Malone after entering city hall headed straight to the prosecutor's office. Once inside informed the secretary they had made an appointment earlier, "And we are here to see Attorney Radcliff."

And may I ask, "What is the name?" Al Dillinger.

"Yes, I see your name and that you do have an appointment. Let me inform Attorney Radcliff that you are here. Please have a seat, He's busy at the moment with another client, but will be with you shortly."

Both Digger and Malone sat down, and several minutes later out walks Attorney Max Radcliff along with a client. Attorney Radcliff shook hands with his client as he was leaving and told his client, "Good bye and I hope to see you again in a week or so. Be sure to make an appointment before leaving." Will do," said the client.

Attorney Radcliff then turned to Digger and Malone who were sitting in the waiting room, Radcliff recognized Mr. Malone, walked over to where he was standing by now and shook hands with him then introduced himself to Digger, asking, "What can I do for you?" The lawyer told Attorney Radcliff, "My client received a communication from the prosecutor's office he needed to visit the prosecutor's office for some kind of interview concerning extortion and embezzlement."

Attorney Radcliff said, yes, I've been expecting you, "Follow me." They got up and followed him into his office and were seated.

Attorney Radcliff reached over and picked up a large file laying on his desk. Opening the file and skimmed over the first couple of pages. After reviewing the file looked up at Digger and asked, "Do you know any one by the name of Thomas Freeman?"

Digger answered, "No." Max Radcliff told Digger, "You may want to reconsider if you know that name or not. Don't want you to perjure yourself right off the bat by lying."

Frank Malone looked over at Digger and told him, "If you know this Thomas Freeman you need to acknowledge it now; save yourself a lot embarrassment and legal mumbo jumbo later."

Attorney Max Radcliff agreed with Digger's lawyer, telling Digger, "It would be better to admit it now than later."

Digger looked back at his lawyer, "Okay, I know this gentleman, but what's this all about?"

Attorney Radcliff gave Digger a brief explanation of why knowing Thomas Freeman was so significant. "We have reliable information Mr. Freeman was known to be removing moneys from the bank where he's presently employed. He's been taking money from certain inactive accounts for some time. Learning of his illegal activities at the bank, we were informed by city council member Raymond Lockhart you and he had been using Mr. Freeman as a cash cow. And after convincing him if he did not share part of the ill-gotten funds with you two, you were going to expose him. We know you and councilman Lockhart have been receiving a portion of the stolen money for at least the last six months, isn't that, right?"

"But how did you find out about me and Councilman Lockhart?" Digger asked.

Prosecutor Radcliff replied, "Everything will be revealed to you in time, but right now you need to tell us everything you know about Thomas Freeman and how he carried out this unscrupulous activity at the bank, I mean everything."

Digger looked back over at his lawyer Thomas Malone who shook his head and told Digger, "It's in your best interest to give a detailed account about what you know and how you became involved with Mr. Freeman and councilman Lockhart.

Lawyer Malone told Digger, "I've previously spoke with Attorney Radcliff on the phone before coming here and he has given me his word if you cooperate fully with him in this investigation, he will ask the court to go easy on you, maybe even drop the charges, but I leave that up to you."

As Digger sat contemplating his options, he said, "Okay, okay, I'll tell you all I know, but I have to have your word before I do, that I receive full immunity. No if's, and's or butt's, total immunity."

Attorney Radcliff looked at Digger and said, "I'll talk to the judge handling this case and get his opinion granting a full immunity in your case. But I'm sure he will take it in to consideration if you're able in exposing Mr. Freeman and how he was able in obtaining the money he stole from the bank. And how none of the other bank officers or employees of the bank or accounting firm was aware of the potential crisis. I cannot guarantee the judge's response for total immunity, but I'll run it by him and get his view on your offer if you turn state's evidence in the case."

Chapter 24

After the meeting ended, Digger and his lawyer Frank Malone left prosecutor Radcliff's office, and returned to Frank Malone's office to discuss their next step, on how Digger was to be Radcliff's star witness.

Meanwhile, Attorney Radcliff headed straight over to Judge Goodfellow's chamber to talk to him about Digger's request for immunity if he were to testify against Mr. Freeman and Mr. Lockhart.

Arriving at Judge Henry Goodfellow office, Attorney Radcliff approached Judge Goodfellow's secretary who looked heard him enter, immediately looked up and saw Attorney Radcliff coming over to where she sat, and said,

"Good afternoon, may I help you?"

"Yes, my name is Max Radcliff, Attorney Max Radcliff, is the Honorable Judge Goodfellow in? If so, would you be so kind as to ask him if he had time to see me?"

"Please have a seat Mr. Radcliff, "I'll let Judge Goodfellow know you are here and wish to speak with him."

The secretary returned from the Judge's chamber, and informed Attorney Radcliff, "Judge Goodfellow will see you now."

Attorney Radcliff rose from his seat and followed her back to the judge's chamber where he was warmly greeted by the judge who graciously asked, "What do I owe this unexpected pleasure?"

Sorry to bother you like this Judge Goodfellow, "But, I talked to you earlier over the phone about a Al Dillinger, better known as Digger."

"Yes, I remember our earlier conversation about this Dillinger." The good judge responded.

"Is it that case you want to discuss?"

"Yes," replied Attorney Radcliff.

"Okay, tell me what it is that's on your mind."

Well Judge Goodfellow, "After meeting with Mr. Dillinger and his attorney Frank Malone, Attorney Malone has agreed in letting Mr. Dillinger testify against Mr. Thomas Freeman and councilman Lockhart, the other defendant misusing funds from the bank."

After meeting with Attorney Malone and Mr. Dillinger Attorney Malone has assured me, Mr. Dillinger would testify against both Mr. Freeman and Mr. Lockhart, but there is a catch: Mr. Dillinger wants full immunity if he testifies.

"I told him I would run it by you and get your input on his request if he testified against both Freeman and Lockhart."

I see, "And what do you think the chances are of a full disclosure by Mr. Dillinger against Freeman and Lockhart? Do you think this Mr. Dillinger has enough evidence on both you'll be able with his testimony, convince a jury of their involvement and get a guilty verdict in return?"

"I do your honor."

Your honor, "Mr. Dillinger has given me an in-depth accounting of Mr. Freeman's and Councilman Lockhart activities, and with that information, it should be enough to convince a jury to convict Mr. Freeman and Councilman Lockhart."

"If you think your case is solid enough with this Mr. Dillinger's testimony against Freeman, and Lockhart, I would say, your Mr. Dillinger has a good chance of being absolved of the charges against him, but the case will have to be played out in court first, and all the facts presented before I would even consider recommending a full pardon for this Mr. Dillinger. I'm sure you understand my position in this unusual set of circumstances?"

"Yes, your honor, I fully understand your situation and position on the issue."

"Okay, I have your word Mr. Dillinger, a convicted felon, has adequate information on Mr. Freeman and Councilman Lockhart and is willing to deliver to the court a resounding verdict of guilty against the two defendants. I'd be more than happy in recommending a full pardon on his behalf. But if his evidence is not enough in convincing a jury of the guilt of Mr. Freeman and Councilman Lockhart, then all bets are off the table and Mr. Dillinger will be tried and if found guilty will be sentenced to the full extent of the law for his part in the embezzlement scheme along with Mr. Freeman and Councilman Lockhart. Understood?"

"Yes, your honor."

On that note, Attorney Radcliff left Judge Goodfellow's chambers, and returned to his law firm. First thing he did was assemble his legal staff together and told them what Judge Goodfellow and he had discussed in the judge's chamber after court. Attorney Radcliff made sure he and his staff had all their ducks in a row before saying anything else to Digger.

He and his staff spent the remainder of the afternoon going over information in the case against Mr. Freeman and Councilman Lockhart and Digger. Slowly and methodically assembled information gathered earlier against Mr. Freeman and Mr. Lockhart and Digger. As the time slowly passed, more and more of the information against the three began falling into place. Once the information had been thoroughly reviewed, sequenced, and placed in chronological order to their liking, the remaining documents were shelved in case they were needed later.

Mr. Radcliff, pleased with the way his staff worked in tandem as they finalized the cases against Mr. Freeman and Mr. Lockhart and Mr. Dillinger

Attorney Radcliff felt he had made the right decision in helping Digger in return for his testimony. He knew how important Digger's testimony was, and felt in his hearts of hearts it would be a slam-dunk case against Mr. Freeman and Mr. Lockhart. But, a conviction of the two defendants were solely in the dirty hands of Digger and his testimony.

Once Attorney Radcliff called Digger to the witness stand, he would give it his best shot before the court, and afterwards, it was up to Mr. Freeman and Councilman Lockhart's defense team as to the outcome of the trial once they were able to cross examine Mr. Dillinger.

Attorney Radcliff at this moment was pleased with his legal team, and chances of a full conviction against both Mr. Freeman and Councilman Lockhart was not only possible, but almost a given with Digger's testimony.

Attorney Radcliff, along with Digger had to wait until the trial finished before knowing if his case against Mr. Freeman and Councilman Lockhart was solid enough or if the legal argument Attorney Radcliff presented to the court was sufficient and the right choice.

Mr. Dillinger, Attorney Radcliff's star witness, who's faith lay in what he exposed about what he knew of Mr. Freeman's extracurricular activities at the bank. The outcome of the trial was to be a test of patience's and fortitude for everyone involved, particularly Attorney Radcliff.

After jury selection and trial date set, it was time to get the show on the road.

On the day court began, the prosecutor along with a small contingency of his legal staff entered the courtroom. Once situated on the right side, opposite the defense team Attorney Radcliff briefly looked over to where Attorney Brubaker and his staff, and defendants, Mr. Freeman and councilman Lockhart sat, and nodded.

It appeared to Attorney Radcliff that Attorney Brubaker appeared a bit apprehensive this morning. But Attorney Radcliff knew Attorney Brubaker had done his homework and was ready for a legal free for all.

It was not long until Judge Goodfellow appeared through a side door and into the courtroom. The bailiff immediately announced the judge's arrival and for everyone to rise. After Judge Goodfellow was seated, those in the courtroom were told by the bailiff, "You may now be seated."

Judge Goodfellow began the proceeding by explaining to the prosecution and defense teams what he expected from them once proceeding began.

He told them in no uncertain terms, "I will not tolerate any shenanigans or questionable practices or conduct unbecoming in my courtroom from either the prosecution or defense teams. Do I make myself clear?" There was an affirmative answer from both sides.

After his spiel to the prosecution and defense legal teams; turned his attention to the gallery and addressed the onlookers in the audience, and told them his expectations concerning their behavior.

After capturing everyone's undivided attention, looked over at the prosecution's table and asked, "Is the prosecutor ready for your opening statement?"

Immediately Attorney Radcliff stood and answered in the affirmative, Judge Goodfellow acknowledged.

Attorney Radcliff reached down and picked up a folder off the table and approached the podium. Standing next to the podium, he placed his notes on top then looked up at the judge, then turned his attention to the jury. Attorney Radcliff began by saying, "Good morning, ladies and gentlemen of the jury, I'm here representing the State vs Mr. Freeman, and Mr. Lockhart.

I hope to present the facts to you the jury, showing the defendant Mr. Freeman knowing and willfully stole moneys from the bank he was employed. And how he was underhandedly hood-winked by my client Mr. Dillinger, and Councilman Lockhart. Mr. Freeman was caught in a catch twenty- two, paying hush money to both city council member Lockhart and my client Mr. Dillinger. Mr. Freeman was kept silent by my client telling him he would be exposed if he stopped sharing his illgotten funds.

This is a highly unusual case involving money embezzled for one's own personal gratification, with equal portions of the money distributed under duress to [Mr. Dillinger my client and Councilman

Lockhart] who absconded off with a portion of the stolen money for self-gratification, and selfishness also.

My client (Mr. Dillinger) though in the wrong himself has since stepped forward and willing to testify against the defendants, Mr. Freeman and Councilman Lockhart. This is a case for all intents and purposes of deception, dishonesty and fraudulent practices including all three. A case where both the defendant and witness are guilty of similar crime's but with a twist. Not only are both presumed guilty of the crime they are accused of, but one thieving from the other? Is my client Mr. Dillinger or Councilman Lockhart guilty of a crime? Or, is Mr. Freeman the only guilty party in this case?

These are just a few of the question you must ask yourself, as I present you with the evidence. It will be up to you to decide the faith of the accused. Thank you.

Judge Goodfellow turned to the defense attorney and asked, "Is the defense ready for their opening statement to the jury?"

"Yes, your honor."

"Then proceed."

"Thank you, your honor."

After the defense's opening statement to the jury and court, Attorney Brubaker felt he had had given what was necessary in such a perplexing and confusing case. The defense's opening statement was brief, but to the point.

Now that the jury had heard both sides, it was time to get down to brass tax and go for the jugular.

Attorney Radcliff drew first blood by having the bank president Mr. Young take the stand. After an hour of questioning, the prosecution finished with Mr. Young, and there was a brief pause in the hearing as the prosecuting attorney, Mr. Radcliff removed his papers from the podium, and asked one of his associates to remove the prop used in making a point of clarification; then returned to his seat.

The judge turned to the defense Attorney Brubaker and asked, "Is the defense ready for cross examination of the witness?"

"Yes, your honor."

"Proceed."

Attorney Brubaker grilled the witness with unabashed furor trying to provoke him at every turn. The witness, calm, cool, and collective demeaner stuck to his guns, and the facts of the case as he knew them.

And, to the defense's dismay in his diverging or opposite view points tried to persuade the jury of Mr. Young's testimony as misleading and not to be acknowledged as fact, only hearsay.

Mr. Young's testimony of embezzling of such a large amount of money from his bank or any bank was hard to fathom, and only had only recently discovered by happenstance. The newest member of the accounting department, double checking the books one day, and notice what he thought had been a clerical error. After discovering the clerical error, immediately brought it to the attention of the accounting firms chief accountant.

The accounting firm immediately launched a complete audit covering the last couple of years. It did not take long before uncovering many misdirected or deceptive entries which lead to the thievery of the bank's monies by Mr. Freeman. Hence, providing the bank with a paper trail.

The bank was lucky, if the new accounting employee had not discovered what he thought was a clerical error, it could have gone on for a very long time and cost the bank thousands or even millions in the future.

Chapter 25

With the first day of the trial coming to a close, it was time the jury, and attorneys returned to their respective work places or sanctuaries to reflect back on the day's proceedings. It had been a fruitful day for Attorney Radcliff and his staff.

Returning to his office, Attorney Radcliff had a staff meeting to discuss the court proceedings and what they needed to accomplish this evening in order to prepare for the following day's presentation.

Time was of the essence.

With no time to waste, they immediately began preparing for the next day's court appearance.

Knowing they must follow proper protocol or they could possibly lose the case in a slip-up or of establishing a wrong estimation or conclusion in haste.

Attorney Radcliff also had to be on his game, anticipating each move and how the defense team responds to his introducing questions off the cuff while demonstrating skillful knowledge in presenting evidence into the trial detrimental to the defense, but beneficial to the prosecution. With several witness's testimony and affidavits obtained earlier, Attorney Radcliff was ready to hammer the defense's arguments. He could not deviate from the facts thus allowing the defense team access to certain information the defense team could use against them, and therefore allow new and damming information to surface.

Attorney Radcliff and his staff must cross every T, and dot every I if they were to be successful in this high-profile case.

Several weeks passed as the case moved slowly, and methodically, point by point by both prosecution and defense teams. It was not looking good toward the end of the trial for Attorney Radcliff, but he saved his biggest surprise for the finale. The last witness on the docket for the prosecution was Mr. Al Dillinger (Digger) with irrefutable knowledge Attorney Radcliff believed was ample evidence in convicting both Mr. Freeman and Councilman Lockhart.

As the trial was winding down, it was time for Digger to take the stand. Once Digger had been sworn in, Attorney Radcliff quickly approached the witness box where Digger was seated.

Attorney Radcliff began the afternoon questioning session by saying,

"Good afternoon Mr. Dillinger."

"Hi."

Attorney Radcliff's first question to Digger was, "Have you ever been charged with a crime and if so, were you found guilty and convicted of that crime?"

"Yes."

"Have you been arrested since getting out of prison?"

"Yes."

"On what charges were you arrested?"

"Aiding and abetting."

"Who were you associating with at the time of your arrest?"

"Doc Nelson."

"What relationship did you have with this Doc Nelson?"

"We worked together occasionally, different jobs each time."

"And in what capacity were you two working together?"

"We had set up separate organizations for the sole purpose of intimidation and harassment. And on several occasions, I was asked to arrange a hit on an individual by certain council members on the city's payroll, even by the mayor's office. Also, there were several city inspectors who asked for assistance at different times."

I see. "So, basically you worked with this Doc Nelson in solving the problem of those entities he requested. It was you who was enlisted in helping eliminating those problems that arose in certain construction projects. It was you who took care of those not adhering to the demands of paying payola or stood in way?"

"Yes."

"Okay, is it fair to say that you and this Doc Nelson were in, let's say, unlawful business together?"

"Yes."

"And how long did the two you run this criminal enterprise?"

"Approximately several years all toll."

"Were you still running this illegal activity when you were picked up on this latest minor infraction recently?"

"Yes."

"And why did you decided to turn states evidence, against the defendants whom you were associated with prior."

"I asked you while you were questioning me, if I turned state's evidence against the defendants, if the court would consider dropping the charges against me for my testimony."

"And were you told that if you testified for the state the court would consider your offer?"

"Yes, but only if my testimony was enough to convict the two defendants."

"I see. So that's why you decided to testify against the defendants. Not because it was the right thing to do, but to stay out of prison if convicted?"

"Yes, that's why."

Were you not also told, "If your testimony against the defendants was not totally convincing, you would not be given immunity, convicted, tried yourself and if found guilty sent to prison also?"

"Yes."

"So, the court can assume you will tell the court about the embezzlement of funds from the bank by Mr. Freeman and what part you and Councilman Lockhart played in the appropriation of part of those funds."

"Yes."

With that Attorney Radcliff began his slow methodical questioning of Digger. After several hours on the stand with Mr. Dillinger, Attorney Radcliff had exhausted his line of questioning and sat down.

It was now time defense Attorney Brubaker got his chance to question Mr. Dillinger?

Judge Goodfellow asked, "Is the defense ready to question the witness?"

With a resounding, "Yes, your honor," Attorney Brubaker told the judge, "I have many unanswered questions I would like Mr. Dillinger to answer."

"You may approach the witness."

Attorney Brubaker arose from his seat and as he approached the witness box, began his line of questioning with, "Mr. Dillinger, you said in your testimony you and Councilman Lockhart were part of a misappropriations of funds scheme carried out by my client Mr. Freeman, and yourself is that correct?"

"Yes."

"Can you explain to the court once more how you and Councilman Lockhart became involved such a scheme?"

"Well, I had previously worked with Council Lockhart on several occasions doing intimidation, and terrorizing workers on construction sites for him. At the time I met him, he was having problems with a collection business he ran. During one of our encounters, he hinted to me about a scheme involving embezzlement from one of the local banks and wanted me to check it out. I was told a Mr. Freeman who worked at the bank was the master mind behind the miss appropriation of funds. He wanted me to corner Mr. Freeman and apply pressure, threatening him with exposure if he did not share the proceeds."

"So, councilman Lockhart was your only source into the embezzlement scheme being committed by Mr. Freeman?"

"Yes, how councilman Lockhart knew about the scheme I didn't ask. He only told me, if I could convince this Mr. Freeman by hook or crook to cut us in on the embezzled monies he was stealing from the bank, and we too could share in the bonanza. A couple of weeks later, I cornered Mr. Freeman in a secluded area near his apartment as he was arriving home late one evening. After confronting Mr. Freeman about the embezzled of funds, and I explained to him what would happen if he did not agree with my offer; he was more than receptive to my demand."

"So, I take it, you and Councilman Lockhart threatened to expose Mr. Freeman if you two were not included in this arrangement?"

"Yes, with some bullying by me and threats of retribution by councilman Lockhart."

So, it's safe to say, "You and councilman Lockhart threatened Mr. Freeman exposing him if he did not comply with your wishes?" Is that correct?"

"Yeah, I guess you could say that."

"You do know one's intention of intimidating another human being is illegal and frowned up on, and in this case could be considered a crime of coercion. Just the threat of retribution carries a hefty price or consequence. Were you aware of that?"

"No. But if you say so."

"Mr. Digger, you must know, by threating my client with retribution you could be charged and punished. It's no laughing matter causing such stress and anguish to my client. You too could be charged down the road with your part in the transgressions of this case so don't think you're scotfree yet."

I ask the court to consider, "If the defendants in this case are found guilty, that Mr. Dillinger should be tried in a separate trial and if found guilty, sentenced along with his cohort. He has played a major role in the scheme of things and is just as guilty."

Ending his cross-examining of Mr. Dillinger, Attorney Brubaker returned to the defendant's table where he was given thumbs up by his clients.

When the judge saw their jesters, reminded the defendant's, they were in his courtroom and that kind of conduct was not to be tolerated.

The only thing left in the proceeding now were closing arguments by the defense attorney and prosecutor.

After another long day in court, Judge Goodfellow addressed the jury, telling them they were not to discuss any portion of the case while being sequestered; and court would resume the following morning at 9:00 am sharp.

That night Liam and Darla Sue met for dinner to discuss the case and the impact it would have on the rest of Jersey City's elected officials. If councilman Lockhart was found guilty of extortion, it would not look good for other council members. It would literally turn city hall into a state of uncontrolled pandemonium.

Liam told Darla Sue, "I've been thinking of revealing more information of other incidents where not only retribution, but accusations of wrong doing in my upcoming articles concerning the mayor, city inspectors and council several members, the entire criminal enterprise going on at city hall as I know it. I need to be told."

Darla Sue said, "The only thing I can say at this point is, you best watch your step if you decide to inject more wrong doings concerning those in high places. I will do what I can to help, but do be careful."

After dinner, Liam took Darla Sue back to her apartment and dropped her off.

Since it was late and he had a story to write before retiring. After returning home jotted down a list of things he wanted included in the article. Liam sat down in front of his desk hammered out the article making sure he had all the I's dotted and Ts crossed before calling it a night.

Entering the newspaper building the following morning, Liam headed straight to the editor office, where he presented his latest article to the editor-in-chief. The editor-in-chief read and reread Liam's article, correcting minor errors or mistakes he observe, then asked Liam, "I would like you to return later this afternoon so we can discuss your latest article in its entirety."

"Yes sir."

Later that afternoon Liam was summoned to the editor's office where the editor told Liam,

"After reading over your article again, I hope all the insinuations and unpleasant comments mentioned in your article about the city officials are accurate and will past the smell test. The insinuated adverse results of your article I'm sure will cause major blowback as a result of your latest article. Are you sure you want to run this piece?"

"Yes, I've tried to be as partial as possible. I know parts of the article will be disputed; but I've tried to give the reader insight as to how imperfect, one-sided and unjust the city's so-called elite function and operate on our dime."

"Okay, I'm going to approve the article, but hope you are ready for the injudicious consequences of your article and how it will be accepted hopefully without adverse results by those you've included in your article."

"Yes, I understand the consequences and I'm ready as I will ever be for the backlash of those responsible for the turmoil, they've caused inside city hall."

Now that the article had been approval and the stern warning from the editor-in-chief, Liam left the editors office and hurried back to his desk.

Immediately on his return to his desk, Liam picked up his phone and called Detective Paulson's office to inform him of the peril he was subjecting himself once the newspaper hit the streets the following day.

Later that afternoon Liam arrived at Police headquarters to meet with Detective Paulson. After Detective Paulson heard his dilemma, told Liam, "I'll going to have you followed day and night until this matter is settled."

Reaching over on his desk Detective Paulson removed one of his business cards from a holder, and proceeded in writing something on the back. Handing Liam, the card, told him, "Any time, you feel threatened, call this number immediately, do I make myself clear? These people you're implicating in your article are some of the most powerful people in the city and state. They will not take kindly to what you've written, and will be looking for payback. This will not be a cake walk for you until they get their just rewards or arrested, and put away."

On that note, Liam stood up, shook Detective Paulson's hand, and told him, "I appreciated everything you're doing for me Detective Paulson, thank you." I'll keep in touch.

Leaving police headquarters, Liam drove back to his apartment and spent the remainder of the evening contemplating his next article. He made a few calls to his contacts in the area, to see if there were any new information, threats or changes, he had not been made aware of since their last interaction.

Also looking for additional information for his next upcoming article, and how he expressed contempt for city hall, and its upper echelon, and the way they were taking advantage of the city. In his mind no one in city hall or local government was watching the hen house while the fox was stealing it blind. This corruption had to stop.

Those with authority locally seemed aware of the situation, but did not know how to address the rampant problem. So, they said nothing, kept quiet, and by doing so, kept themselves out of the limelight.

But it had festered too long and Liam was willing to take on the challenge to bring it to the forefront, letting the citizenry know what was going on under their very own noses.

After several calls to contacts, Liam learned one of the local contractors was said to have been involved with a minor disturbance at one of the construction sites recently. The sub-contractor who worked for an electrical company had been accosted by a city inspector and threatened with bodily harm if he did not contribute a donation to some charity he had never heard of. And if he refused, there would be dire consequences. Consequently, he did not heed the warning of the inspector and later was beaten-up by a couple of local hired hoodlums.

Turns out after the beating, a complaint was filed by the subcontractor against the city's electrical inspector and the city of Jersey City for adjudication.

This was the first time Liam had heard of the incident. The electrical contractor working on site where the incident occurred actually filed a lawsuit. This was a first.

Liam, with this new information concerning the lawsuit, carried more weight than just hearsay. Finally, someone had the cojones in bringing the situation to the attention of the those able to apply pressure on city hall. Up until now it had been, "Business as usual."

Maybe, just maybe, this would be the start bring down the infrastructure run solely by crooked and dishonest parties working under the umbrella of Jersey City and Hoboken's elected and appointed administrators.

Liam's faith in the system and people were once again beginning to emerge, and anything he could do to help the situation would be icing on the cake. He began making notes to use in his upcoming article, and soon afterwards began writing a rough draft of what he wanted to incorporate into this latest article.

His latest article started with a simple phrase,

"Has, The House of Cards, built on deceit and conspiracy had finally started to fall?"

Spending several hours writing and rewriting the story, decided it's time to stop and retire for the evening. He would finish the article at work the following day.

Arriving at the newspaper earlier than usual the following morning. Liam, feeling a bit giddy about what he had written so far, entered the building where he continued to the security guards' station. Stopped, showing his credentials, and was motioned through the scanner set up just inside the building near the front entrance. Once cleared to enter, hurried through the building to his desk.

After removing his jacket, and placing it on the back of the chair, sat down and once again began writing. The words flowed like a gentle breeze over and thru the outreaching branches, and meandered its way to the other side, picking up where it left off to continue its journey.

Once his article had been completed, he was off to the editor-inchief's desk once again to get his opinion on his story. Given a green light by the editor-in-chief, Liam was sure this would be the beginning of the end of the swindling, dishonesty, and double-dealing within the ranks of the city administrators and those departments they controlled. At least Liam presumed it would help eliminate a lot of the corruption going on within its ranks.

Following the article's appearance in the newspaper the following morning, Jersey City and Hoboken became a bee hive of irrefutable têteà-tête. It was something most residents had never given thought too. How could something like this continue throughout the city and there not be some type of systematic or formal inquiry into the allegations? You could almost hear a single loud gasp from the populace as Liam exposed the latest allegations trying to establish the truth.

The general masses of its residence had been or under the assumption all city and county officials were elected to work in their best interest, not running a hustler's game on the very populace they swore an oath to and uphold the very laws they now violated without excuse or justification.

The problems associated with the current and past administrators was bigger and wider spread that anyone could have imagined. It was apparently ubiquitous in most jobs associated with a title or label throughout the city or county's municipal employment; from local police departments, and faceless bureaucrats. It appeared, the entire metro area was involved one way or another in some form of exploitation.

Could this injustice of an entire municipality be rectified? That was the question on everyone's mind who read the derisive article that morning. It was the thought of such malicious behavior running ramped, not only its residents, but some elected officials were surprised to learn what was going on right under their noses, causing this magnitude of unimaginable distress and damage to their city. Could it be stop, was the thought running through every one's mind at this point?

Now that the situation in Jersey City and Hoboken had once again been exposed to the masses, steps immediately were being taken by the city and state to rectify the ongoing problem. The prosecutor's office was given a green light by officials under pressure by the state to right this wrong. It did not take long until a full investigation of the city's upper echelon and all departments under their directive was put under the microscope.

Since the genie was out of the bottle, it was up to the FBI to come in using the Hobbs Act to investigate violations by public officials in local governments.

Liam and Darla Sue were surprised by the response the article had had on the community. Including the law office where Darla Sue was employed, seemed overwhelmed with new clients seeking protection from the turn of events caused by the exposure of fraud and lawlessness going on in the metro area.

Everywhere you went, the same conversation was being scrutinized and all kind of theories circulating about what went wrong. Time had runout for those in charge of misconduct, deceptive practices and violence against local contractors and their employees. It was time to pay the piper.

Chapter 26

As the days, weeks, and months passed, the FBI along with local law enforcement agencies compiled mountains of evidence and material pertinent to the case. After many months of intensive work on the case they had gone as far as they could, and ready to present what they had to the prosecutor's office. Those elected officials, department heads, outside mob groups involved in the investigation, each were handed a summons requiring everything from depositions, attending a court hearing or supplying documents evidence in their possession relating to matters in this case.

Once this was accomplished, it was now up to the prosecutor's office to begin sorting through the many hundreds of documents, array of information gathered, then compiling those items relevant to the case in some semblance of order for the monumental task ahead. After such an immense undertaking was finally accomplished, their work was done. All that was left for them to do was get the show on the road.

The prosecutor in charge, Attorney Max Radcliff had been involved in similar cases throughout his career. This was a first. A case against a small number of city officials gone rogue and the violence in which they instigated.

Attorney Radcliff was instrumental in prosecuting cases relating to robbery, fraud, conspiracy, deceptive practices, and last but not least, accused killers. This type of case was unusual and different from anything he had previously been a part of. It was new and that's what intrigued him most, and why he took on the case.

Attorney Radcliff was familiar with how most city offices conducted business. He was fascinated upon hearing of the scheme the city officials had been involved and anxiously looking forward in taking on this new challenge. He had worked diligently on the case alongside the law clerks who served under Judge William Claymore, along with counsel and support. They provided direct assistance in the case writing opinions, researching issues, proofreading, verifying citations, and talking to counsel concerning procedurals requirements, and other administrative duties he required.

The paralegals and legal assistances were the ground pounders. Even though their work and responsibilities differed, they were a necessary entity coordinating all facets of the case. It would have been impossible to maintain scheduling without their help. The paralegals did the scheduling, contacting clients, lining up experts, communicating with witnesses, setting up hearings, meetings, and depositions. A tireless job but necessary in any large case as this.

Once the investigation by the prosecution was complete, and charges against those in the case, it was time for the initial hearing and arraignment. After the initial hearing comes the discovery part of the case, then plea bargaining between the opposing attorneys, ending with a preliminary hearing, last but not least a pre-trial motion and then trial.

After completing the initial phases of the trial, trial date had been set for the first Monday in June.

Now that the difficult part of the investigation was behind Attorney Radcliff, the next hurdle was presenting and arguing the facts of the case in front of a jury and Judge William Claymore, who was familiar with Attorney Radcliff's presentations and impartiality in the courtroom.

Attorney Radcliff was hoping the facts he presented along with witnesses in this case was enough in convicting the jury those accused were responsible for the offenses they were charged with, and found guilty of all charges against them, and sentenced accordingly.

The first day of the trial, Attorney Radcliff and staff entered the court room, and as they sat down at the prosecutors table, immediately began going over their presentation material.

Attorney Radcliff was suddenly distracted by a noisy disturbance coming from the back of the courtroom. Looking back, he sees the Defense Attorney Morgan Bandow, and his group parading down the aisle like they owned the place. Attorney Bandow looking rather dapper, and when their eyes met, nods were exchanged between the two Attorneys.

Attorney Bandow proceeded over to the defense table which was on the opposite side of the courtroom from Attorney Radcliff. Not long after Attorney Bandow's grand entrance into the courtroom, it was soon filled to capacity with onlookers and press alike. Inside the courtroom you felt the tension and saw the strain on the faces of not only the participants, but the audience as well as they waited for the Honorable Judge William Claymore's entrance into the courtroom.

Attorney Bandow and his team, had been brought in from New York to represent the defendants in this case. In due course Attorney Bandow would represent each principal indicted in the indictment. The only defendant inside the court room this day was the mayor. The city council members and department heads were to be tried in separate cases at a later date.

Attorney Bandow, during his time as an attorney, had represented only high-profile clients during his long and colorful career. His reputation proceeded him to Jersey City, and he was looked upon as some sort of a celebrity. It was appalling, to see someone of his caliber representing the worst of the worst. But Attorney Bandow had a reputation that of a rogue attorney. He was dishonest, and an unprincipled individual. But today, after his entry into the courtroom, appeared somewhat subdued in manor and appearance, but gave the impression he was in total control of his responsibility on behalf of his clients.

Attorney Radcliff on the other hand, was the complete opposite. He was straight forward, conscientious, an honorable and decent human being. This trial was to be a war of words and whichever attorney was able convincing the jury, the guilt or innocence of the accused would come out the winner.

Judge William Claymore, as he entering the courtroom, appeared ready to face any and all challenges from prosecution or defense attorneys. Judge Claymore was fair but a no-nonsense judge, and would call out either the defense or prosecution attorneys if he determined they were out of line, with no hesitation.

Upon the arrival of Judge William Claymore, the bailiff asks everyone in the court room to rise (showing respect for judge) and announced, "Court is now in session, presiding in this case is the Honorable Judge Claymore."

Once the Judge Claymore was seated behind the bench, the bailiff told those in attendance to be seated.

Judge Claymore began his open remarks relating to the case and what he expected from the jury and attorneys present.

Judge Claymore after a short a short dialogue looked over at the prosecution Attorney Radcliff and asked, "Is the prosecutor ready for his opening statement?"

Attorney Radcliff stood and answered, "Yes, I'm ready your honor." Judge Claymore told him, "Proceed."

"Thank you, your honor. Good morning, Judge, ladies and gentlemen of the jury. I would like to take this opportunity to give you a short summary of the case, with the hope of clarifying a few misconceptions of the case against the defendant."

Once I've explained what I'm trying to accomplish during this undertaking, and at the conclusion of my opening statement, hope you have a clearer, unbiased and impartial understanding of the complexity and depth of the case. After establishing the crux of the matter I'll call several witnesses to come forward and affirm the accountability against the defendant, Mayor Arthur Wiseman.

Mayor Wiseman is the one sitting over there (pointing to the defense table) in the blue blazer and red tie. He along with several of his cohorts have been accused of illegal activities while serving in public office. It has been brought to the attention of several law enforcement departments of the underhanded tactics and schemes the mayor and several of his cohorts who's taken an oath to serve and uphold the laws of the state and community, but has caused nothing but havoc during their tenure lining their pockets with returns from ill-gotten inducements.

I'm going to walk you through what I believe is one of the most scandalous and outrageous offenses against the city of Jersey City and Hoboken I've been privy too since becoming an attorney. Once the witnesses in this case have testified, it will be up to you, the jury, to determine Mr. Wiseman's fate. Thank you.

It was now Attorney Bandow's turn to give his opening statement to the jury. He began by walking over standing alongside the jury box leaned on the railing, looking at the jury individually showing little or no emotions.

Then he began slowly, and methodically, telling the jury, "Mayor Wiseman had done for the city what no other mayor has been able to do in such a short time. He has been instrumental in getting several projects that had been on the docket for years, fixed, repaired, or built, benefiting each and every person in the community. He is involved with bringing in new industries which provided jobs, he's been an outstanding member of the community helping with charities he believes strongly in, and brought about a leaner and more productive city run government.

He's an honest and hardworking mayor who would in my opinion would never stoop to the level he is being accused of.

I plan proving his innocence and returning to him, his good reputation, and that he's allowed to return to his position as mayor and finish the valuable work he has started. Thank you, ladies and gentlemen of the jury, for your undivided attention."

Judge Claymore told the jury, "Now that you have heard both the prosecution and defense's opening remarks, without further ado it is now time we call Attorney Radcliff to the podium along with his first witness."

Thank you, your honor."

I would like to call my first witness Mr. Anthony Iola to the stand.

After being sworn in, Mr. Iola sat down in the witness's chair. Attorney Radcliff began his enquiry of Mr. Iola which lasted a little more than an hour. After his questioning of Mr. Iola, told the judge, "I'm finished with the witness."

"The judge thanked Attorney Radcliff, then turned to the defense Attorney Bandow and asked, "Would the defense like to question the witness?"

Attorney Bandow stood, and told the judge, "Yes, your honor."

After spending only, a short time questioning Mr. Iola, Attorney Bandow told the judge, "I'm finished with my questioning of Mr. Iola at this time."

Then Attorney Bandow asked the judge, "Could you have Mr. Iola stay in town in case I need recalled him for further testimony if it becomes necessary?"

The Judge said, "Yes. I'll have him standby for future questioning if it's necessary."

"Thank you, your Honor, that's all for now."

The judge looked over at Mr. Iola and told him, "I do not want you leaving town. The court may request your presence for further questioning, if need in the future, for clarification or to shed light on specific sticking point by either the prosecution or defense attorneys. Mr.
Iola, you are free to go, you may step down.

"Thank you, your honor." Replied Anthony Iola.

As the days and weeks continued it was not looking good for Attorney Radcliff. He was at his wits end until a witness for the defense was admitted late in the hearing and took the stand. It was Liam's Street contact which Attorney Radcliff had been made aware of by Liam in the past. When Attorney Radcliff saw Loui approach the stand and sworn in, at which point Attorney Radcliff's demeaner changed. This was his last chance to put a nail in the defense's coffin. He had a staff member call the office where he had kept in a separate file a small dossier on Loui. He wanted one of the staffers to bring it to the court [S.T.A.T.]. It arrived shortly afterwards while Attorney Bandow was still questioning Loui. Attorney Bandow spent a lot of time questioning Loui about his association with city staffers, and pleased at Louis's remarks which helped shine a light on his client the mayor. He made the mayor seem like a father figure and all the good he had done for the city. As Attorney Bandow was finishing up his questioning of the witness; Attorney Radcliff turned and saw one of his staffers enter the courtroom.

After defense Attorney Bandow finished his grandiloquence spiel it was time Attorney Radcliff made this pomposity and arrogant Bandow cower behind his cloak of hyperbole and the embellishment of the mayor's past activities by Loui; which anyone with a lick of sense could read between the lines, and see-through this arrogant and opinionated individual as nothing more than a boasting blowhard.

The judge asked, "Is the prosecution ready to cross examine the witness?"

"Yes, your honor but could I have a moment to confer with staff, there may be new information which just arrived, and possibly relevant to the case."

The judge granted his request.

Attorney Radcliff was handed a file. Quickly opening the file and scanned over the information inside, refreshing his memory about Loui and information contained inside about Mayor Wiseman, in which Loui had earlier related to Liam for one of his articles which for some reason Attorney Radcliff had saved the article.

After reviewing the article, Attorney Radcliff felt a sense of relief and the damming material it contained about Mayor Wiseman by Loui. It confirmed Attorney's Radcliff that Loui's had lied on the witness stand about his revised version of Mayor Wiseman and the earlier events he recalled been involved. The article related to an incident told by Loui, how Mr. Wiseman while serving as Mayor of Jersey City had been involved in the disappearance of a missing witness by the name of "Sammy "the man" Romano. And during the trial of Doc Neeson, Mayor Wiseman had been personally responsible for Sammy Romano's kidnapping.

Loui when asked told Liam, "I heard several rumors on the street about the abduction, and that the mayor had been heavily involved.

That he had to protect Doc Neeson because if Sammy Romano was called to the witness stand and allowed to testify it would be all over for the mayor."

Liam asked, "What did Sammy Romano know at the that could have been detrimental to the mayor?"

I've heard through the grapevine, "He's used not only Doc Neeson for certain jobs, but Sammy Romano as his personal hit man, and had had Sammy remove several people from the streets who become risky to his success. There's nothing the mayor would not do in protecting his position as mayor."

But now Loui testified, Mr. Wiseman as far as he knew had never committed a crime. That he knew the mayor on a personal basis and had nothing but respect for him. That he would never do anything to dishonor the position he held as mayor.

With his new information now in his possession, it became Attorney Radcliff's smoking gun, and the time had come to use it. As he began cross examining Loui, Attorney Radcliff was ready to bury the defense attorney and all the rhetoric which had been spewing out so persuasively concerning the mayor, and how the mayor had been a man of the people while serving in that capacity.

It was time to step up to the plate and hit a home run.

Attorney Radcliff laid down the file and approached the witness stand. Said to Loui, "Good afternoon."

And started right off the bat by asking Loui about certain questions he was asked by the defense and if his answers were the same as when he had been quoted in the Jersey Journal a year or so back about your association with the mayor. What you were quoted as saying at that time, and what you told the court today, under oath, are total conflicting answers. I'm going to ask you the same question the defense attorney asked you, and then show you the article from the Jersey Journal you espoused to back them.

As he drilled Loui over for the next hour about what he admitted to under oath, Loui was at the place where he had nowhere to turn or hide. The testimony he had given previously when questioned by the defense attorney meant if he now changed any part of that testimony, he would be committing perjury.

Louis had no choice; he was now between a rock and hard place. If he answered the question Attorney Radcliff asked truthfully, it would open the case wide open against Mayor Wiseman, and his band of faithful cohorts.

Notwithstanding Attorney Morgan Bandow's credibility, and seal the prosecution's case. He had no choice but to answer Attorney Radcliff's question. Loui knew if he did not answer the questions candidly while under oath, he would face additional consequences.

In a trial such as this, [a federal trial], a person convicted of federal perjury and found guilty, would be looking to serve a minimum of five years in prison. This was not what Loui had in mind to do, when he admitted bending the truth under questioning by Attorney Bandow. Loui told Attorney Radcliff all he wanted to do was reflect in the record Mayor Wiseman was nothing more than a criminal like those he associated with. But Attorney Bandow convinced him to testify just the opposite and he would be well rewarded.

Once Louis let the cat was out of the bag, Attorney Radcliff lightened up with his questioning. Loui was not about to perjure himself any further in protecting the mayor or his lackeys or political supporters no matter the consequences. Loui's testimony continued the rest of the afternoon and into the following day.

Attorney Radcliff after wrapping up his questioning of Loui, told the judge he was finished with Mr. Loui Montana, but asked the judge, "If I have further need to question Mr. Loui Montana, will he be available if called on later?"

The judge immediately looked over at Loui and told him, "You are not to leave the county until the trial is over, do I make myself clear?"

"Yes, your honor."

Finishing up his questioning of the witness, Attorney Bandow walked over to where Attorney Radcliff sat and ask if they could talk in private before leaving the courtroom. Attorney Radcliff was surprised and puzzled at hearing Attorney Bandow's unusual request.

But agreed to meet with him afterwards in Attorney Radcliff's office where Attorney Bandow told Attorney Radcliff, "After the disastrous bombshell Mr. Montana dropped on my client, he's decided to change his plea.

After talking it over, Attorney Bandow asked Attorney Radcliff if he would be willing to drop one or more serious charges against his client Mayor Wiseman, and therefore reducing time he spends incarcerated?"

By getting Attorney Radcliff to drop one or more serious charges against Mayor Wiseman. Attorney Bandow felt Attorney Radcliff would provide a small concession to his client, in exchange for his plea of guilty?

Attorney Bandow ended by telling Attorney Radcliff, "As we both know, it's contingent on Judge Claymore, and his willingness in granting the request. Would you be agreeable to such an arrangement?"

I think my client would consider it somewhat a personal if not a legal victory.

Attorney Radcliff told Attorney Bandow, "Give me a little time to think about it. I'll let you know my decision prior to the hearing in the morning."

Attorney Radcliff already knew his answer to Attorney Bandow's question, but wanted him to stir in his own excretion overnight before agreeing to his terms.

Both attorneys arrived in court the following morning, Attorney Radcliff approached the defense councils table handing Attorney Bandow a yellow manilla envelope. Inside a memo, a typed message stating he was willing to drop the felony charge against Mayor Wiseman, if Mayor Wiseman plead guilty to the other charges, that of perjury and bribery.

Judge Claymore entered the courtroom the bailiff called out, "All rise, The Honorable Judge William Claymore presiding."

After the judge and jury were seated, the bailiff announced, "Court is now in session, you may now be seated."

Once court was called into session, the defense Attorney Morgan Bandow stood up and asks the judge, "May I approach the bench your honor?"

The judge then asked both attorneys to approached the bench. Once the defense and prosecutor were in front of the judge's bench, the judge looked down, and over at Bandow and asked in a low voice, "What is it you need to discuss that could not be discussed in open court?"

"It concerns my client your honor, Mr. Wiseman. He has indicated to me he would like to change his plea from not guilty to guilty if such arrangements are approved by you."

"In that case, I'll need to call a short recess in order to discuss this issue further."

"Thank you, your honor."

The judge immediately called for a short recess, telling the jury, "There's a new set of circumstances which has been brought to my attention and before continuing with this hearing this issue must be resolved."

The judge rose from his chair, and he along with the attorneys proceeded back to the judge's chamber to discuss this latest turn of events.

Attorney Bandow told Judge Claymore, "The mayor as you know is facing multiple counts of fraud, greed and abuse of power, and saw no chance of winning his case after Mr. Montana's testimony. My client has decided the best thing to do going forward is change his plea. I have discussed it with Attorney Radcliff and he is on board. All we need now is your opinion and recommendations in this matter."

After Judge Claymore heard Mayor Wiseman's offer, he seemed to be in agreement with the attorneys, but his offer needed to be reviewed further before granting any type of leniency to the mayor.

The judge and attorneys returned to the courtroom where the Honorable Judge Claymore explained to the jury there had been an important development in the case which had been brought to his attention and was sorry for the delay.

Soon after, the judge dismissed the jury, and postponed the hearing until Judge Claymore could reviewed the case one again against the defendant.

Once trial resumed several days later, Mr. Wiseman was found guilty, but received a lesser sentence after changing his plea.

This was not what those involved wanted to hear, but they had no choice in the matter. Once Mr. Wiseman changed his plea, he was rewarded by a more lenient sentence.

Later that month, court was in session for the sentencing phase. The sentence given to Mayor Wiseman was basically a slap on the hand, compared to what it would have been if he had been found guilty on all charges. He was sentenced to eight to ten for aiding and abetting. Although serious crimes he would still spend time behind bars for his role of criminal activity while serving as mayor.

As Mr. Wiseman was leaving the court room had this big smile on his face even though he was handcuffed and shackled. Surrounded by police and quickly escorted through a side door to a holding cell to wait until they came to loaded him on a bus along with several other convicted individuals for their ride to the big house.

Justice was not swift like those who harmed by his actions, but Mayor Wiseman had been removed from office where he would no longer be dictating what went on in the streets and community around Jersey City and Hoboken. This time in the pokey would give him time to think about all the harm he had done to his community and fellow man.

It was back to the drawing board for Liam and Detective's Paulson and Callahan. They had lots of investigating to accomplish before the next trial came up; concerning several more major and minor players associated with the mayor and his band of thieves.

Chapter 27

Several months later, Jacopo Gallo nicknamed [Jonesy], a local brute working out of New York was arrested along with several others in Hoboken. They were caught red-handed trafficking in prostitution in one of the local brothels along the waterfront.

Shortly after their arrest, Police Captain Cahill was found murdered along the docks in Hoboken near one of the brothel Jonesy ran. An inquiry into his death by detectives Paulson and Callahan quickly turned up evidence connecting Captain Cahill and his involvement with this Jacopo Gallo. It was learned later through the rumor mill, Captain Cahill also worked with Angelo (the mob boss out of New York) prior to his being murder.

The web of deceit and their exposure, those appointed and elected individuals began to surface indicating the involvement of public servants and individuals of importance had been deeper than anyone knew or was aware of. The small community of Hoboken found itself involved in allegations of unparallel and unrivaled consortium of crime groups working the area. Upon learning of Captain Cahill's involvement rocked the hard-working people working and living in the area.

Violence and greedy gangs once again slowly began creeping back, causing havoc throughout the neighborhoods, as city officials and police officers turned a blind eye as the greed and selfish desire of a few grew in intensity. The money was readily available to those willing to take the plunge.

Jersey City and Hoboken once again wound-up with egg on their faces. How could these communities plagued with such atrocities and lack of disorder survive? A daunting task as the two cities thought to be somewhat free of organized crime, suddenly out of nowhere, more serious and heinous violation of the law once again ran wild.

Liam, and Darla Sue met for dinner one evening after of learning of Captain Cahill's involvement with local organized crime. They talked about this latest outbreak, Liam reiterated his intentions to hold steadfast supporting his belief of one day it was possible crime could be less obtrusive, and more manageable, while wondering all the while, when and how?

He expressed to Darla Sue "I'll not stop until this unrestrained activity of tainted faith and deadly consequences of greediness is once again under control, and or quashed."

Liam knew when he expressed that to Darla Sue, it was nothing more than a pipe dream. But in his heart of hearts recognized it was an unattainable fanciful hope he had. If those elected or appointed to power in the metro area would only do the right thing most of the anarchy would disappear on its own. But as long as the upper crust of the communities continued working with and feeding organized crime fantasies would continue to endure.

Liam, with Darla Sue's help, began a campaign of all-out assault on local crime. With her position in the law office and information she was privy too, and his clout with local CIs on the streets and daily editorial's, it was possible making a difference in his attempt in curbing such violence. As the days and weeks waned, more and more violence occurred. The hysteria amongst law enforcement agencies was reaching a crescendo, the intensity of crime continuously spiraled out of control. Police with several agencies from the outside assisted in the effort of rounding up and arresting individuals believed to be responsible for this latest wave of mayhem. When found, those individuals were arrested on the spot on whatever charged the police could think of to get them off the streets. With many of the crime figures now out of the picture, the efforts of police ate slowly away at the fabric of the community and unrest. As more information was gathered from those arrested, a bigger and more repugnant picture was emerging.

Mob activity around the area went deeper into the fabric of local leaders than anyone imagined. It appeared half the police force and city officials were involved one way or another in protecting those undesirables causing all the havoc. It turned into a long and arduous battle between good and evil, but with help from those honorable, and decent people working for the betterment of the community eventually would prevail.

Everyone, associated with the problem worked diligently to correct the situation. A few months later the status quo of the cities were once again somewhat manageable. It was time to bring those responsible to justice. The justice system now clogged and overburdened, but as the wheels of justice slowly turned, one by one those individuals found guilty were convicted and removed from society.

By now, Liam had no shortage of material in which he could expound on daily about lawlessness and corruption which plagued the area.

With Darla Sue's help, they became a team, a force to be reckon with. Eventually they were able exposing the interworking's of organized crime locally. It was difficult at times on Liam, as he was constantly harassed, threatened, terrorized, and stalked on a daily basis. But the promise he made to himself earlier became the driving force behind his latest push for justice, and would not stop until this disaster was laid to rest.

As things finally began to settle down and troublemakers defying authority were captured, convicted, and sent to prison, a few of the lucky ones were able to slip through the system and fled town. It was once again safe for Liam and Darla Sue to walk the streets without having to constantly look over their shoulders.

After this latest and painful experience was behind Liam and Darla Sue, they were able in spending more time together and thinking of a future together. Soon afterwards Darla Sue learned of her pregnancy. She informed Liam immediately and he proposed and the immediately began making plans to marry as soon as possible by a justice of the peace there in Hoboken.

After Liam learned of her pregnancy, he became ecstatic at the prospect of becoming a father.

The following day Lima asked Detective Paulson and Detective Callahan and significant others to be witnesses at the marriage ceremony. Both accepted readily and told Liam, "We would be honored to be part of your special day."

On the wedding day Darla Sue and Liam along with Detective Paulson and Callahan and their wives met outside the courthouse on Saturday morning. Found their way up the stairs to the justice's office. The ceremony started on time and soon vows were exchanged and just before pronouncing them man and wife; the judge turned to Liam and said, "You may now exchange rings."

Liam turned facing the justice of the peace, told him, "Sorry, judge, I forgot to pick up the rings when I left home." Liam bent down and kiss his new bride."

Afterwards Darla Sue looked back at Detective Paulson's wife and down at her ring, which she immediately covered her gold band with her right hand and shook her head as if to say, "No, I'm not giving up my ring."

Without the rings all the judge could do was conclude the ceremony by pronouncing them man and wife.

After the ceremony Liam and Darla Sue invited Detectives, Paulson and Callahan to lunch to celebrate their happy occasion.

Arriving at Amanda's on Washington Street, one of the more upscale restaurants in the area, were quickly escorted back to a private room just off the main dining room, which had been reserved earlier by Liam.

After being seated, a rather questionable character came out of nowhere into the private room, and without introducing himself, told Liam, "I saw your group enter and wanted to warn all of you, there's been a contract place on your heads, and if I were you, I would not become too relaxed after leaving here. The talk on the streets is, all of you are responsible for sending several key people of their organization to the big house. I'm referring specifically to a local Faction group out of New York known as [The Family]. They'll stop at nothing to settle a score no matter how long it takes."

Oh, and by the way, "Congratulations are in order on your recent marriage." He then turned leaving the room and returned to his table in the main dining area.

This was not the way Liam, Darla Sue, Detectives Paulson and Callahan had envisioned the afternoon. It was to have been a happy occasion, but spoiled by what a stranger out of now where passed on to the group about a contract placed on their heads. It was a wake-up call, but with a new twist, it now involved the two detectives. As they sat around the table discussing the situation it was clear, [The Family] did not play favorites. They were out for revenge and would stop at nothing until victorious in their endeavor.

The next few days were uneventful for Darla Sue and Liam, but things began to emerge which were not normal. Darla Sue was accosted and confronted while entering the law firm one morning by two men whom she did not recognize. They told her in so many words that she and her husband Liam, were going to regret getting involved in matters that did not concern them. Their lives were in danger and not to involve the police. Then turned away and walked slowly down the street, where they quickly ducked into a nearby alley and disappeared.

Once inside the safety of her office, Darla Sue called Liam and told him what occurred.

Liam told her, "Do not to leave the office, I'll drop by and pick you up after work."

Leaving the newspaper that evening Liam headed straight over to the law firm where Darla Sue stood just inside the entry door, and when she saw Liam, hurried outside to the car and got in. Liam was driving toward their condo when Liam noticed a car following closely behind them. The longer he observed the individual driving, finally recognizing the driver, it was Kenny Dugan, a close friend of Loui

[Liam's CI]. Remembering back, as Kenny was working when someone pushed him from the fourth floor, breaking his back and almost died from his injuries.

Kenny Dugan began flashing his headlights several times, with Liam at his wits end, and a tremendous amount of trepidation finally pulled the car to the curb. Kenny pulled in behind, and got out of his car and walked to where Liam's car had stopped.

As he approached the driver's side of the car, Liam with apprehensive and anxiety was asked by Kenny, "Roll down the window I have important new.

Once Liam rolled the window down, Kenny told Liam, "The talk on the streets was [The Family out of New York] are planning a hit on your place this evening. I wanted to warn you of the possibility of the incursion later. If I, were you, I would not go home this evening, they will be waiting for you?"

Liam thanked Kenny, drove Darla Sue and himself straight down to the police station where they met with Detective Paulson and gave him insight into what was going down this evening.

Chapter 28

Detective Paulson along with several other police officers followed Darla Sue and Liam to Darla Sue's unoccupied condo. Liam parked his car in the garage as usual, he and Darla Sue and waited on Detective Paulson and his fellow officers to join them. They did not immediately stop and meet with Darla Sue and Liam. They drove around the area looking for any suspicious activities, anything out of the ordinary.

Finding none, parked their squad cars in front of the condo, where they exited. Once again looking around for anything dubious going on or caught their attention before entering. A couple officers took the stairs while Detective Paulson, Liam and Darla Sue took the elevator. Stepping from the elevator, it was a tense moment sensing someone was hiding either in the stairwell or Liam's unit. With much caution, two of the policemen who rode up on the elevator with Darla Sue, Liam and Detective Paulson made their way back to the stairwell door, quickly opening the door heard footsteps running down the stairs. They made an attempt to follow but by now were too far behind to catch up.

Meanwhile the two officers running up the stairwell soon confronted the two men as they were descending. At which point the two officers drew their weapons when the two were spotted, and yelled, "Stop, raise your hands and lean up against the wall."

Once the two thugs realized it was the police, quickly changed directions, and almost immediately were met by the two officers descending the stairs behind them.

They immediately stopped, raised their hands, turned and assumed the position on the stairwell wall. They were quickly patted down and handcuffed. They were escorted down the stairs to the main floor and taken to one of the parked squad cars in front of the condo, and placed in the back seat and restrained with seat belts.

Meanwhile Detective Paulson and his small contingency entered the condo, searching high and low for anyone who might be hiding inside. It did not take long before locating two more men inside the master bedroom closet hiding behind the clothes that were hung inside.

After their arrest they too were handcuffed, and read the Maranda act before being removed from the condo. Eventually all four men were loaded into two police cars and taken to police headquarters.

The four were book on several charges including breaking and entering, resisting arrest, along with conspiracy to murder.

This was the beginning of the end of The Family out of New York. The four arrested were dispensable as far as [The Family] was concerned. Having fallen out of favor with The Family, the four were left to defend for themselves. It did not take long for them to realize they were on their own and began singing like yellow canaries.

Even though [The Family] in New York had been implicated, with no proof, only hearsay from the four ex-members, it was impossible to arrest or extradite any of [The Family's] higher-ups mentioned. None would be coming to Jersey City to testify or stand trial. This was the end of an era in Hoboken and Jersey City for [The Family] out of New York, but not the end of corruption.

There was always that element of aggression and competition willing to enter any fray at the drop of a hat. Organizations and lowlife's were always waiting in the wings for the first opportunity to enter the battle grounds due to the failure of others and take hold of the reins. Exploitation, fraud, bribery and dishonesty was part of the fabric of most major metropolitan areas throughout the world and Jersey City and Hoboken were no exception to the rule.

Now that another catastrophe had been averted, it was time for Liam to move on. After several months appearing at the court house while watching the trials, and his many editorials concerning the trial, the witnesses, and the four from New York. Trial finally came to a close after the four were found guilty and sentenced. Ending a long and exhausting process for justice, it was now time for Liam to take a break.

Liam decided it was time for Darla Sue and himself to take a long and deserving vacation. He made reservations for the two of them to fly down and stay in Aruba for a couple of weeks. Here they could relax, take in the sights and sounds of the Island, away from the hustle and bustle of city life. Since they had not had a honeymoon, and both looked forward to getting away and enjoying what would feel like being free, even if for only two weeks.

On the day they were to leave for Aruba, Liam received a phone message at work, telling him, "If you know what is good for you, you need to rethink what you are doing stop writing those nasty articles or change profession. If not, your life will become very complicated."

He did not know what to think of this latest threat, but decided not to take it seriously. It was possibly another crank call, one of many received since starting to work at the newspaper.

On board the aircraft on their way to Aruba, Liam felt good as he reclined back in his seat, able to relax and think only about Darla Sue and himself once they arrive on the island.

Relaxing on the sunbaked beaches, swimming in the warm blue waters of the Caribbean, snorkeling along the white sandy shore line, excursion trips around the island, maybe a half-day trip on a sailboat, and just hanging out. It was a dream come true for both. This was the first real get-away since being marriage.

Arriving in Aruba, they deplaned, through customs, picked up their luggage then a short taxi ride to their hotel where they had reservations. It was at one of the All-Inclusive resorts, The Holiday Inn Aruba. With its unique ambiance, its restaurants, a spa, large casino, a fitness center, close to the local shopping mall, and water sports. It was just a hop, skip and jump from an abundance of night life in walking distance, just minutes away.

After being dropped off at the hotel, signing in, were escorted by the bell hop along with their luggage to their room. Both began by putting away clothes from their individual luggage into the dresser drawers and hung the rest in the closet. Finished with the unpacking both laid down on the large king size bed and rested for a short while.

After resting, decided to freshen up a bit and hit the casino located inside the hotel. Taking the elevator down to the main floor, found the casino and after an hour of playing the slots and a few games at the blackjack table they were getting hungry, it had been a long day and they were ready to have a bit to eat and relax. It was time to find a restaurant and have a late lunch. By the time they finished it was late afternoon, time for a nap before showering and dressing for and dinner. They were ready to check out the island's night life.

Leaving the hotel, they heard and felt the heartbeat of the island as calypso, reggae, and modern pop-music resonated softly in the breeze from the different venues along the beach front.

The Bungaloe Beach Bar & Grill, not far from The Holiday-Inn Aruba was their destination that evening to have dinner. Dara Sue had asked the concierge before leaving where to go for dinner, he suggested the Bungaloe on the beach. Departing the rear entrance to the hotel saw a large thatched roof building which extended half of its length from the beach into the blue waters of the Caribbean, and had its own distinctive trade-mark (a thatched roof). With a slight breeze off the warm waters lapping the shore line around the beach bar, felt like the perfect way to spend their first evening on the Island.

It was Tuesday evening and as they entered the beach bar noticed a band was setting up for the evening's entertainment, and as they made their way farther back through the bar toward the open deck at the rear of Bungaloe, it was something they would remember forever.

They learned earlier from a fellow tourist, the band playing tonight at the Bungaloe was one of the three best bands on the Island who performed once a week at the Bungaloe. There were two other bands which alternated, Friday and Sunday nights, along with the entertainment of the Bungaloe employees themselves who sang and entertained every day during Happy Hour.

Finding their way through the maze of tables and chairs, made their way back to the open deck and eventually were seated near the water, with an unobstructed view of the upcoming sunset scheduled later that evening which they were told was spectacular.

Once seated a server approach to the table where Liam and Darla Sue sat enjoying the warm tropical evening under a clear blue sky.

The server stopped at their table, and as he did, both Liam and Darla Sue looked up.

"Good evening, my name is Karel, I'll be your server this evening.
Can I get you started with something from the bar?"

"Yes", Liam looked over at Darla Sue and asked her, "What would like to start with?"

"I believe I'll have the Bugaloe, sounds delightful."

"A good choice on such a lovely evening," Karel agreed.

"And for you sir?"

"I would like one of your local beers, a Balashi, if you don't mind." "Very good sir".

Karel left and returned shortly with their drinks.

Then said, "When you are ready to order, catch my attention and I'll return and take your dinner order. As you can see, we are getting busy. The sooner you decide what you want for dinner, the sooner your order will be served. But if you are not in a hurry, I would suggest waiting until the rush is over."

"Thank you," said Liam, we'll let you know.

As the two sat on the aft-deck mesmerized and enjoying the sights and sounds the island, you could hear the murmur of the sea gently rolling as it lapped against the pilings and shore line with a gentle rippling sound. With an occasional splash or slap on the water from one of the many species of marine life from below the water's surface. The sounds of fish jumping and splashing, they could not tell if it was a sign of contentment or panic, and they would never know.

As things started settling down as night was quickly approaching, everyone's attention turned to the west as the sun was ready to take its last bow of the evening. Slowly it began its disappearing act, once again to the amazement of those witnessing the daily event. A beautiful sight for those who never witnessed this phenomenon up close and personal.

Everyone including the locals marveled at is short-lived beauty as it appeared to momentarily stop and sit on the water's edge before disappearing into the night sky. Once the sun began its disappearing act, it sank quickly out of sight over the western horizon and simply vanished. It was a first for Liam and Darla Sue, they were amazed how fast it disappeared once it started its descent. In less than a minute it went from full sun sitting on the skyline to only a faded memory. Again, something that would remain with them the rest of their lives.

Karel returned after things settled down and took their food order. Darla Sue decided on the Club Salad, while Liam ordered the Bungaloe burger and a side order of Jalapeno peppers and a Broodje Frikandel (deep fried curry flavored sausage served in a bun), only because it sounded interesting. Curry was something he heard of but never tasted.

After dinner they sat a while listing to and dancing to the local band which played many different genres of music, a taste of hip hop, jazz, pop, rock, country a small taste of each to whet one's appetite. It had been a great evening but was time to call it a night and head back to the hotel.

Chapter 29

Liam, as he opened the door to their unit, noticed a letter laying on the carpet just inside the room. Immediately he reached down and retrieved the white nondescript envelope, and carried it over to the couch where he sat down.

Opening the letter carefully, took out the letter inside to read its content. It was from Captain Paulson. It read as follows:

"I hate to be the one to inform you of the murder of Loui Montanan." I know he was someone you relied on and had been special to you in the past. His body was found last night at the construction site by foreman Anthony Iola as he was checking the sixth floor for things that could possibly cause a problem with some building or electrical inspector deciding to make a surprise visit to the construction site, and possibly causing a delay.

As he carefully checked the finished work for any problems, notice a small extrusion or bulge in one of the freshly poured concrete columns. Since everyone had gone for the day, he would wait until tomorrow to find what had caused the unusual protuberance or bump inside the concrete column.

The following day foreman Anthony Iola had a one of the crew jackhammer the concrete from around the column exposing an elongated sealed plastic container. Once the container was removed from the column, he could not tell what it contained, but looked suspicious and immediately notified police.

After the police arrived, were shown the plastic bag and saw what they believed was blood. They immediately contacted the local coroner. After the coroner arrived, he too became suspicious and picked up the plastic container and took it back to the morgue for further observation. It was there the coroner opened the dark red stained plastic container, and inside he found a mutilated body parts stuffed inside which were beyond recognition. searching thoroughly through the mass of wet sticky body parts and blood, the coroner eventually found several items inside, and eventually retrieved a pair of blood-stained work pants. Carefully removing the blood-stained pants from the container, the coroner examined inside the pockets and found several items; a set of what looked to be house key or car keys, a blood-stained billfold, handkerchief, a rabbit's foot and small pocket knife. Cleaning each item meticulously and then labeled each item. Further searching of the wallet found it contained a pictured driver's license belonging to a Loui Montanan.

This sent shockwaves through Liam and Darla Sue as he finished reading the letter. How or why had this happened to Loui? He was not your typical CI; he was a hard-working individual just trying to make ends meet.

Loui worked as taxi driver, able keeping an open mind and eye out for the unusual thing's going on around town. Loui was interested in at one time in helping Liam quash the ramped upheaval happening around Jersey City and Hoboken. Same as most law-abiding residents living in the area. That's why he felt it his duty at the time assisting Liam whenever he could in any startling or previously unknow criminal acts circulating throughout the illicit world of crime. In his line of work, he was often afforded or provided information freely from those riding with him on a daily or weekly basis.

They too were tired of the killings, the violence, the threats and fraud by the local officials and their counterparts. It had become an entire network of human endeavor, unknowingly working together to rid the community of carnages without realizing they too were contributing to the eradication of a growing problem. Loui's demise was just another setback for those trying to clean up the city's lawlessness and the anxiety of what to expect next. The strife which covered the city was never ending, something or somebody was constantly raising its ugly head. Apparently, Loui had become mixed up with the wrong people and had become a liability and no longer wanted.

Liam and Darla Sue concluded their last day of their island honeymoon, and anxiously awaiting their return to Hoboken to learn more about what happened to Loui. It was a somber trip back knowing what they faced when they arrived.

Landing at Newark Liberty International Airport took a cab back to Hoboken. Arriving at their condo found several messages on the answering machine and one from Loui. He sounded panicky as he mentioned being stalked by Zenoah Ricci (Hatchet Man) and Jacopo Gallo (Jonesy) both had recently been released from prison and made their way back to town. He did not know who hired them or for what reason; only that they were closing in on him and he was frightened.

Loui also question if Liam had heard who was behind this shit? Liam could tell he was discernably shaken by the way he spoke. Loui, before hanging up told Liam, "If anything, happen to me before he and Darla Sue returned, I'm going to give you gave a contact number, they can fill you in on the status quo."

Immediately up on hearing Loui's plea on the answering machine, immediately called the number Loui gave him. On the third ring a female answered, "Hello".

Liam asked, "To whom am I speaking?"

"This is Marlene Montanan; may I ask who is calling?"

"Yes, Liam Drake a friend of your late husband."

My wife and I have been out of town this last week and after our return home found a message on our answering machine from Loui asking me to call this number.

"Yes, he told me he left you a message. He wanted me to tell you, he had been stalked recently and feared for his life., He was sure the people behind the stalking were city officials. Did not the names only there was a plot to silence him. He wanted you to find out who they were and have them put away for life."

"Did he tell you anything else?"

"No, only they were stalking him and he did not have much time left."

"Thank you, Mrs. Montanan, I will do my best to expose those responsible for your husbands' demise. Keep in contact, if you learn of new information don't hesitate in calling me."

"I will, thank you for calling." Good luck.

Liam hung up the phone and told Darla Sue what transpired after talking to Loui's wife. Both Liam and Darla Sue were surprised to learn Loui had been married. Liam said, "You know it's funny, he never spoke of his wife all time I knew him. Guess he did not want her involved with what he was doing."

Back at the newspaper the following morning, Liam found several notes concerning Loui's demise. Most were from his faithful followers of his newspaper articles or friends who they thought they knew who could be responsible for Loui's early demise.

Some blamed Loui personally for being a snitch and deserved what he got while others could not believe someone would do such a thing to a taxi driver. Why, they wondered would kill someone like Loui for a couple of dollars?

Liam decided to start the by morning calling each person who sent him information. He wanted to get a feel for the reason or motivating force inspiring such response from his readers and friends.

Learning as much as he could from feedback of his readers and friends; might just spur a new light on the situation and encourage those interested to continue their own inquiries and if new information was learned, to inform him or police of their discoveries.

After contacting several readers whom he received notes from, and learning what they knew, he had a better understanding of the challenge he was up against. Finished with calling several on his list, and while the information was still fresh in his mind, Liam began his article for the following day.

As he wrote his thoughts down, he could not help thinking about Marlene, Loui's wife. Why had Loui never mentioned her; he found that strange.

Finishing the article later that afternoon and submitting it to the editor for changes [if any] and approval; Marlene kept popping-up in his thoughts. He needed to learn more about her and why Loui never mentioned her. After all the time Liam and Loui had known each other, Loui should have mentioned her, but why had he kept her a secret?

The article was approved, and sent to publication to be placed on the front page once again. It was another controversial article, but needed published. This was the only way the lawlessness surrounding the city could be brought to light, and eradicated.

Later that evening while at home conversing with Darla Sue, Liam decided to do some research on his own on his home computer to see what he could find out about this mysterious Marlene. It did not take long until her name surfaced, and certain aspects of her past came into play. She was not the sweet thing she appeared when he talked to her earlier over the phone.

His research was turning out to be a treasure trove of information, and not what he expected to unearth.

Marlene had a checkered past including, several run-ins with police and had been incarcerated at one point for several months refusing to testify in a murder case involving [The Family] working out of New York.

She had been a key witness in a former trial for the prosecution, but refused to take the stand and testify when ordered by the judge. At which point she was held in contempt, given six months in jail, and fined several thousand dollars. Later Liam discovered she had been associated with not only Doc Neeson, Angelo but Kenny Dugan. She was one that needed watching now.

He went to see Captain Cahill at police headquarters the following morning, to explained in detail what he found while searching Marlene's records on his home computer. Captain Cahill was just as surprised as Liam at his new findings. They had no idea

Marlene Montanan had been involved with most of the notorious crime figures in and around city.

Her run-ins with law enforcement earlier in her career, was apparently kept from the lime light after marrying Loui, who had never been arrested, and lived a typical straight, uneventful life, prior to meeting up with Marlene.

Unknowingly to Loui he confided to Marlene as being an informant to Liam. It was important to him in helping Liam informing him of certain information vital to his scathing articles he came across from street talk and fares. A lot of rumor and idle talk went on outside and inside the taxi, and occasionally a real valuable piece of information was leaked. He would tell Marlene in confidence, not knowing she would immediately pass on what he told her to those she associated with, but only after Loui had left to go to work.

This passing on of information had been ongoing for three years since their marriage. That's why it was so hard at the time for law enforcement to catch or entrap those responsible terrorizing the citizenry and companies around town. By knowing ahead of time [with Marlene's help], those in power could easily slip below the radar or wait for things to settled down before continuing their evil deeds.

The higher up were willing to pay any amount of hush money to get things accomplished, while they themselves stayed at a safe distance away from the media and public attention. That's why it was with Marlene as their informant, such a lucrative business for those running the show.

As long as they themselves stayed off the radar, and behind the scenes, business continued as usual. Lawlessness and terrorizing continued unabated with outside help from the streets, as long as they received their daily and weekly updates from Marlene by Loui.

This was the perfect arrangement. As long as Loui [unknowing] supplied Marlene with pertinent information, about things they needed to know, kept them on top of their game and out of the limelight. once Loui was murdered, the material supplied by him to Marlene dried up. She now became a liability. No longer an asset to those she confided in. Knowing the active players locally, she herself now had to be removed.

It was only be a matter of time until her usefulness as an informant was no longer desirable. Information provided by her was the only purpose for her existence within the group, once her info dried up, she was no longer required.

Meanwhile Liam, Darla Sue, Detective's Paulson and Callahan followed up with their search for vital information concerning Marlene past. They could not believe Marline had been such a find. With her inside knowledge of different organizations, she was associated, was possible to crack the case wide open if only they could convince her to assist them in their investigation.

It was agreed by all those involved in the case that Liam was the one to approach Marlene, since he was the only one who knew her personally. His job would be to convince her to give-up what she knew after explaining to her the court system would go much easier on her down the line if she was would testify about her involvement with those undesirables she had associated with in the past. This would not be easy, and Liam was not looking forward to his role in persuading Marlene, it was in her best interest to do so.

Marlene had always treated him with respect while in her presence. This was going to be one of the hardest things he ever done. But something needed to be done, and those individuals responsible for the unrest and terror plaguing the community had to be put away.

Marlene was their only conduit; the only insider with access to names, dates, and whereabouts of those who were accountable.

It was contingent on Marlene's willingness to assist the prosecution in its case against those members of city hall's elite and their subordinates. With Marlene's connection and knowledge to the criminal element locally, plus her association with the individuals responsible for most of the illegal activity around town. Her testimony would be a game changer. It was up to Liam to convince her to play hard ball with police and prosecutor. If not, she too could be facing prison time as an accomplice or coconspirator.

Everything rested on Lima's shoulders, convincing Marlene to give up the names of those responsible. If Liam could convince Marlene to turn state evidence, it would be a feather in his hat, and over for those in charge of the carnage and misdeeds. It would bring an end to an era that had been going on far too long, and heading in the wrong direction.

Marlene was their one and only hope getting a conviction of those in authority and ridding the community of corruption and wrongdoings.

Liam, was briefed by Detective Paulson and Callahan on how to approach Marlene, gaining her trust, getting to her to tell of her involvement within the organizations she worked. It took several days of intense coaching from the two detectives, instructing Liam on the finer points convincing Marlene's assistance in the investigation. Soon he became all too familiar with the values of being persuasive; it was time to turn him lose. Now, that Liam was up to speed, felt he was ready to take on the challenge.

Chapter 30

It was time he called Marlene.

Liam while sitting at his desk at the newspaper office, picked up the phone and dialed Marlene's number.

Marline answered after several rings, "Hello."

"Good afternoon, Marlene this is Liam Drake, a friend of your late husband."

"Yes, I remember you. You, on occasion visited Loui here in our home."

"Yes, that's right. I was wondering if I could talk to you sometime in the near future about circumstances surrounding your husband's demise? I have a few questions only you know or could possibly clarify. It would be helpful to me in getting your input or response to certain questions concerning those he believed was responsible for some of the havoc going on around town. Would you be up to me interviewing you next week? Of course, and at your convenience."

"Don't know what it is I could possibly help you with, but yes. You can all me next week and we'll make arrangements to meet and if I can
be of help, I'd be more than happy to be of assistance."

"Great, I will call you early next week to set up an appoint for the interview. Looking forward to seeing you again, good bye."

After hanging up talking to Marlene, Liam picked up the phone again and dialed Detective Paulson.

"Good morning, Detective Paulson, this is Liam Drake. I wanted to let you know I got hold of Marlene Montanan. I made arrangements to call her back next week and set a time and place to interview her. I wanted to let you know ahead of time, that way you'll be able keeping her under surveillance and witness any unusual activity between her and her cronies before my interview. She seemed to be upset when she answered her phone, but otherwise she seemed quite amiable.

Now that Loui is dead and no longer supplying her with information; she serves no vital purpose to those groups or associates. I'm sure they no longer require her assistance and maybe weighing heavy on her mind. She's become a liability not an asset any longer.

With the information she's collect over a three-year period could cause immense trouble within the organizations she's connected. You may want to think about placing her in a safe house later if I can get her to testify on behalf of the state until this is over. As we both know without her testimony, it would be almost impossible to convict those individuals involved."

"Yes, I agree. I will get to work on this matter right away."

Liam hung the phone up and settled in to begin his daily routine, composing an editorial article for the following day. He did a bit of snooping around the office to see if there were any new stories or information, he could use in his upcoming article scheduled for tomorrow's editorial page. As he searched, he just happened to see something tacked on the bulletin board that caught his attention.

A simple note stating, Kenny Dugan missing?

Liam thought to himself, [Kenny, Dugan, a friend of Loui's suddenly comes up missing? What gives?]

He started searching the local archives to see if he could come up with more on Kenny Dugan's past. So little was known of him, maybe there was a story here too. The more he searched the more he learned of Kenny's past and found it checkered but colorful. After several hours of searching found more and more information on Mr. Dugan. Before long he had enough material he thought for a new article.

After his research on Mr. Dugan, returned to his desk, where he sat down, spending the next several hours compiling his research, and when he had them in order, began writing his next article. After finishing his latest article, thought to himself, *[This is a* real *game changer, can't believe I just happened up on this Dugan out of the blue]*. With the completed article in his hand, walked it over to the Chief Editor's desk where he placed the article on the editor's desk, then asked, "Do you have time to read my new article, then give me your opinion?

After reading the article, the Chief Editor was taken aback by the all the new information Liam provided about this Mr. Dugan and his connection to organized crime.

Kenny Dugan was not your typical small-time hoodlum or thug, his specialty as Liam learned was torture, carnage, and murder. Not once in all the delving into Dugan's past had Liam discovered any type of long-term conviction, although having been arrested several times, but no formal declaration of guilt was ever found.

Somehow, Kenny Dugan was able in avoiding conviction on lack of evidence or some off the wall minor technicality by his high-priced lawyers. Mr. Dugan somehow had been living under the radar due to his introversion personality, focusing on his inner feelings and ideas, and not what was going on around him.

Those powerful people he worked for keep him out of the limelight and jail, paying off their high-priced lawyers, with clout with an unlimited expense account. They were hired because they were the best. Dugan, each time he had been arrested had been immediately surrounded by the best lawyers available in the area or brought in from the outside. He was one of a kind, a prize possession for those who demanded his specialized services. They did whatever it took to keep him safe and available at their beckon call.

He was one you seldom read or heard about. But when brought to the public's attention, one could not ignore his audacity in his respect to human life. One of a kind. A hired assassin. And when presented before the community, the focus of public interest was always reached its apex, and necessitated a lot of attention and curiosity.

After the story ran the following morning in the Jersey Journal, it put a whole new light on the meaning of hired gun.

Not only did the police department and prosecution team confronted with two murders, how were they ever going to be able in tying them together. It was to be a monumental task trying the two murders to Mr. Dugan let alone a conviction. But with time on their side, they hoped justice would prevail. At least that was the hope of those involved in this case.

Meeting with Marlene the following week, Liam was able in convincing her it was in her best interest to turn state evidence, admitting her guilt in the matter, and testifying as a witness for the state against her accomplices in exchange for leniency or possibly immunity from further prosecution.

Detective Paulson after hearing of Marlene's commitment to Liam, assuring him she would testify for the prosecution; Detective Paulson sent two patrol officers to picked her up and drive her to one of several safe houses locally run by law enforcement.

Detective Paulson was ready to take the bull by the horns and begin the long laborious task of locating individuals associated or thought to have involvement in the two latest homicides. When found, they would be rounded up, brought back to police headquarters for additional questioning and investigating.

Once the questioning of those who were believed to have knowledge of the murders, statements would be taken and later recorded. At that point, the paperwork would be handed over to the prosecution's office to be scrutinized by their legal staff. The prosecution's office could then begin focusing on what to do with the information received from the interrogations of those brought in for questioning, prior to filing the case with the court.

A lot of leg work and mental effort trying to piece each part of the puzzle together, before going forward and charging each individual litigant.

But, the second murder by Kenny Dugan [if it could be proven], only made things more complicated. The charge of the second murder now doubled their efforts, and suddenly found themselves back to square one. How were the police and prosecutor's office going to combine forces and separate fact from untruths of information gathered from the liars and hooligans that were questioned? It was a daunting task no matter how they sliced it, for those assumed involved somehow with information into the murders.

After months of investigation, and piecing together bits and fragments of known facts, the case was finally taking shape and coming together.

Both murders had a similar modus operandi (MO), in the way they had been carried out, and concluded Kenny Dugan's was the murderer, because it had all the classic signs of a hired assassin, but quickly dropped because Kenny Dugan been found dead shortly after his egregious act on the two women.

The million-dollar question now, who was this new hired assassin?

Chapter 31

With no new clues as to who they were now looking for, asked help from all the agencies associated with police departments locally and nationally. Again, they came up short with only a few signs as to the identity of the would-be assassin. Exhausting all avenues at their disposal, Detective Paulson and Callahan were at wits end as they searched high and low for the new elusive trigger man who had shot and killed Kenny Dugan.

Not long after running into this brick wall, out of nowhere a person of interest had been arrested on a minor offence and brought to police headquarters where he was booked for misdemeanor.

As he sat in a cell along with a former associate, he told his cell mate the story of how the infamous Kenny Dugan (which they both knew) had been taken out by a person of little importance.

Kenny Dugan, happened to be visiting a local gin mill late one evening in Hoboken where he had struck up a conversation with a regular (named Leon) who happened to be sitting next to him at the bar. After a time, Kenny who soon felt comfortable talking to Leon, began spouting about how he snuffed out someone by the name of Loui Montanan a while back and police he heard still had no clue as to who did the killing.

Unbeknown to Kenny Dugan or Leon, a friend of Loui's arrived about that time and sat down at the only seat left at the bar. And it just happened to be next to Kenny Dugan as he continued espousing his story of killing Loui.

Travis Beno's a lifelong friend of Loui, having grown up together in the same neighborhood in Hoboken, attended the same schools and served in the military together. Had kept in contact after serving together and still got together on special occasions.

After hearing Kenny acknowledge killing his best friend, Travis decided to follow Kenny out of the gin mill when he left and confront him. When it came time for Kenny Dugan to leave, he told Leon not to mention this to anyone that he was the one responsible for killing Loui.

As Kenny got up to leave, shook hands with Leon and told him he hoped to see him around. As Kenny was leaving, Travis finished his drink then got up from the bar and followed Travis outside. Once outside and as Kenny began walking down the street, Travis called to him. Kenny stopped in his tracks, turned around, and by now Travis was just one or two steps away. Travis confronted Kenny about killing his best friend Loui.

Kenny Dugan who was highly intoxicated at the time, became loud and boisterous, could not believe what was happening. Told Travis, "Get out of my f…king face or I'll do the same to you."

At which point Travis took one last step toward Kenny, quickly pulled out an 8-inch switchblade knife from his back pocket, and began stabbing Kenny Dugan in the midsection, each time twisting and turning the knife in all directions cutting anything it came in contact with. After Kenny Dugan fell to the sidewalk, Travis bent down and wiped off his knife on Kenny's shirt, stood back up, turned, and quietly walked away. It did not take long until Kenny Dugan bled to death there on the dark, damp, and deserted sidewalk. End of an era for Kenny Dugan.

After hearing Leon's story, Joey Langhart (Leon's cell mate) convinced Leon to give it up. He would never be able in living with himself knowing what Kenny Dugan had done. Joey Langhart finally convinced Leon to tell the story Kenny Dugan told him the night he was murdered.

When Detective Paulson heard Leon had personal information about Kenny Dugan murder, he wasted no time having him delivered to one of the small interview rooms and confront him.

That afternoon as Leon was brought to the interview room, was met by Detective Paulson who were waiting by the door of the small cubical. After the two entered the small cubical and seated, Detective Paulson asked about what he had learned in the cell after talking to Leon? Leon told Detective Paulson the story of his meeting Kenny Dugan one evening a gin mill. How he, Kenny Dugan, told him about snuffing out Loui Montanan earlier. Kenny explained to Leon that Loui Montanan had to be silenced because of certain information he had been privy to and had passed on to his wife. Loui was unaware at the time his wife had been passing this confidential information back to those who carrying out acts terrorizing local contractors and employees, and occasionally murder. He told his wife everything, even the names of persons responsible for committing such a reprehensible act? It was getting too hot for those Kenny Dugan worked for, and Loui Montanan they declared was dispensable.

Detective Paulson, after questioning Leon and hearing how and why Loui had been murdered had more than enough to keep himself and Callahan busy for the next several weeks.

Three murders now, with no responsible party to pin them on become a nightmare.

Continuing with their investigation, it was not long until the name Travis Beno's was brought to the forefront. But only after questioning the bartender at the gin mill who was on duty that night, were they able in learning of Travis Beno's involvement. Detective Paulson along with Detective Callahan made a major break in the investigation and now were able tying Travis Benos to the scene and possibly the murder of Kenny Dugan.

The only thing missing was Travis Benos. He had to be found and questioned before their only lead in the case turned cold. Travis Benos, now the main suspect in Kenny Dugan's death must be found, and brought in for questioning as soon as possible. It now became a race against time for Detective Paulson and Callahan. With their latest lead, it was all hands-on deck until Travis Beno's was located and brought in.

After talking to the bartender and learning of Travis Benos, went back to the police station and looked up Travis Benos's file in their computer data base, where they found his mug shot and a short rap sheet.

He had been arrested a half dozen times on minor offenses, ranging from petty theft, loitering, and fighting. Nothing serious. With his last known address listed on his rap sheet, the detectives decided to drive out to see if he still lived at that address. After their arrival, located the landlord whom they questioned him about a tenant named Travis Benos.

The landlord informed the two officers, "Mr. Benos had moved out only a couple of days prior to their arrival, and had not left a forwarding address. He paid his last month's rent in cash and left."

They asked the landlord, "Would it be possible to inspect the room Mr. Benos rented?"

"Yes, let me get you the key."

After an extensive search of his room, found nothing beneficial to the case with the exception of a discarded birthday card signed, "From your friend, Loui."

Detective Paulson and Callahan looked at each other and both thought to themselves, *[Was this be the same Loui that had been found murdered recently?]*

This was the first solid lead they had come across while searching for Travis; it was not much but significant. If they could tie Travis Benos to Loui Montanan, it would establish a connection and hopefully a motive for Mr. Lenny Dugan demise. A lot was riding on finding Travis Benos.

They knew Travis Benos had been at the gin mill the night Kenny Dugan was murdered, as several witnesses had step forward and verified seeing him there. Each of the witness detectives talked to at the gin mill that particular night substantiated the fact that it was Travis Benos who sat next to Kenny Dugan prior to his leaving.

The bartender recalled Travis Benos having only one drink and finished drinking it before paying his bar tab and left around the same time as Kenny Dugan.

Another patron of the bar by the name of Joe Bryant, sitting alone at one of the tables not far from the bar, remembered this Travis fellow sitting next to Kenny Dugan, and that Travis Benos seemed upset as he followed Kenny Dugan out the front door.

If it was Travis Benos who followed Kenny Dugan out that night; had Kenny and Travis know each other previously? Could it be possible they had a prior beef with each other and that's why Travis followed Kenny Dugan outside to confront him? There were many questions needing to be answered before the real reason for the killing would be fully known.

With no other evidence found inside Travis's apartment, (other than the birthday card) and Detective Callahan had carefully picked up and placed it inside a plastic zip lock bag to turnover to forensics for analysis. Finding nothing else of interest, finished with their investigation of Travis's apartment, and drove back to police headquarters.

Was the birthday card the smoking gun they were looking for?

Arriving back at headquarters, and handing the birthday card over to forensics, hoping it contained other mysteries such as DNA or fingerprints, tying Travis to the homicide. With all the new techniques and scientific test used in police laboratories today it was almost certain the card contains some trace of DNA or other vital information that could be used in this case. If nothing else the detectives maybe get lucky and locate which store the card had been purchased, and by watching an old surveillance tapes (If available) spot Travis. The possibilities are endless, every lead no matter how minor was worth following up on.

The Police Forensics Department would go over the birthday card found at Travis's apartment with a fine-tooth comb, in hopes of finding something of interest, a finger print, a strand of hair or minute piece of fiber and be used to enhance the results of similar evidence stored in their collection of evidence. If confirm, their hypothesis as to Travis's connection with Loui Montanan was correct, it would be an open and shut case.

Chapter 32

As the detective's investigation slowly moved forward, day after day, the bits and pieces of information started to confirm their suspicions. The mystery person behind the killing of Kenny Dugan pointed more and more to Travis Benos. With what evidence the detectives had collected up to this point, clearly pointed to Kenny Dugan as the one who killed Loui Montanan, and Travis Benos killing Kenny Dugan. With the volume of evidence in this case now, it was thought to be enough in charging Travis Benos with Kenny Dugan's murder.

With the evidence compiled by Detectives Paulson and Callahan was sufficient and ready to be handed over to the prosecution to file a pretrial brief. It was time for the prosecution to do the arduous task of taking the information given them by the two detectives and perform their magic.

From the assembled information they received consisted of only the known facts. It was their job to assemble those facts into legal issues, decisions, (holdings), reasoning, separate opinions analysis and principles in the case, then present those facts to the court providing the judge enough evidence and cause to rule in favor of the party represented by the writer of the brief, motion for a pretrial hearing on the merits of the brief.

A couple of days after learning who was responsible for killing Kennedy Dugan, Travis Montanan was found hiding in his stepfather's basement. At which point Mr. Benos was arrested, read his rights, then removed from the basement and taken to the local jail, where he was eventually book for murder. While awaiting a hearing Travis Benos had been appointed a Defense Attorney since he was not able to afford one himself, named Alexander Thompson.

Freshly out of law school, this would be Attorney Alexander Thompson's first attempt at representing a client actually accused of murder. Hastily Attorney Thompson gathered together a small defense team and began his brief to present to the presiding Judge Henry Goodfellow. Once the prosecution and defense teams presented their briefs to Judge Goodfellow they were told, "I will notify you of the date I need you to appear to discuss the legal arguments of both sides before setting aside the jury selection process. Once the jury process has been completed, I will then set the time and date to begin the trial.

When the day came to begin the jury selections, jurors were notified and selecting of jurors begin on the following Monday. One by one, the jurors were brought forward answering questions from both sides of the isle, and only those jurors who satisfied certain criteria were selected. A juror who was considered leaning or gravitating one way or the other were immediately disqualified and dismissed. Those jurors who seemed creditable and without prejudice were carefully chosen to sit in on the trial. Once the jury selection had been accepted by both sides, the second phase of the trial was ready to begin.

Opening day of trial, the prosecution began parading witness after witness to the witness stand. After a few days of questioning each witness by prosecution and defense teams, witnesses who took the stand and seemed to be truthful, gave full accounting of what they saw or could recall; all the while the defense attorney or prosecution attorney tried poking holes in the others witness's testimony.

Time had arrived that the defense side was to place Trevor Benos on the stand. After being sworn in he was told, "Be seated."

The defense attorney approached the podium and before questioning Mr. Trevor Benos, turned to the jury pointing at Trevor Benos and told them,

"Mr. Benos, happened to be an innocent bystander (at the time) of the alleged murder of Mr. Dugan, he happened to be at the wrong place at the wrong time. While sitting at a bar relaxing that particular evening, overheard a conversation between a Mr. Kenny Dugan and a Mr. Leon Everhart. He heard Mr. Kenny Dugan admit to Leon Everhart killing his best friend, Mr. Loui Montanan.

This apparently was the catalyst which triggered his reaction to follow Mr. Kenny Dugan outside when he left the bar. Once outside the bar and without fully thinking what he was about to do, confronted Mr. Kenny Dugan, when suddenly, my client over powered by anger at Mr. Kenny Dugan for killing his friend, his military background kicked in. With his persistent PTSD (posttraumatic stress disorder) suffered during the Iraqi war. Had battled it on a daily basis since leaving the military; and without warning my client Mr. Trevor Benos went off the deep end.

Mr. Benos quickly provoked by Mr. Dugan and in a rage of anger, withdrew the switchblade knife he carried from his back pocket, pressing the button on the handle, exposing the sinister razor-sharp seven-inch blade and stabbed Mr. Kenny Dugan in a fit of ire. After the short episode on the sidewalk, Mr. Trevor Benos calmy closed the blade back into the handle of the knife, turned calmy from the victim lying on the sidewalk and slowly walked from the scene.

Still facing the jury, young Attorney Allen Thompson communicated to the jury,

"Ladies and gentlemen of the jury, Mr. Travis Benos has been receiving treatment and counseling through the Jersey City VA clinic since leaving the military, and has been a model patient and progressing well with the programs and treatments offered. But Mr. Travis Benos upon hearing his lifelong friend had been killed by this hired assassin could not constrain his emotions and feeling any longer, and no one is beyond doing things that are outside his or her rational realm of reasoning from time to time. This was one of those times Mr. Benos I'm sure wishes he could take back; but unfortunately, as regrettable as this act had been, it can never be undone.

Ladies and gentlemen of the jury, put yourself in his shoes. I'm sure some of you would have done the same thing. He will always be fraught with this heinous act for the remainder of his natural life. Something any of us would be capable of if the tables were turned. We all act or react differently to any given situation and that is exactly what Mr.

Trevor Benos did. Killing Mr. Dugan was not the right decision, but one Mr. Benos was faced with at the time. With little or no control of his emotions or feelings about what he was about to do, did killed Mr. Dugan in cold blood."

Turning back, facing Mr. Trevor Benos, said to him,

"I understand you and Mr. Loui Montanan grew up together and had been lifelong friends? And you were beside yourself when you learned that this Mr. Dugan took your friends life, is that correct?"

"Yes Sir."

"And you visited him at home on special occasions or he had asked you over for dinner? And, was his wife usually present when you were there?"

"Yes, she was always present when I went over."

"Had you been privy to accounts given by Mr. Loui Montanan about certain illegal activities occurring throughout the city by elected officials and some of their department heads?"

"Yes, we often talked about the illegal activities going on throughout the city."

"At the time do you recall his wife being present when he revealed certain illegal activities going?"

"Yes."

"And is it true, his wife unknowingly to you and her husband passed information he gathered on a daily basis from passengers in his cab, friends, and strangers on the street to the criminal element she working with?"

"Yes, that's correct, as I've learned since his passing."

"In your opinion, how long had she been secretly informing these illegal groups she was associated or worked with?"

"I'm assuming, as long as she and Loui had been married, for at least three years I know of."

"Were you aware of her ties to organized crime at the time?"

"No, that came as a complete surprise to me. When I first heard of her activities working with those groups, I could not believe what I was hearing."

"Is it your belief that Mr. Loui Montanan was unaware also of his wife's affiliation with the mob?"

"As far as I know he was oblivious of the fact."

"Were you aware that the group she worked for was responsible for having your friend Mr. Montanan killed?"

"No Sir, not until the night I learned of it while sitting at the bar and overheard the conversation between Kenny Dugan and Leon Everhart. That was the first time I had heard of either Kenny Dugan or Leon Everhart."

"And when you heard that this Kenny Dugan had murdered your best friend, what went through your mind?"

"I really don't recall. I think I was so distraught finding out that I was sitting next to the person who killed Loui that I lost it."

"What do you mean, you lost it?"

"Don't remember anything after hearing Kenny Dugan admitting to killing Loui, until after I had stabbed him on the sidewalk. I looked down and saw him lying on the sidewalk bleeding to death, trying to breath and was mumbling something, but could not make it out what he was saying. At that moment, I realized what I had done. It was not the first-time killing someone, I've killed several people while in Iraq on patrol, and I've became hardened at seeing people die. When I realized what had happened, that's when I went to my stepfathers and hid in his basement. I needed time to think."

"Did you tell your father-in-law the reason you wanted to use his basement?"

"No, it was a place I could lay low for a couple of days until I could get a handle on my faculties. I was confused and needed to regroup and think about what I had done."

"I see, and what happened after you were found in the basement?"

"I was arrested and booked for the murder of Kenny Dugan."

"Are you remorseful at the heinous act you committed?"

"Yes, but it was something I had no control over. I thought I was back in Iraq; he was the enemy and needed to be silenced."

"Have you been suffering with the PSTD since you've been incarcerated?"

"Yes, I have flashbacks on a daily basis. I have asked several times while incarcerated to see a case manager about sending me a therapist, but my request has been denied each time."

"I presume a therapist is able helping you cope with everyday situations and the stresses of normal living?"

"Yes, they have the means to help with the evil thoughts that go on in my mind daily. Without having a therapist available; I find it difficult coping with the real world at times."

"Then it can be assumed you are not 100% since your return from
Iraq?"

"You can say that."

"Your Honor, I have no further questions."

"Thank you, councilor. Does the prosecution wish to question the witness?"

"Yes, your honor."

With that, Attorney Jared Leibovich, hired hatchet man for the group takes to the podium.

"Good afternoon judge, ladies and gentlemen of the jury. I'm Jared Leibovich representing the state in this case involving the murder of one Mr. Lenny Dugan."

Turning toward the witness stand, looking at Travis Benos, then asks the judge,

"May I approach the witness?"

"Yes, you may approach the witness."

Slowly Attorney Leibovich reaches down and picks up a photo of Lenny Dugan. Then slowly walks out from behind the podium and approaches the witness stand. Once he is next to the witness, places the picture of Mr. Kenny Dugan on the counter in front of Travis Benos, then backs up a couple of spaces.

"Mr. Benos, do you recognize the person in the photo?"

Travis looks down at the photo?

"Yes,"

"And where do you know this person from?"

"I saw him the first and only time at a gin mill."

"Had you seen this individual previously?"

"No, not to my recollection."

"So, you had no idea who this person was, but later that evening followed him outside and murdered him, is that correct?"

"That's what I've been told."

"Had he been a threat to you that evening while sitting at the bar?"

"No, but hearing him admit to the murder of my friend, I became numb and was no longer thinking rational."

"Why did you not report the incident to the police?"

"Was not thinking clearly, I only wanted to confront him, but was not able in controlling my emotions once outside."

"So, what you are telling me, you did not know this person, only over heard a conversation at the bar with another bar patron, at which time you decided to kill him.?"

"No, that's not what I thought at the time, I wanted to confront him. I wanted to know what my friend had done that was so bad he had to him to kill him."

"Again, you only heard a conversation between two men? Made up your mind it was the person who killed your friend, and you decided to walk outside when he left and confront him? That's all? Is that what you are telling the court?"

"At the time I was sitting at the bar, that was my intentions, yes."

"But what happened between leaving the bar and confronting Mr. Dugan?"

"That remains a mystery. I don't recall following him out and certainly don't remember stabbing him to death."

"But you do remember going to your father-in-law's and hiding in his basement after the incident?"

"Yes."

"Then you knew what you had done, correct?"

"Yes, after I stabbed Mr. Dugan, I remember what I did, and my first thought was to run away and hide. Don't know why I chose the basement at my in-law's, but that's where I wound up."

"Did your in-laws know what you did before hiding in their basement?"

"No. I had access to the house and sneaked in the back door. They apparently did not hear me enter and walk down the basement steps to the basement. I was going to try and get my thoughts together before going to the police. But police found me before I had time to turn myself in."

"No further questions your honor."

"You may step down Mr. Benos."

Judge Goodfellow looked around the court room and declared, "Now that the jury has heard testimony from witnesses on both sides; I'm going to adjourn court and resume again tomorrow morning for closing arguments. I'd like to see both councilors in my chambers once we finish here to go over the details of what I expect from you concerning your closing statements."

With that statement from Judge Goodfellow, court was adjourned.

The following day after court resumed, the prosecution and defense attorneys gave their closing arguments. The trial for all intended purposes had run its course, and all the evidence given and it was now up to the jury in determining the faith of Mr. Travis Benos.

Chapter 33

After several days of serious debate and deliberation, the jury finally reached a verdict. It was time to reconvene court and hear the jury's verdict.

Court was once again convened and called to order by the Honorable Judge Goodfellow who looked over at the jury and asked "Has the jury reached a verdict?"

The jury foreman stood up and said, "Yes, your honor."

"Will the bailiff bring me the verdict."

After Judge Goodfellow was handed the verdict, he read what had been written on the note, then handed it back to the bailiff who returned the note back to the jury foreman. Then Judge Goodfellow asks the jury foreman to read aloud the verdict.

Yes, your honor, "The jury finds the defendant Mr. Trevor Benos, not guilty, due to SMI or serious mental illness."

There was an immediate outburst in the court room by onlookers and prosecution team and those they represented.

The judge hearing the disturbance, immediately picked up his gavel, pounding it on his desk, sternly warned those inside the courtroom causing the ruckus, "I'll have order in the court."

Calm, quickly returned to the court room. Then Judge Goodfellow looked in the direction of the defense's bench and told

Mr. Trevor Benos, "You're free to go." With that said, Judge Goodfellow adjourned the proceedings.

It came as a complete surprise that the jury found Mr. Benos not guilty of murder, but his serious mental illness caused by his PSTD affected the uncontrollable emotional and psychological rage. Under the circumstance the verdict fit the crime in the jury's eyes. It had been a case of coldblooded murder, but with extreme extenuating circumstances attached.

Now that the trial had concluded, it was back to square one for Liam. He left the court house, returning to the newspaper for his next article.

Sitting at his desk began writing, and totally taken aback at the same time, he too was surprised at the outcome of the trial. He expected Mr. Trevor Benos, at the least would be found guilty and placed by the court into a VA mental facility for long term care. He definitely needed psychological because of his PSTD, which had affected his emotional state. But in Trevor Benos's case he gained back his freedom?

Finishing with his latest article, he turned it in to the editor, left the building and drove home. After such a long and vexing day and totally exhausted, he was ready to sit and relax while thinking back on today's events.

The following day Liam made several calls after arriving at work. First was a call to Detective Paulson, a follow up call to Darla Sue requesting seeing her later, and then a close friend by the name of Allen. Liam was worried about the outcome of the trial and the verdict. Would it cause more unrest by those accountable for the discontent and disorder around the city? He had had several threatening calls while at home and now at work. All were about the verdict and a couple of calls congratulating him on his tenacity pursuing those taking advantage of their positions. It had been a long and scary mission, but one Liam was willing to endure in trying to change the system.

Darla Sue called Liam before leaving for work and told him, "I have some good new, we need to talk later."

He said, "Okay, meet me at our favorite haunt."

Their favorite haunt was a local restaurant in Hoboken, where they could have a quite dinner and she could share her good news with Liam. Liam was due some good news, since his life had been in turmoil for the past several years.

While at dinner, Darla Sue reached over and picked up a folder she had placed on the chair next to her and handed it to Liam. Told Liam, "You can read it later, it contains damaging information on the mayor and vice mayor of Jersey City." I received through the mail this morning from an anonymous sender.

As they sat discussing not only the letter, but the trial and how the jury found Trevor Benos not guilty of murder; also, the state of politics in Jersey City and Hoboken. And how the illegal activities seemed to bounced back as city hall reverted back to their old ways, that of corruption and kickbacks. With little or no self-control in city hall after everything possible had been done to rid the metropolitan area of its ravages by the elite, it continued to rage out of control.

What had been done in the past to curtail the havoc and chaos, the surrounding areas were still hot beds of violence and criminal activity. It was like the wild-wild west, with violence and mayhem found under every rock turned over in the city's assembly. *[Could it ever be stopped]*, Liam questioned himself?

The next day Liam visited the police station where he met with Detective Paulson. He questioned Detective Paulson about what the police were doing at present in to stop this madness going on within its own ranks and city hall?

Detective Paulson gave Liam a rundown on what his department and other departments locally and state wide plus several honest city officials were doing, and the overall success they were having restraining the state of affairs locally. It was working, but would take time slowing down this menacing dilemma facing the city.

As the weeks, months and years passed, things slowly began turning around. There was less violence and corruption within the metro area, but continued at a snail's pace and getting better. As those in city hall were targeted as violators they were quickly arrested. Most were removed or replaced by local elections, which helped weed out some of the riff raft previously plaguing the community as they went about their business serving themselves as well as their constituents.

Things in the city were nowhere near normal, but seemed to be on the mends. The construction groups working in the area were basically free of the turbulence at present, which so often had hindered their work in the past. A feeling of peace and tranquility had semi-returned to the city and it felt good.

Detective Paulson and Callahan on occasions meet with Liam and bring him up to speed, plus congratulating him on the success his articles had had helping stem the tide of those who once roamed the streets with total immunity. Those days were over. But they knew it was not over, but curtailed or reduced for the moment.

With local groups and centralized enterprises run by the criminal elements, they were always on the prowl. Ready in a moment's notice to engage in any and all illegal activities that popped up. It was only a matter of time before they again enter the bowls of the city in force.

Lawlessness, had been a staple of the community over the years, and had no intentions of going away anytime soon. These organized groups prayed on the general public with as much reprisal as those who opposed them. It was a cat and mouse game gone awry. This type of activity had been going on since the dawn of time in one form or another.

Chapter 34

With the bulk of those causing trouble and turmoil having been convicted or had left town seeking refuge or greener pastures. Once again it was safe walking the streets without fear of reprisal.

Liam, continued his articles on organized crime, still prevalent, but working underground and for the most part out of sight; while keeping a tight lid on their movements and activities. It was hard finding anyone who knew where they were and what they were up to. The police, at the helm, kept watchful eyes out as they continued their war on persons of interest and objectionable.

Darla Sue and Liam, had combined forces and making arrangement for their future. It had been a long time coming, but their time to be together had arrived.

They began making plans for future, to wed, and start a new life together. Deciding to tie the knot, and prior to the big day, Liam had discovered an envelope taped to his front door as he arrived home from work one evening. He opened the envelope before entering and found a short note inside threating his life.

It read as follows:

"Your life is in serious danger and you need to take this message serious. This is your final warning."

After reading the message a couple of times as he stood outside in the hallway visibly shaken. Finally, after gathering his thoughts, opened the door and went inside, closing the door behind him. Then proceeded over to where the phone was, and called the police department. He again called for Detective Paulson. After several rings the desk sergeant answered. "Could I talk to Detective Paulson?" The desk sergeant informed him that, "Detective Paulson had left for the day."

Liam then asked the desk sergeant, "Would you please leave him a message that Mr. Liam Drake needs to speak with him at his earliest convenience?"

The following morning at work, Liam received a call from Detective Paulson asking, "What can I do for you Mr. Drake?"

Liam told him, "I received a note as I returned home last evening from work. It was a threat on my life if I did not stop writing my articles about the criminal dealings going on around city hall. And I'm taking this latest threat very seriously."

Detective Paulson said,

"Why don't you bring the envelope with the note to my office, I'll have forensics analyzed both to see if there's any evidence still on either of the items. There could possibly be hair, fiber or prints. If anything shows up, we may be able to follow up."

Liam left work as soon as he could, delivered the envelope along with the note to the police station and gave it to Detective Paulson.

Liam was informed by Detective Paulson,

"It will take the lab a few days to check for DNA and other telltale signs, if they exist at all; no guarantees, but worth a closer look."

Several days passed when Liam received a call back from Detective Paulson telling him the results of the test had been returned, but no significant evidence had been found on either the envelope or note inside. Whoever sent you the warning apparently wiped the contents clean prior to taping it to your door frame of the apartment.

Liam, disappointed at hearing nothing had been found connecting those who had written the note, or who left the envelope and where it might have come from. The threat was still a priority; Liam had to be caution and vigilant once again, each time he left the office or apartment.

Darla Sue hearing of the note later, felt she too was under the microscope even though she had not been mentioned or included in this latest threat.

A couple of weeks passed, when Liam was abducted leaving for work one morning. Two men had rushed out of the stairwell while he waited for the elevator. One of the abductors pointed a gun at his head and told to follow them or he would blow his F*****g head off. With Liam in tow, walked him to the stairwell and down to the first-floor landing. Opening the stair well door, one of the men took a looked and without saying a word, walked Lima out into the parking lot and shoved him into a waiting car.

At which time they not only blindfolded him, but hog tied and strapped him securely in the rear seat of the car with one of the seat belts. Then drove him around what seemed to be forever. It was really closer to a half hour or so to another part of town, where they stopped the car when Liam heard one of them say,

"Okay Hector, let's get him inside before anyone sees us, you know how many eyes are out there and could be watching."

"Yeah, I know."

Once Liam was removed from the car and hustled into a building, and led up a flight of stairs to a room somewhere on the second floor. Here they left him blindfolded and tied up laying on the floor.

Then warned him,

"Do not get up or try to escape, if you do, you'll be sorry."

Liam, heard them as they left the room, closing the door and locking it.

They left him lying on the floor all night, and it was not until the following morning Liam heard several voices, he assumed it was his captors walking down the hallway. Soon he heard the door unlocked, as several men entered.

He heard this Hector say,

"Is he the one you wanted me and Carlos to kidnap?"

"Yes, you boys did a fine job in finding him, and bringing him to me."

At which time, the boss Lefty told Hector,

"Remove the blindfold and let me see his face."

Once the blindfold had been removed, Liam slowly opened his eyes but was having difficulty adjusting to the bright light in the room; when he heard this Lefty say, "So, Mr. Drake you are the one that's been writing and harassing me and my organization in your daily editorials? Why do you continue to hound me, I've not done nothing to you have I? I'm a business man doing a job I'm hired to do, just like you. 1 I think I've had enough of your s**t to last me a life time, so today I'm going to put a stop to it, do I make myself clear?" Liam did not answer.

Okay Hector, go get me the black bag I left in the hallway, and bring it to me.

"Okay Boss."

Hector left the room and soon returned with a black bag which he handed to Lefty. Lefty placed the bag on a table nearby and opened it quickly. Reaching inside, removed a pair of pruning shears and walked slowly back to where Liam was now sitting up on the floor. Reaches down and cuts the restraints off Liam's right wrist, then tells Hector,

"Stuff this rag in his mouth and restrain him so he's not able to get up or move around. Once everything had been done according to Lefty's demands, Lefty reaches down and takes Liam's right hand in his left and hold it high above Liam's head, and without warning snips off his right pinky finger.

Liam tries to screams, but only muffled sounds are heard.

Lefty asks Liam,

"Did that hurt? That's how I feel when I see those lies you write about me and my organization in your daily column."

Lefty had Hector remove the rag from Liam's mouth once he settled down and stopped screaming. Liam looked up at Lefty and very softly said in between sharp pains still reverberating from the severed finger, and said, "But I did not mutilate your body parts, only wrote about organized crime."

"I know, and I'm one of those you write about and it hurts."

With Liam's hand still high above his head, still bleeding profusely, Lefty tells Hector to replace the rag back into Liam's mouth. Still in pain from the removal of the first pinky finger, Lefty once again proceeds to snip off Liam's index finger.

Liam tries screaming a second time, but with the rag stuffed far back into his mouth, and the pain so great, he soon passes out.

When Liam woke up the following day in the hospital. Opening his eyes slowly, the first thing he saw was Detective Paulson and Callahan standing by his bedside. As he slowly looks around the room and realizes where he's at; looks back up at Detective Paulson who then asks,

"What happened to you?"

Liam, after hearing Detective Paulson's question; quickly looks down and at his bandaged right hand, and remembering the excruciating pain as this Lefty held his right hand and arm above his head, sitting there on the floor and began sniping his fingers off.

"I remember being kidnapped by two men, one was named Hector, the other Carlos, if I remember correctly. They drove around town and eventually stopped the car where I was escorted blindfolded up a flight of stairs to a second floor and into a small room where I was left overnight. I was awake the whole night, I was not able to sleep wondering what was going to happen to me. When the following morning I heard several men enter the room. They returned with their boss a man by the name of (Lefty) who chastised me for writing stories about him and the different criminal organizations. When suddenly without warning began snipping off my fingers. I remember the pinky finger as it was sniped off, and how excruciating the pain was. Moments later he sniped another finger off, that's all I remember until I woke just now.

"Yes, the doctor here at the hospital told us they found you out front of the hospital's emergency entrance on the sidewalk where you were apparently dumped off after your ordeal."

"Guess I should be grateful they did not kill me."

"Yes, but don't think it's over. These people are playing with you. If you step over the line again, it may spell disaster. You need to take their warning seriously and leave well enough alone at least for the time being."

"But as you know I can't. It is my job to inform the public of such people and stopping this madness in its tracks. I've accepted the challenge and I'm not backing down now."

"Do what you must, but be aware of the consequences if you overstep your bounds," Detective Callahan said.

"I appreciate your concern, but this incident only incentivizes me more to get these scum bags off the street.

The more I can do in removing the individuals one at a time, leading to groups and ten organizations down the road, the better off the citizens of the community will be."

"Thanks for the information."

Detective Callahan and I are going back to the police station and look up those names you supplied us with, maybe we'll get lucky and find the culprits sooner rather than later. I'll be stationing a policeman outside your room until you are released, then I'm going to keep you under surveillance a while longer until this latest episode settles down. Maybe by then we will have this case in the bag.

The Detective Paulson told Liam, "Be mindful of what going on and above all else, be careful once your discharged. Both detectives turned and walked out of the room.

Liam, once again looked down at the large bandaged covering his right hand trying to determine which was the last finger that had been sniped off. But with the huge bandage covering his hand could not tell. He hoped it would not be too much of a burden when it came to doing his work. But any time one loose a finger, it made a difference. He was sure he would overcome his latest impairment, no matter how difficult it turns out to be.

Liam's work, revolved around typing and with the loss of two fingers on his right hand, would certainly put a burden on his ability to type. But with Liam's grit and determination he was not going to let this latest setback stop him from what he did, and again accepted the new challenge. It took longer to become somewhat proficient at typing than he envisioned, but over time he was able to type well enough to continue his daily articles. He continued exposing those taking advantage of the system, noting in a few of his articles, the American system of laws was not always perfect, but still the best legal system in the world and it worked.

Chapter 35

Detective Paulson and Callahan put in a lot of overtime after this last run in Liam had with this Lefty. Searching for the individuals responsible for Liam's assailants, when after several weeks had gone by, finally got a break they'd been looking for, and able in arresting Hector Alverez. After weeks of tireless effort were able in linking this Hector Alverez with Lefty (the boss of a small group of local followers). With a lot of persuasion Detective Paulson and Callahan were able in convincing Hector Alverez in giving up the location of Lefty and Carlos.

Not long after supplying Detective Paulson and Callahan with Lefty's and Carlos's last known addresses, both were found and arrested, brought downtown where Carlos was were booked and charged with kidnapping, and Lefty with bodily harm and kidnapping.

Lefty with the additional charge of causing bodily injury without provocation. All three men were eventually tried and found guilty. Lefty received the maximum sentence and sentenced to East Jersey State Prison for 30 to life. While Carlos assistance in the bazar case received lighter sentences. Since Carlos's corroborating, was sentenced to 10 years' probation. Hector received 10 years for his role in the kidnapping.

Liam, returned back to work, and none the worse for wear. He eventually overcome his handy cap and was back typing daily articles for the paper. With some difficulty, he learned by making minor adjustments to his typing, he was able in completing his work. But, like everything else in his life, had to overcome his adversity and accept his job.

After his latest setback, several things began happening to them.

Darla Sue was promoted at the law firm, giving her more understanding into the inner working of the firm, along with fringe benefits and an increase in salary. This would improve her quality of life and the extra income came along at the right time too.

While Liam had been given more leeway and freedom at the paper, along with a substantial increase in his weekly pay. The increase in salary's came as a complete surprise, and with the increase in pay, would certainly help. The old adage or axiom, [two could live as cheaply as one] does not hold water in today's economy.]

With Darla Sue's promotion and his bump in salary, life was good. It would help them as they readied themselves for their next step in a busy but chaotic time in their life.

After all that had happened since Liam and Darla Sue marriage, they finally were at a point where they began planning a long, but deserved vacation on the Island of Crete. The law firm Darla Sue worked for and the newspaper Liam worked presented them with a check covering the expenses for their flight, vacation arrangements while on their vacation, and extra spending money came along with the packaged deal.

Liam with a strong Greek heritage (on his mothers' side) had always dreamed of going to Greece and learning about his Greek heritage. Not only to Greece, but the island of Crete itself, where his mother was born. He wanted to meet his extended family along with introducing himself and new wife to his Greek relativities living on the island. It had been a lifelong dream of his to return to the birthplace of his mother and meet his family. And while there, learn as much about his mother's side of the family as possible.

Arriving at Athens international airport, they had booked a hotel downtown Athens where they planned spending a few days taking in the sight and sounds of the city before continuing their short flight over to Heraklion, Crete.

The first full day after arriving in Athens, first thing on the agenda was visiting the famous Acropolis. It was a beautiful experience to visit this site where the ancient building known as the Parthenon still stood impressively a top of a huge rock. Darla Sue and Liam could not visualize how such a structure could be constructed so high above the city without modern machinery. It remains a mystery to them and many others even today.

Next day they visited the National Archaeological Museum downtown Athens, and saw the many of the ancient sculptures, artwork and pottery was on display. Later that afternoon they visited the Port of Piraeus and had a late lunch at one of the outdoor dining facilities called Refene. A small but inviting outdoor dining facility and food worth dying for.

Next day they packed their bags and headed back to the Athens International Airport for their short flight to Heraklion, Crete. Arriving at the small airport, they rented a car and drove east along the picturesque and scenic view of the blue waters of the Mediterranean Sea to Malia beach where they had reservations at the High Beach Resort.

Upon reaching the resort, Liam checked he and Darla Sue in and were immediately escorted to their room. After settling in, Lima called his Uncle Adonis who waited anxiously by the phone for a call from his nephew arriving from America. After dialing Adonis's number, Adonis picked up and answered, "Yassou." Adonis after hearing Liam on the other end of the line say,

"Yes, Uncle Adonis, this is Liam."

"Ah nai', yassou Liam, so good to hear your voice.

Sorry for answering the phone in my native tongue, but did it out of habit. Hope you understand? My family and I have been waiting for your call. Where are you and your new wife staying?"

"We are staying over here on Malia Beach at the High Beach Resort."

"Yes, I know the resort."

"Glad you finally arrived, can't wait to meet you and the newest addition to the family."

"Would you like me to drive over to the hotel and pick you up this afternoon?"

"Yes, that sounds great, but if you don't mind, give me and Darla Sue a little time to freshen up."

"Good, see you in a couple of hours, will call when I arrive."

Later that afternoon, Lima after he and Darla Sue had freshened up, heard a knock at the door. Lima walked over, and opening the door, there stood his Uncle Adonis with a wide grin on his face beside his wife Selene. They entered the room and Liam and his uncle Adonis embraced, afterwards Liam introduced his uncle and aunt to his wife, Darla Sue. Whom immediately embraced and welcomed her into the family?

"Sorry I did not call after we arrived here at the hotel, but was not thinking. I was over joyed at meeting my nephew from America and wife, forgot all about notifying you of our arrival."

After a brief meeting, were on their way back out to the parking lot where Uncle Adonis parked his car. It was no time until they were heading down the road on the way to the small town of Kastelli (Kastelli) where Liam was to meet several more members of his immediate family.

The other members of his family he was to meet had either driven or walked from their homes nearby or neighboring villages to Uncle Adonis's. They had come to meet their extended family from America. Soon after their arrival at Uncle Adonis's and Aunt Selene, the gathering turned into a festival.

Uncle Adonis told Lima and Darla Sue, "Any time we have a chance to gather and celebrate, it becomes a holiday. It's not often we have visitors from America and we shall celebrate the occasion with fervor."

Now that everyone had been introduced, it was time to enjoy the memorable event. Lots of wine and goat cheese were consumed while sitting outside under a small olive tree around a large wooden table set up for just such an occasion. They talked nonstop for hours.

But, as the sun slowly began sinking into the west, everyone but Uncle Adonis and Selene and oldest daughter Athena remained. Other members of the family had said their goodbye earlier and gone home.

While Liam and Darla Sue sat outside around the large wooden table, unwinding from their afternoon of eating and drinking with their extended family, had eaten so much cheese, and drank a bit too much wine and ouzo; decided it was time to head back to the hotel. Uncle Adonis told them he would drive them back to Malia Beach to the hotel if they were ready. Both Liam and Darla Sue agreed they had enjoyed their visit and meeting the many family members, but it was time to head back.

Saying good bye to Selene and Athena, Uncle Adonis, Liam and Darla Sue returned to his car where Uncle Adonis drove them back to their Malia Beach hotel. Uncle Adonis stopped at the drive thru entrance of the hotel and dropping them off, but before leaving said, "I wish to see you again before you leave."

"Yes. We will meet again before we leave. Darla Sue and I would like to invite you and Aunt Selene along with Athena to lunch here at the hotel tomorrow if you are not busy."

"That would be something we all would like very much. Call me tomorrow and let us know what time and we will drive back."

"Great, see you tomorrow."

After dropping Liam and Darla Sue off in front of their hotel, Uncle Adonis drove his car around past the parking lot, waving goodbye as he headed out of the parking lot to the main road in front of the hotel.

After a busy day visiting and relaxing with relatives, it was time to clean up, and get ready for another wonderful day on Malia Beach. After showering, took a leisure walk on the beach while listening to the soft murmuring sounds of the Mediterranean waters gently lapped the shore line. It was memorizing as they walked and listened to the sounds and watched the waters as it ebbs and flowed. Faint sounds of bouzouki music could be heard off in the far distance, as tourist and locals sang, danced and enjoyed themselves as the cool breeze blew off the Mediterranean.

After having Uncle Adonis and his family for lunch the following day, their days on the island was running its course. The last couple of days were spent driving around the eastern part of the Island taking in the local culture, ruins and the many sights unfamiliar to them. It had been a marvelous adventure for the newlyweds. So many antiquities and ruins to see and locals who were so hospitable, not like Hoboken or Jersey City. It was like going back in time. After seeing and learning as much about the island and its traditions where his mother's side of the family came from. Both he and Darla Sue had a better understanding of his Greek heritage, and its culture, and the enormous contribution it had given to the world.

Returning from the eastern side of the island, it was time to pack up and head to Heraklion before jetting back to America. The following day checked out of the hotel on Malia Beach and drove west to Heraklion.

They had the concierge at the call ahead, and make reservations for them at the Capsis Astoria Heraklion, near the Heraklion Archaeological Museum which just happened to be on their bucket list to visit.

After checking in at the Capsis Astoria, they head out to visit the famous Minoan Palace of Knossos. It was still early in the day and the weather was perfect for a trek around the country side and the famous Knossos ruins. Knossos ruins was the oldest and most famous ruins in the Mediterranean basin which includes portions of Europe, Africa, and Asia with varied contrasting topography.

Knossos just happens to be the largest Bronze Age archeological site on the Island. It's been referred to in the past as Europe's oldest city. Its location, south of the city of Heraklion and considered the most important archeological site on Crete. Knossos is nestled among the slopes of Kefalas Mountain and was the seat of King Minos. In its heyday, was the heartbeat of the Minoan cultural development and organization. It's considered one of the most advanced cultural societies during the period which began somewhere around 1900 BC.

After spending the day trapsing through the ruins of Knossos, and the encapsulation of wonders contained within; it was time to return to their hotel, to freshen up, and relax before heading out for dinner.

Looking at several brochures which had been left in the room, decided to visit one of the local restaurants in Paralia (meaning "beach"), known for is airy seafood and wonderful sea view.

After a delightful dinner took a walked through the surrounding area where Darla Sue purchased a few souvenirs to take back home, reminding them of their vacation on Crete.

Departure from Crete was approaching fast and their vacation quickly drawing to an end. With one day left before their flight back to Athens, and the long flight back to the states.

Since they had not gone to the Mediterranean for a swim (which had also been on their bucket list), decided the last day they would put on their bathing suits and head down to the small beach area set aside for swimming along the waterfront.

Reaching the beach which was not crowded, found the perfect spot. As they placed their belongings on the towels taken from the hotel, once that was accomplished, they quickly proceeded to the water's edge. At the water's edge, walked into the water up to their knees and to their amazement, found it to be cold but invigorating. Standing in the cold water, looked at each other, and decided on the spur of the moment, the only way to enter the frigid waters was to take the plunge. Both dared each other to jump head first, and before you could count to three both jumped head first into the cold but clear Mediterranean. After their initial shock of the frigid water found it to be alluring.

Once acclimated to the cold water, were soon enjoying the clear blue waters in which they found themselves very stimulating. After spending some time frolicking around in the water, enjoying the beach and its surroundings; it was time to head back to the hotel and start packing for their return trip home.

Reaching their room at the hotel found it had been ransacked. As they searched the contents left strewn over the room, discovered their moneys and a small amount of Darla Sue's jewelry missing. Immediately notified the front desk of the incident.

It was not long until police arrived along with the manager of the hotel. Telling the police, they had locked the room before leaving for the beach, and a late afternoon swim. And upon returning to their room found it had been entered and several items missing.

An hour or so later, dusting for fingerprints, checking for unusual anomalies left behind by the thief. Once the room had been cleared, the local police inspector told the Drakes' they would be contacted if anything turned up or learned of the identity of the intruder. Before leaving, police and manager of the hotel were apologetic and showed much concern about the break-in.

Liam and Darla Sue were shaken by the experience, but now had to find a local bank before closing time and request their bank in the states wire them money needed for their return trip. Once a local bank had been found and notified of their dilemma. The local bank put a call to their bank back in the states requesting they wire them money along with a new credit card directly to the hotel A.S.A.P.…The next morning the hotel informed Liam the money and credit card requested had been sent, and picked up at the front desk. Liam wasted no time going down to the front desk and picking up the money and credit card.

Returning to the room, he found Darla Sue busy packing. As he entered the room, Darla Sue told him her wedding ring was missing. Remembering she removed it before going to the beach, and laid it on the bedside table in the ashtray. While packing she glanced over at the ashtray and discovered her ring was gone. Liam returned to the front desk and informed the manager that his wife's wedding ring was also missing. In turn the manager called the local police, and included the ring to the other items listed as missing.

That morning, prior to leaving the police paid them a second visit and told them, "We still have no leads on the person or persons who entered your room and absconded with the moneys, credit card and wedding ring. But if we find any of the articles, they would be returned. Again, I would like to tell you how sorry we are for your loss. But, with so little to go on, it's almost impossible tracking down the where abouts of the jewelry or who the perpetrator or perpetrators were."

With that, the manager and police excused themselves, leaving the room and closing the door behind as they exited.

When Liam and Darla Sue came down to check out, the manager spotted them approaching the counter to settle their account. He walked out from his office to where they stood and told them, "The hotel management is deeply embarrassed by the incident and have absorbed all charges for your stay. That's the least the hotel and management can do for your loss and inconvenience."

Thanking the Hotel manager, Liam reached out and shook his hand, and expressed his thanks for the hotel's consideration and concern. Liam, bent down, grabbing both pieces of luggage, and proceeded outside with Darla Sue to the rental car. Opening the trunk, Liam loaded the luggage inside the trunk for their short drive back to Nikos Kazantzakis or Heraklion International airport.

Arriving at the airport, the weather had turned gray, and was overcast, with strong prevailing winds blowing in from north Africa. The air strip ran east/west and with wind blowing from south to north the strong crosswind made it difficult for take offs and landings. But this was a common occurrence, and expected for flights in and out of the airport.

Liam, after arriving at the airport, dropped their baggage off at the front entrance along with Darla Sue, then returned the car to the rental office a short distance away. Darla Sue had one of the porters on duty carry their luggage inside to the check-in counter where she presented her passport and ticket to the check-in clerk. After checking their luggage and receiving her boarding pass took a seat in the waiting area.

Liam after turning in the car, returned to the check-in counter where he went through the process of checking in. Then met Darla Sue who he spotted sitting in the lobby. Since it was going to be a little while before they were to board, decided to go to one of the small restaurants inside the terminal and grab a bit to eat before boarding their flight back to Athens.

Sitting at a small table along the west wall of the restaurant, talking and reminiscing of past events of their trip to Crete; felt a bit of sadness having to leave. They had had a wonderful time, meeting family and touring sites of a world once known as the Centre of Europe's most ancient civilization, the Minoans. It had been the vacation of a life time and a sad occasion having to return to the fast pace life style they had become accustom to back in Hoboken. But they had memories and pictures that would last them a life time.

Arriving back at New York's Newark Liberty International Airport, collected their luggage and headed to the long-term parking area to pick up their car and drive the eight miles back to Hoboken. It seemed so different, the traffic, super highways, people everywhere in a hurry, not the slow pace they had been part of the last two weeks.

Back in Hoboken, Liam parked the car in the underground parking facility at their condo. Removed the luggage and took the elevator to the third floor. Exiting the elevator, Darla Sue reached inside her purse and retrieved the entry key, but as they neared their unit noticed that the entry door ajar. Had they forgotten to close it when they left? Upon entering the unit found it to be in disarray. Found it had been ransacked, pillaged of everything valuable. They were devastated at seeing the destruction left behind. This was the second time in a week they had been burglarized, how often does that happen?

Liam immediately called police station to report the break-in. Detective Paulson and Callahan who happened to be working. Arriving at the scene, was filled in as to what they had come back to. After the police forensic team finished their investigation, Detective Paulson and Callahan, headed over to talked to Darla Sue and Liam, who were sitting quietly on the couch looking dejected and disappointed at what they had come back to. Nothing had changed, it was still chaos everywhere they turned.

They seemed to be lost in thought thinking to themselves, [Would this madness never cease? Who were these people trying to destroy their lives on a regular basis? This lunacy had to stop.]

With what little evidence police located at the scene, was bagged, tagged, and later dropped off at the police lab where it was handed over to the crime scene investigators who would document, and catalogue each piece of evidence for future reference if called to do so. All the evidence from the crime scene like photographs which were taken, any physical evidence, along with documentation.

Several key pieces of evidence had been located at the scene, including several tiny bits of fabric not found anywhere else in the unit. A fragment of red hair, a partial fingerprint, enough of a print to work with. A footprint was later discovered on the bathroom floor. It appeared as if someone had been trying to cleaning up and let water drip on the floor and the perpetrator unknowingly stepped in the water, and after the water dried on the floor, left a faint, but visible and viable footprint. All items collected at the scene were placed in plastic containers along with photos of the footprint. Each item removed from the unit would be examined in hopes the evidence would lead to the person or persons involved with the break-in.

Darla Sue and Liam were asked after the police's initial search to check the bedroom for any missing items such as jewelry or items of value. Darla Sue and Liam meticulously went through the bedroom and found several irreplaceable items missing.

Listing the items on a sheet of paper then gave the list to the chief crime investigator. The items missing and presumed stolen were two diamond rings belonging to Darla Sue and Liam's prized possession a watch he left behind because he did not want to lose it during his overseas trip.

The two diamond rings had been given to Darla Sue by her mother. One was her grandmothers wedding ring, the other belonged to her great grandmother. Darla Sue's grandmothers and great grandmothers' gifts were irreplaceable. She had a great deal of sentimental attachment to both rings.

They were her most prized possessions in the world. The 1930's Blairstown ring wedding her grandmother bequeathed her mother before her passing along with a 1900 Westbury ring belonging to her great grandmother, who gave it to her grandmother before passing.

Liam discovered that his rare 1957 Earnest Boral 366400E Men's/ unisex gold Kaleidoscope watch his father gave him before his death was also missing. It was the only thing he had of his late father and it would be sorely missed if not found.

It took time for the evidence collected and examined, but in time the forensic lab would present their findings to the investigators who would then try to piece together the facts, and in due course unravel the secrets contained within. Eventually fitting the puzzle pieces together, one piece at a time and eventually solve the mystery.

Chapter 36

Several months had passed, and the evidence found at Liam's and Darla Sue's residence had been studied and scrutinized, and a few clues found at the condo were found to be quite relevant to the case. Both the fingerprint and partial foot print pointed to an individual not readily known to the local police department, or to Liam or Darla Sue. The only finger print found, plus the partial shoe print were the only clues of known quantities matching an individual found after an intensive search of police archives. Which by chance turn up in one of the old cold case files.

This individual had been on the run for several years, after skipping out on bond for burglary and petty larceny. It was nothing major, but still a fugitive and needed to be located and face charges for his crimes. There would be two new charges added to his record, which had now grown exponentially, and added to his file. Which now included additional charges of burglary and additional grand larceny charges.

Since the crimes had been committed on separate occasions, the fugitive faced other charges and multiple years in prison if convicted on all counts.

The police had a positive ID, one Albert Slone, a small-time hoodlum with a foul mouth, a brute of a man, and ties to organized crime. If located he was capable of busting some of the most disreputable local crime figures around New York City, Jersey City and

Hoboken, but only if the police could entice him to rat out some of the organizations and higher ups he worked for in the area.

It was time to hunt him down and bring him in. The police began their search for Albert by visiting the last known address they had on file, which turned out to be a dead end. He had moved from that location over two years ago and of course not left a forwarding address.

Police caught a break from an informant at the jail of a possible second location. Fortunately, the detectives after interviewing the landlord, was told of a note left inside the apartment listing a couple scribbled addresses which appeared to be addresses of apartments he had visited recently.

The landlord as he was searching the desk in the unit after Slone moved out, found the note. With this new lead, it did not take the police long in locating the elusive Albert Slone who now lived in a small unobtrusive room along the water front in Hoboken.

The police arrested Mr. Slone without incident, and returned him to jail where he was booked for his previous outstanding warrants and the two new charges. After booking Albert Slone, he was taken into one of the interrogation rooms and left for almost an hour letting him stew over his apprehension before the two detectives returned. Once they returned to the interrogation room, found Albert Slone fidgety and looking uneasy about his confinement, and what the future held for him.

The two detectives entered the interrogation room and introduced themselves, "I'm Detective Paulson and this is Detective Callahan," prior to sitting down.

Then asked Albert, "Would you like something to drink before getting started?"

"Yeah, a coke I guess," Albert replied.

Having one of the clerks fetch a cola for Albert, it was time to get down to business and question Albert about the break-in and burglary at the Drakes' while they were away on vacation. But first they read him the Maranda act.

Then asked him, "Do you fully understood what I just told you?"

"Yeah."

"Do you wish to be provided council before we began?

"Nope, I understand my rights."

"Okay, let's see what we have here?" That's when Detective Paulson began looking over the file in front of him and his first question of Albert Slone was, "Mr. Slone, where were you on or about the 8th of June of this year?"

"Let me see, June 8th? That was at least four weeks back, I kan't recall."

"Let's see if I can refresh your memory. There was a break-in and robbery at a condo over on 1st Street around that time. Do you know anyone who lives in a condo on 1st Street?"

"Nope, that's out' a my league."

"Well, we found several items of interest at the scene of the break-in. And a couple of items found at the scene contained DNA and we also found a fingerprint and partial shoe print. After running those items though our lab, we were able in linking both the DNA and fingerprint and shoe print located in our data base back to you. Can you explain how your fingerprint, shoe print and DNA wound up in the condo if you've never been there? And not aware of the person or persons who lived there?".

"Must' a been a mistake, I've not been near that place as I can recall. Kan't tell you how my DNA, fingerprint or shoe print were found there unless someone's trying to frame me."

"Mr. Slone, we know it was you who broke into the condo, and stole personal items belonging to the owners and we are charging you with that break-in along with a grand larceny charge. Considering the evidence linking you to the break-in and grand larceny charges; it will not be difficult for the prosecution if and when it goes to trial, to prove you were there and it was you who broke-in and stole several valuable items belonging to the occupants while they were away. The evidence against you is substantial, and will be easy convincing a jury of your guilt. Even if certain charges in this case are not allowed; we still have those previous charges of robbery and burglary from previous arrests. Oh! And don't forget, skipping bail which I'm sure will brought up during a trial. You are not out of the woods yet. If I, were you, I think I would think long and hard about what your chances are at this point being convicted of all counts? To me they don't seem to be too good."

After several hours questioning Albert Slone, he decided to come clean and expose those he worked for and the reason behind the break-in.

He explained to detectives, "The reason for the break-in, I was told was, teach this Liam Drake a lesson and hopefully stop the mudslinging in the Jersey Journal about illegal activities he was exposing around the city."

Once Albert Slone told the detectives the whole story surrounding the break-in, told Albert, "They would try and help him since he had been upfront and truthful concerning the break-in and burglary, and exposing those behind the incident." Albert had given them a treasure trove of information which they would use in eradicating certain illicit or moral causes still running ramped throughout the city.

Several months later after several trials and those responsible for the incident were found guilty, Albert Slone was exonerated. After due consideration of his wrongdoing in the case he was absolved by the court, and released from jail and immediately fled the city.

Liam and Darla Sue along with the help of the local police were able locating the stolen items at a local pawn shop in Hoboken, where Albert Slone had pawned the items the very same day, Slone took them.

Happy to get the rings and watch back, Liam and Darla Sue immediately took their precious heirlooms to a local bank down the street from where they lived, and rented a small deposited box in which they deposited the items for safe keeping. They were not going to risk losing them again, once was enough. Leaving the bank, once their valuables were safe, headed back to the condo to freshen up and celebrate by having an early dinner and a bottle of bubbly.

Chapter 37

While serving time in the big house, Lefty met up with a well-known crime figure named Zenoah Ricci. Even thought they had never met personally, knew each other by reputation. One day while exercising in the prison yard, happen to meet, and realized they had several things in common.

Top of their list was Liam Drake, who had a hand in fingering them, and leading to their arrested, resulting in a conviction. Both had been charged and found guilty of different crimes involving strong arm tactics against individuals working for construction sites. With the help of his editorials, they had been exposed as local hitmen by a snitch named Albert Slone. Lefty learned later that the low life came clean during an interview about stealing a truck containing liquor. As he was being interrogated, Albert slipped up with his story fingering the two.

After several months meeting and talking in the exercise yard at the prison, Lefty and Zenoah decided to get even by putting a contract out on both Liam, and this rat Albert Slone.

After a lot of discussion about this low life Albert Slone and what he did to them, decided to have Sammy (the Man) Romano who served time with both Lefty and Zenoah in the past, but since released and was back on the streets in lower Manhattan, just across the river from Jersey City and Hoboken.

Sammy, after his release from prison went to work for one of the large trucking companies operated by a large New York syndicate in lower Manhattan. It was Sammy's job delivering stolen merchandise throughout the northeast corridor from New York City to Vermont and all points in between. He was known in the trucking business as a (henchman) who engaged in crime practices selling his service to the highest bidder. A person with no scruples, a real tough guy.

Sammy was called on occasionally to make sure the drivers working for the syndicate towed the line, and did he did not spare the rod when it came time to divvying out punishment for any infraction large or small. He was feared by everyone around him; a force to reckoned with.

After contacting Sammy (the Man) Romano through channels available from the outside, Sammy eventually sent word back he would accept the job of taking care of Lefty's and Zenoah's problem.

After several weeks, Sammy (the Man) Romano with a couple of his best cohorts crossed the river into Hoboken and began asking around about this Liam Drake and Albert Slone. It was not long until Sammy had an address on both. Immediately putting the two henchmen shadowing Liam and Zenoah 24/7.

Once Sammy had them in his sights, he quickly tries to take care of business, but his first attempt did not go as planned. He had been waiting at a local hangout where Slone frequented daily, but that particular day Slone was a no-show. So, Sammy had to regroup. The following day Sammy and his henchmen arrived outside the establishment; this time Slone arrived at his usual time. Sammy nervously waited outside for Slone, but again Sammy's plan had to be aborted.

By now Sammy was at wits end and decided to whack Liam Drake and leave Slone until later.

Once again Sammy planned his attack very carefully as he waited in the parking garage at Liam's condo. When Liam arrived, his game plan was to approach Liam's car prior to him exiting, shoot him through the car window, and hightail it out of the garage to a waiting car outside of the parking garage.

Liam arrived at the garage and before exiting the car, someone came up shoving a gun against the car window and pulled the trigger. At the very same moment Sammy pulled the trigger, Liam aware of his surroundings, his instinct kicked in as he tried to ducked. He was not fast enough and was shot on the left side of his head, but the bullet glanced off his skull and stopped by the door glass on the passenger's side of the car.

Sammy did not stick around to see if he had killed his mark, but ran back to the waiting car and sped away. The following day Sammy learned Liam had miraculously survived the attempt on his life with only a superficial wound in front of his left ear.

Sammy's attempt on Liam's life quickly and Slone's found its way back to Lefty, who was not impressed with the two failed attempt. Sent word to Sammy to return to New York that he had failed and was finished in Hoboken.

Lefty was not looking for notoriety floating to the surface involving him in a botched attempt on either Liam's life or Slone's. Lefty, a known crime figure, known to Liam and local police, and if they put two and two together could possibly link him as the instigator for this latest attempt in snuffing out Liam and Slone.

Liam, was forced again to look over his shoulder every time he left the condo to go to work, run errands or go to dinner. This latest fiasco put a terrible strain on Darla Sue's and his relationship. But somehow, they overcame the debacle and got back on track with their lives.

Liam was terrified at knowing some low life might harm Darla Sue, it would truly devastate him if anything happened to her. It was he who brought this problem to the marriage and he alone was responsible for ending it. But he had no idea how to stop this madness, other than quit the newspaper. But quitting the newspaper would not solve the problem. The damage he caused inside the criminal element around town was taking on a new sense of direction.

Several people were now serving time in prison who had a legitimate beef with Liam. No matter what he did he could never be free of the stigma attached to his name by those he'd been instrumental in sending away. He had to live with the thought, *[Someday, someone will approach me and say, "Remember me? You helped send me up the river. While there I had a lot of time to think about what you did to me and what I could do to repay you when I got out. Well, I'm out and I'm going to make your life miserable, a living hell."]*

With that thought, the only thing he could think about was someone attempting to hurt Darla Sue. He had to think of something before that day arrived, but what? He was a writer, a small fish in this big pond, advising the citizens of the corruption and danger going on in their city. He was not a street fighter, which left a lot out of the criminal equation and those responsible. Liam was being held accountable for all the unrest among the criminal element locally.

Wrestling with that burden all he could do was continue and hope he would not be backed into a corner with no means of escape.

One evening after dinner decided to talk with Darla Sue to get her feedback about what he should do going forward. After dinner, they sat at the table where he proceeded to explain to her this latest catch-22 he faced.

She told him after hearing of his latest encounter, "I will talk to a couple of lawyers down at the law firm and get their advice as to what course of action or direction you should take."

Threats, were a common occurrence in case after case that lawyers dealt with on a weekly basis. But threats of this nature were not something to be ignored. Sometimes the problem of coercions could be solved by agreement between individuals which on occasions could induce the desired response. But in other cases, this type of response was not applicable or considered relevant or appropriate. In Liam's case it is the latter.

Chapter 38

Liam, after his lengthy discussion with his wife about this latest threat, decided to go it alone, and find out who was behind this aggressive activity against him.

He vowed to himself, [*I will find and take action against the persistent offender no matter how long it takes. But where do I start and who do I pursue? Was this a person or group looking to cause bodily harm to me and my wife? I need to get to the bottom of this and now.*]

The following morning, he showed up to work, and first thing he did was locate his boss. Meeting face to face with his boss, Liam explained to him, "I cannot continue doing my job if every time I leave home, I have to look over my shoulder and wondering if today is the day, when someone was going to do bodily harm to me or my wife. I need to find out who is behind this latest ultimatum one way or other. I have to stop this madness or face the dire consequences. I can't live like this any longer."

After his gave his spiel to his boss, then asked for an extended period off work so he could begin his inquiry into this latest peril he now faced.

"Well," his boss said. "I know you've been under a lot of stress lately and understand the situation you face on a daily basis. But I don't understand your reasoning behind your intentions, but since you're so damn adamant on pursuing this matter, all I can say is, "Good luck,

I'll grant you your leave of absence, but expect you to call me occasionally and let me know what's going on."

With that, Liam left without any further fanfare. He walked out of the building not sure what the future held in store, but had to get to the bottom of his menacing problem before something really bad happened to him or Darla Sue.

No sooner leaving the building, he headed straight toward the docks to see if he could find out the latest scuttle butt going around the docks. That was where he felt most comfortable, talking with dockworkers and loaders about the complexity and temperament of the area.

After a couple of hours talking to those he knew and meeting with a few of the local dockers, came up with nothing of interest or noteworthy. So, he decided to head home for the evening and talk with Darla Sue again. Maybe she could ask around the law office and shine some light on the issues or at least find out if there were any new ideas or leads, he might follow up on.

After dinner, Liam approached Darla Sue with what had transpired earlier. He explained to Darla Sue what he had planned on doing for the foreseeable future, and needed her assurance it was acceptable to her. She was taken aback after hearing this new course of action Liam had embarked upon. She immediately began questioning his ability in carrying out such a divisive plan.

She told Liam, "Why don't you let Detectives Paulson and Callahan and do the detective work and you continue with what you started with exposing those in the illegal business?"

"I have reached the point of no return, and have to finish what I started myself. It was me who's been instrumental in uncovering local crime and fraud, and it will be me who brings down those who are threating my life and livelihood."

"I think you are taking on more than you can handle, but if that is what you need to do, there is nothing more I can say or do to stop you. I will do what I can to help, but you need more than my help. Wish you would let the police handle the situation."

After their lengthy discussion on his future goal, they called it a night and went to bed. The following morning Darla Sue got dressed, and before leaving for work told Liam, "Please be careful and if you needed me, call."

Darla Sue left the house, as Liam finished getting ready for another trek around the docks. This time beating the bushes for all it was worth, and was able in coming up with a name, Cocco di ometto (Cocco the little man). Liam had never heard of this Cocco di ometto or any one referring to him in the past. It was going take some smart detective work in finding this individual, but it was a lead he had to follow up on.

That afternoon he visited police headquarters and was able in talking with Detective Paulson who was more than willing to help Liam in looking up this Cocco. When Detective Paulson brought the name up on the screen of the computer, the information was sparce, but this Cocco had come out of Chicago, with several priors for kidnapping, adding and abating in commission of several crimes locally in Chicago. Looking over his rap sheet, Cocco appeared to be a highly dangerous character and considered a real threat.

Detective Paulson told Liam, "If I were you and this Cocco has been hired to do you bodily harm, I would be very careful and avoid any personal contact with him. He's not someone to mess with or interfere with. In my humble opinion if you are confronted by this individual, I'm telling you you'll come out on the short end of the stick, no if or butts about it. He's a hired assassin and I would not go out looking for trouble, but looks like trouble has come looking for you. My suggestion is you need to make application as soon as possible, and get yourself a concealed weapons permit. At least you'll have a fighting chance in case of an unexpected meeting with this Cocco." Do I make myself clear?

"Yes. I and I appreciate the information' and words of wisdom. I'm going to take your advice and head over to the court house right now and make that application for a concealed weapons permit post haste. Thank you for your time and understanding. Will keep in contact, and let you know what's going on from time to time."

Liam left Detective Paulson's office and headed over to the courthouse which was just down the street and around the corner from police headquarters. Entering the office, he met the young clerk working the permit section.

Walking up to the counter she asked, "Yes, may I help you?"

"Yeah, I would like an application for a concealed weapons permit."

The clerk reached under the counter, selected the form Liam needed to fill out.

Then told him, "Take this form over to that table, fill it out, and when your finished, bring it back to me and we will go over it to make sure you answer all the questions."

Liam, with the form in hand, proceeded over to the small table and filled out the form. Once he completed the questionnaire, returned it back to the clerk. After looking over the form and making sure it was filled out correctly, the clerk told Liam, "Now I need to take your picture and fingerprints. Once the process in verifying your application is confirmed, it should not take more than two to three weeks. Once your application has been approved, you will be issued a permit. It should arrive by mail no later than two weeks from tomorrow. If it has not arrived by that time call us back."

"Thank you."

Liam paid for the permit and left the office. Leaving the courthouse, Liam felt relieved he had taken Detective Paulson's advice and applied for a concealed weapon permit. It would make his life a somewhat less stressful knowing if he ran into Cocco, at least he would have a fighting chance.

In less than two weeks his permit arrived. Now with his permit in hand, drove over to a local gun dealer and purchased a small weapon which could easily be conceal on his person when out and about. After purchasing the weapon, found a gun range where he could be taught the proper use of a firearm. For the next few days, Liam visited the firing range religiously, and soon became very proficient at shooting and handling his firearm. He felt after a few days of mastering his weapon, it was time to seek out those who wanted to destroy him, it was payback time.

Chapter 39

With the information obtained from several dock workers about this Cocco, began his search in earnest. While canvassing the dock scene, he'd been informed Cocco had been seen hanging out at one of the local dives near the waterfront. This was his first real break locating this Cocco.

Liam had been letting his hair grow long and his beard, trying to conceal his real identity as much as possible, hoping it would give him an edge. A couple of days later while sitting in one of the local establishments, a known hangout for Cocco, a strange little man came in, cautiously looking around, eventually seated himself at the end of the bar where he had a full view of the bar. He had looked at Liam a couple of times as if he recognized him, but had quickly turned, and sat silently drinking his beer.

Liam, a short time later heard someone say, "Hey Cocco, want to play a game of pool?" That sent a cold chill up Liam's spine.

At that moment Liam wanted to confront this Cocco, and get it over with, but something told him he had to be patient. Before Cocco finished his game of pool, Liam got up and left the bar. Knowing now what Cocco looked like, and where he hung out, needed to know where he lived. He hung around the neighborhood until he saw Cocco leaving the dive, and appeared to be heading home. He followed him for a block or so, when suddenly Cocco disappeared.

How did he vanish so quickly, he had him in his sights until he rounded the corner, and like magic, he just disappeared? Since he had lost sight of Cocco he decided to head home himself for the evening. After all it had been a long and grueling day, but successful in many ways. He had found his man, but it was time to figure out how to take care of this major concern of his, Cocco.

Liam needed a strategy, that of putting him in control of any given situation that came up in which he needed self-discipline, also direction. Both these thoughts were beginning to weigh heavily on his mind. His self-confidence and optimism lay within his own willpower and his destiny was on the line. Whatever he decided at this point going forward had to be total commitment fighting the establishment. He had a lot to do and so little time in which to prepare for this monumental endevor. Not only how to deal with Cocco, but those forces surrounding his own survival and city hall.

After Darla Sue arrived home that evening, Liam told her, "I ran across this Cocco at a local dive along the water front earlier, and as I tried tailing him, somehow, I lost him, he seemed to simply vanished into thin air."

Darla Sue related to him, "I heard through the grape vine at the office, this Cocco has been snooping around trying to locate where you live."

One of the lawyers at the office told me, "He had a phone call inquiring about you, and wanted to know if I was your wife and where we lived. He told him needed to come to the office so they could discuss this issue in private."

But whoever it was, immediately hung up.

"Looks like he's getting close, we both need to be extra careful any time we are out or get a phone call. I would hate to have him find us, no telling what he would do. What do you think about telling Detective Paulson about what you've learned and you spotted this Cocco at one of the local watering holes along the waterfront? That he called the law office trying to get information about the two of us?"

"Good idea. I will call him in the morning and give him a heads up at what I'm doing and see if he has any suggestions."

"Yes, I think that's the best bet, letting him in on what's going on, maybe he can give us some advice, maybe an answer to our problem, and what we need to do next."

"Darla Sue, I'm sorry I got you involved, but hopefully all this will end soon and we can get back to our own lives. I miss not working and I'm worried about you."

"Don't worry about me, just take care of yourself and let's get this problem behind us."

"Okay, how about we retire for the evening and get ready for another round of confusion, lack of understanding and uncertainty at what tomorrow may bring? I feel I'm in a state of bewilderment about this whole affair, want it over and over soon before I go off the deep end. Don't know how much more of this I can take."

"I know, it's more than either of us ever dreamed of when we started down this path. But, hopefully in the end it will prove to be the right thing we've set out to do."

The following morning Darla Sue got ready and went off to work, leaving Liam to contemplate his next move in finding this Cocco. It was around noon before he got around to calling Detective Paulson about what he observed, and Darla Sue found out who it was that called the office inquiring about her and I.

With what information he was able supplying Detective Paulson it gave him insight as to what was going on in Liam's world. Detective Paulson thanked Liam for the follow up and to be careful. By now it was time to get back to the docks and see what he could find this Cocco.

Detectives Paulson and Callahan also decided to drive around the waterfront to see if they could uncover any new information on this Cocco.

With Liam and the two detectives beating the bushes, maybe they could shake out this Cocco, and get him off the streets before he did something foolish. After a couple of hours of pounding the waterfront, the detectives suddenly spotted Cocco walking the docks. Slowly the two detectives approached him and extra cautious not to spook him. With the stealth of an owl in flight, quickly apprehended him, handcuffing and removing him from the street and into their unmarked car, then downtown for questioning.

After several hours of questioning Cocco, he was book on several outstanding charges, then placed in isolation. At least this would take the weight off Liam and Darla Sue having to looking over their shoulders every time they were out.

Liam learned later that day Cocco had been apprehended and was sitting in jail awaiting his turn to appear before the judge for charges and a bond hearing.

The following day Cocco was bonded out of jail and back on the streets. Liam's and Darla Sue's reprieve from Cocco was brief and it was back to square one.

Liam was not going to give up on finding this Cocco, and taking care of business. Time had come to end this madness and end this insaneness going on around him. He once again began his journey along the waterfront to find Cocco. It took several days, but Liam finally located Cocco at the flop house he was staying.

He entered the downstairs and found out from the superintendent what room he was in. Taking the stairs up to the third floor, after exiting the stair well, Liam slowly walked down the dark corridor to Cocco's room. As he stood just outside the door, he hears something that made his hair stand up on end. It was a muffled cry of a woman pleading for her life coming from Cocco's room.

With out hesitation he rushed the door, busting the lock from the door jam, finding himself face to face with Cocco. Cocco had a knife, and was bending over a woman laying crossways of the bed. He suddenly looked around and saw Liam standing in the doorway near the entrance to the room. Taking his attention off the woman, now on him. Cocco suddenly got up off the woman, then rushed toward Liam with the knife in his right hand above his head, making a sudden lunge at Liam, dropping him like a rock to the floor with the 8-inch knife blade now embedded in his left shoulder. Cocco immediately ran over Liam and down the hallway to the stairwell, never looking back.

Liam lay on the floor with excruciating pain radiating from his left shoulder, but slowly regained his faculties, and realizing what just happened; roll over on his right side and raise himself off the floor with the knife still buried deep in his left shoulder. As he turned and saw the woman still lying on the bed, he asked, "Are you okay?"

"Yes, thanks to you."

Liam knew he had to locate a phone to call an ambulance. He quickly left the room and went back downstairs where he found the superintendent of the building, then had him call an ambulance. He told the superintendent that there was a woman in Cocco's room who may also may need assistance.

It was not long after that the ambulance arrived and placed Liam on a stretcher where they took him to the emergency room at a local hospital where the staff on call was able in removing the embedded knife from his shoulder.

Before leaving the hospital, Detectives Paulson and Callahan heard about the incident and dropped by to question him about the latest episode encountered with this Cocco. Liam, gave them all the information he could recall about the attack, and how when he busted in the room found this Cocco with a knife raised above his head ready to do bodily harm to a woman lying cross ways on the bed. After Detectives Paulson and Callahan finished questioning Liam, Detective Paulson told him, "Go home and stay there until your healed, and we will take care of this Cocco in due time."

After Liam was released from the hospital, he had the nurse call him a taxi for his return home.

Chapter 40

Hearing nothing from Detective Paulson or Callahan, after a few days, Liam called police headquarters and was informed they were out of the office and would not be back for the rest of the day.

He got ready and drove over to talk with some informers along the waterfront. After talking with a couple of individuals found Cocco had not been seen in the area for a few days. Apparently, Cocco had gone into hiding and was nowhere to be found. Liam continued his search the rest of the day without success.

When Darla Sue returned home from work that evening, was greeted at the door by Liam who gave her a big hug and kiss on the cheek.

She asked, "What's that's all about?"

"Thought I would surprise you by you cooking dinner."

"That's a pleasant surprise. Why are you being so kind and hospitable all of a sudden?"

"Nothing special, just wanted to tell you how much I love and appreciate everything you have done for me lately. You have been a godsend during my recovery and I wanted to show my appreciation to you, being there for me."

"I value your feelings, and understand the pressures you've experienced lately, just glad I was available to help."

"You will never know the respect I have for you, and will always be beholding to you for your kindness and understanding."

"Now, lets have dinner, hope you like what I've prepared? I know lamb rib chops; are among your favorite meals when we go out. I've tried to prepare it just the way you like them, hope I've done it justice?"

Sitting down at the table, Darla Sue was in awe to see how well Liam had done in preparing her special dinner.

She looked across the table and told Liam, "It's perfect."

After dinner, Liam told her to go in and sit in the living room and rest until he cleaned the kitchen. He would join her afterwards.

Once the kitchen was cleaned, and dishes put away, Liam joined his wife on the couch.

Liam told her, "I went back to the waterfront, and inquired about Cocco, but he has gone underground and has not been seen or heard of since our encounter. I also call Detective Paulson, but was informed he was out for the day.

I was told by the Desk Sergeant, "Detectives Paulson and Callahan had not been able in locating Cocco, but as soon as they did, they were going to call."

"I'm going out again tomorrow, and search a different part of the waterfront. He may have taken up residence in one of the homeless shelters near there. It's worth a look."

Do be careful if you go, remember, "He is dangerous and will stop at nothing. He reminds me of an injured animal, and would do anything to avoid conflict or capture."

"I'm going to do my best to find him and when I do, I'll not be so careless as to let him have a free existence to fight another day. I seek vengeance against him, and what he has done to us. I'll not stop until I have him out of the picture, one way or other. He's someone I've developed such a hatred for, I need retribution for the harm and hardships, he has caused us. You do understand, don't you?"

"Yes, I do. But don't want anything to happen to you in the meantime." With that they went to the bedroom to get ready for another day.

The following day Darla Sue went to work at her usual time, leaving Liam home alone. As he was getting ready to head out for another day of searching, he heard a strange noise on the balcony. He got up off the couch and walked over to the balcony, opening the drapes just enough to peered out onto the balcony. At first, he saw nothing, but then an explosion blew both sliding glass doors off their tracks. Liam was blown back by the force of the explosion, and found himself lying flat on his back near the coffee table on the living room floor. The glass of the two sliding doors had shattered into a million small pieces and had littered most of the living room carpet. Still confused as he rolled over and eventually able in getting up off the floor. His head felt like it had exploded, and the ringing in his ears was excruciating.

Making his way over to the couch, sat down and tried to make sense of what just happened. It was not long until he heard a siren, then someone knocking on his entry door. He was able in getting up, and made his way over to the door and unlocked it. Standing outside was a neighbor from down the hall asking him, "Are you alright, and what happened inside your unit?"

"I don't know. All I remember was I heard a noise on my balcony, when I went to check it out, all hell broke loose."

As the neighbor peered inside, he could see both sliding glass doors had been blown off the tracks and lay inside the unit along with the broken glass littering the floor.

About that time there appeared several firemen exiting the elevator in full gear rushing to his unit. Both Liam and his neighbor moved out of the door way as the firemen rushed inside to assess the damage. Luckily there was no sign of a fire only a large, mangled opening where the sliding doors and curtains once existed. The firemen went through the opening out onto the balcony, making sure it was safe and secure.

Returning to the living room, assessing the damage caused by the explosion, deciding there was nothing else for them to do but began collecting their gear laying around the unit as police and paramedics started arriving. At which point Liam was escorted back inside by paramedics where he was examined, finding he suffered only superficial wounds by the flying shards of glass from the windows as they exploded and rained down inside.

As things settled down and Liam began to collect his wits once again, could not believe at what happened. It was not long before the phone rang and when he answered, it was Darla Sue calling to see what had happened. Liam told her, "Don't you worry, I'm okay, a bit shaken, with a few minor cuts from the flying glass, but otherwise in good shape." She thought about leaving work to check in on him, but after hearing he was okay; told him, "Since you are okay, I'll see you after work," and hung up.

Later that morning after everyone left, and the maintenance crew from the complex came in and help clear the debris away, and boarded up the large opening that now existed. Liam sat down on the couch and soon he had dozed off to sleep and when he awoke heard Darla Sue as she opened the door and entered. Turning to greet her, he felt a sharp pain in his right temple area and winced. Darla Sue seeing this told him, I need to take you to the hospital and have the hospital check you out. I saw you wincing when you turned when I entered. That tells me something bad maybe going on and you may need help.

Later that evening returning from the hospital after being poked, prodded, and scoped, was given pain pills to help ease the pain, and trauma he had experienced earlier. Darla Sue helped him into the bedroom where he undressed himself, and crawled into bed. Darla Sue before he went to sleep gave him a glass of water, and a pain pill so he could rest. It was not long before he was asleep, and slept the remainder of the night.

The following morning, he awoke as the alarm clock went off. Both he and Darla Sue got out of bed, took individual showers and dressed for the day. Before going to work Darla Sue told him, "I want you to rest today and don't do anything that requires physical exertion. You need to take it easy, if you need anything, anything at all, call me."

"Okay, but you be careful, and if you see anything out of the ordinary, call the police."

"I don't expect anything unusual to happen, but if I feel threatened, I will do what I have to do to avoid any type of conflict, I promise." Darla Sue left for work, still worrying about leaving Liam alone. But knew if he needed her, he would call.

Later during the day, the phone rang.

"Hello."

"Yes, just checking on you, sorry you are not feeling well, but that's what happens when you don't listen."

"Who is this?"

"Some one who has tried to get you to be reasonable. I've given you many chances to redeem yourself, and next time, I'm going to have the last word. Understand?" And hung up.

Liam, sat rattled on the couch trying to recall the voice on the phone, but was unable in putting a face with it. He'd heard that voice in the past, but for some reason could not put a face or name with it at the moment. He continued for the remainder of the afternoon trying to recall that voice.

Suddenly it came to him, it was the voice of Raymond Lockhart, one of the city council members who had been involved with a certain aspect of organized crime around the city. He tried disguising his voice, but was still recognizable to Liam, because of Lockhart's distinct dialect. that of someone from Massachusetts or that area.

Since having been found guilty of retribution, Lockhart along with Digger, were given a smack on the hand and sentences of five years' each, then probation for two. Why had he broken probation, again intimidating by threating Liam? What was he thinking?

Why, all of a sudden had he become hostile? Had Lockhart become involved again with the underworld criminal element? This time Liam was not going to let let this slide; so, he immediately contacted Detective Paulson and Callahan to help him get to the bottom of this new alarming and aggressive situation he found himself.

Lockhart, surely must realize, if he carries to carry out his threat and is caught will be taken back to court, at which time his life would cease to exist. Since he was on probation, and if he breaks probation, then found guilty would be sent to back to prison, no ifs, ands, or butts about it. And would face years behind bars.

The following day, Detective Paulson and Callahan visited Council member Lockhart and ask him to come downtown to police headquarters they needed to ask him a few questions. The next day Lockhart showed up at police headquarters where he was questioned about his role with "The Family", and if he knew of new threats against Liam Johnson. Once Liam's name was mentioned, Lockhart immediately requested a lawyer.

The question-and-answer session ended as quickly as it had begun.

Detective Paulson and Callahan got up from their chairs, walked out of the interview room scratching their heads. Detective Callahan asked Detective Paulson, "Why do you think Lockhart clammed up and requested an attorney if he had nothing to hide?"

Detective Callahan replied,

"I'm sure he has some dark secret to hide or cover up, but what?"

The next few days passed and Liam went about his work with no outside interference from those who wanted to do him bodily harm.

Suddenly, one afternoon while at work, Liam was contacted by an individual who said he had evidence about a new contract being put out on him. Once again, his life and possibly Darla Sue's life hung in the balance.

Thinking to himself after the call, *[Why? Why is Lockhart and or the organization he's working with so unyielding in doing me harm?]*

This question remained a mystery and the answer would not be forthcoming until the people responsible for this cowardly act had been arrested, judged by a group of their peers in a court of law and convicted.

The following day Lockhart along with his lawyer Nate Brown entered police headquarters and escorted to one of the interviewing rooms where they were eventually joined by Detectives Paulson and Callahan.

Lockhart along with his lawyer made it difficult on the detectives by not answering certain questions about who it was behind the contract put out on Liam. They explained not only to the lawyer, but Lockhart, if he did not cooperate and work with them, he could possibly be charged with civil contempt. At that point, Nate Brown told Lockhart not to say anything else that this interview was over.

Chapter 41

Again, the two detectives were disappointed having to end their session and walk away with no resolve.

Liam's daily routine had become a night mare as he was constantly looking over his shoulder not knowing when someone would approach out of the dark try to kidnap or kill him. His life had become a total disaster as well as Darla Sue's. They continued as normal as possible as they went about their daily activities, but at a cost.

One day while searching for anyone who had knowledge who put the contract out on him, Liam was getting desperate enough at this point, and willing to put his life on the line. Putting himself in danger, but it came with the territory he had chosen. He had to find out who the party was behind this insanity, and confront whoever it was even if it meant someone would not walk away.

Liam, eventually located a CI along the waterfront willing to contact that individual for a fee, and set up a meeting between the two. Liam had become desperate at this point; he was willing to pulled all stops out; and put his life on the line no matter the outcome. Later, learning from his CI where and when a rendezvous was to take place, but not given the name of the person he was to meet.

It was now or never thought Liam, *[I need to prepare myself before heading out to meet this low life.]* After Liam was informed of the time and place the meeting was to take place; had done all he could do to ready himself, and was prepared for the challenge. With his gun tucked inside his waist band, headed out to the car and drove to where he was told the individual would be waiting.

Driving over to the George Washington Bridge, Liam reminded himself he was not leaving until this problem was settled once and for all. Arriving under the busily traveled George Washington Bridge as the sun was going down, and night quickly approaching; drove to the south end of the bridge where he was to meet his latest nemesis.

Slowly approaching the area where the meeting was to take place, noticed not one but two vehicles sitting silently, both with occupants inside. One was parked on the outer aspect of the area, the other near the third column from the end. This he was told would be the site of the meeting place. Liam was told to come alone, but expected his archenemy to arrive alone also. But at this juncture, suddenly feeling trapped, things started ramping up, and Liam had to decide quickly if he was ready to fight or take flight.

Liam brought his car to a stop near his nemesis's car. Rolling down the driver's side window of his car, stuck his head out and yelled,

"If you want to talk, I want you to inform the other group in that car to leave or I'm leaving."

When unexpectedly the other car started up and began heading toward Lima's car picking up speed as it approached Liam. Seeing what was about to happen, Liam quickly putting his car in gear, turned his car sharply to the right, heading in the direction of the vehicle holding his archenemy. Without warning, slammed his vehicle into the side of the car pushing it up against the column, pinning the driver inside with no means of escaping. Immediately Liam climbed out of his car, gun drawn, approached the car and fired two shots inside the car hitting the driver. In the meantime, the second car veered away after seeing the crash and gun fire, and immediately drove away from the area.

Returning to his car, back it away from the side of the vehicle pinned against the column, proceeded to drive back home. Shaken as he opened the door to get out of the car, slowly walk up the steps onto the porch and stopped. He heard someone yell and looked back toward the street. As he turned around, saw a local police officer get out of his patrol car with gun drawn. As the officer slowly approached where Liam was standing, yelling at him to put his hands above his head.

Liam dropped his keys on the porch and did as the officer ordered. With hands above his head, the officer quickly traversed the stairs, grabbing hold of Liam and turning him around handcuffing his hands behind him.

He asked,

"What's the problem Officer?"

The officer did not answer his question, but read him his rights, then asks, "Do you understood what I just told you."

"Yes, but on what charge am I being arrested?"

"You'll find out soon enough."

The officer led him down the steps and into the waiting patrol car, strapping him in with the back seat seatbelt, and quickly headed toward police headquarters. Arriving shortly afterwards at the police station, Liam was booked and placed in a holding cell.

Liam was astonished at how fast they had found him, and how slow the system had worked when he needed help in finding someone.

A while later an officer came and opened the cell door, and led him back to an interrogation room down the hall where he was shackled to a chain attached to the metal table he was sitting at, when in walks Detectives Paulson and Callahan. They looked at Liam and smiled, then sat down.

Detective Paulson asked,

"You've been read your rights, so I'll not go through them again. Just want to talk to you about what happened earlier this evening under the George Washington Bridge?

A witness who happened to see what happened, called us, and gave us a detailed description of the car and tag number. So, if you wouldn't mind explaining what happened, we're listing?" I don't know where to start.

"Let's see. After I found out from a local CI about who put the contract out on me, I decided to take it the next level.

I asked the CI, "Can you help set up a meeting, so I can meet this person face to face?"

He said, "I'll see what I can do about setting a meeting up, I may or I may not be able help."

Then I told him, "I would like for you to set it up as soon as possible, but just me and him."

The CI called me back as soon as the meeting had been arranged. At which time he told me, "It's all set up. You are to meet down by the Hudson River later this evening." And after I arrive at the rendezvous site, I saw he was not alone. There was a second car with a couple of his henchmen parked a short distance away.

Stopping my car near the person I was to meet, I immediately rolled down my window and told him, "I'm leaving if you do not send your compadres over there in the second car away.

That's when suddenly, the other car started up and was heading straight toward me at a high rate of speed. Realizing it had been a set up all along, I floored my car, turning the steering wheel sharply to the right, spinning the car around ramming into the car in which the scum bag sat. Pinning him against the column he was parked alongside. I quickly jumped out of my car, with my gun drawn. That's when I saw him come up behind the steering wheel and pointed his gun toward me. I immediately raised my gun and shot through the front window twice, hitting him in the head. I know I shot him, because I saw blood splatter on the driver's window. I got back in my car and returned home. As I walked up on to my porch, I heard someone yell put your hands up. That's when I drop my keys turn around, that's when a policeman handcuffed me, and I was brought downtown.

"Is there anything else you would like to tell up about the incident," Detective Callahan asked?

"Only that you call my wife and tell her I'm okay and where I am."

"We have notified her already and she is on her way down at this moment."

With the interview over and a signed statement by Liam Johnson concerning the killing of Luke Weatherman, it was now time to take Liam back to the holding cell to wait his wife arrival.

Darla Sue's arrival at police headquarters and taken back to the same interview room Liam had just confessed killing Luke Weatherman (a hired assassin) contracted by "The Family" out of New York, to silence Liam Johnson.

Once Liam entered the interrogation room, she rushed over and hugged Liam and was immediately restrained and taken back to the other side of the table and told to be seated.

Looking forlorn, and dejected Darla Sue aske Liam,

"What did you do? Why are you in jail handcuffed to the table like a common criminal? Are you okay?" She had so many questions to ask but so little time.

"I was to meet with a hired gun this evening down at the river under the George Washington Bridge. But when I arrived, he was not alone, and immediately I spotted a second car carrying two of his henchmen. Stopping my car near the hired gunman's vehicle, rolled down my window and told him I was going to leave if they did not clear out until our meeting was over. Suddenly out of the corner of my eye I saw the car began coming toward me, that's when I floored my car spinning around to the right, ramming my car into the hired assassin, pinning him against one of the giant column's. I then got out of my car with gun drawn and shot him."

"Oh Liam, what are we going to do?"

"I need you to find me a good lawyer. Since you work for a law firm, I'm sure you shouldn't have any problem finding me one."

"I will call when I leave and talk to my boss, see who he would recommend, and get back with you. I'm so sorry it's come to this. Is there anything else I can do?"

"Not at this time, just find me a good lawyer."

Visitation time had run out, and Darla Sue was escorted out of the interview room, leaving Liam alone, sitting handcuffed to the table, and thinking to himself, *[What are my chances being found not guilty of murder?]*

He now had time to think about what lead up to this, and how he was going to get out of this murder charge. Being a writer for a local newspaper was one thing, but a cold-blooded murderer he was not. Time will tell if he was thinking rationally when he stepped over the line.

Chapter 42

The next day Darla Sue had a conference with her firm and they all were in agreement, the best attorney to represent Liam was Attorney Fletcher O'Neal.

The following day, Darla Sue contacted Attorney Fletcher O'Neal, explained to him the situation her husband was in and asked, "Would you be interested representing my husband Liam Johnson who's now sitting behind bars awaiting his court hearing and charges?"

After a brief hesitation of the circumstances and what was at stake said, "It would be an honor representing your husband Mr. Johnson, whom I recognize by name, from the many articles he's written for the Jersey Journal against local corruption. It would please me immensely to help this journalist out because of all the good he has done in the past for the community.

Tell him, "I will see him tomorrow and not to worry about a thing, I'll represent him pro bono, that's the least I can do for someone of his moral character and convictions. To me, your husband is a giant among men, taking on a corrupt system single handily; it takes a lot of courage and firm conviction to do that."

Now that Attorney Fletcher O'Neal was on board and agreed to take on the murder case against Mr. Johnson, a lot of work was necessary in order to get ready. Attorney Fletcher O'Neal and staff gather as much information about the murdered victim Luke Weatherman as possible. It was not an easy task since so little was known about this Luke Weatherman. But researching the local and national archives of police data bases, shaking a lot of bushes, and calling in IOU's, Attorney O'Neal was able in accumulating a great deal of information about this case, and by the time Mr. Johnson's case went to trial, Attorney O'Neal would be ready to argue Liam's case.

Liam, sitting in a single cell was beside himself, as he waited for his court hearing and subsequent trial. As time slowly dragged by, he beginning having not only major health, but psychological problems relating to his mental and emotional state at present. He was becoming a basket case.

With all the stress in previous encounters with corruption and threats to his life, and now this? It was more than one person could handle. How was he able in coping with a long-drawn-out trial of this magnitude in such an emotional state?

As time drew nearer for his court hearing, Liam was at his wits end. He had become remorseful at what he had done to his wife and himself, causing him sleep deprivation, little or no appetite which led to him having high blood pressure, and eventually leading him to being a borderline diabetic; while he continued losing weight. The last doctors visit indicated he was on the verge of developing other chronic problems associated with sleep deprivation. His mental capacity was deteriorating in general Liam was dying from the inside out. Darla Sue on her many visits to jail noticed the subtle changes as he was slowly deteriorated mental and physical along with other numerous health issues.

After months of waiting and wondering the outcome of the trial and his fate, which hung in the balance of what the jury would decide after hearing his case. The day finally, arrived and trial was officially underway.

Liam arrived in a wheel chair now too weak to walk. Sitting at the defense table it was all he could do was hold his head up. Judge Nicole Anderson the presiding judge in this case noticed a time or two, Liam closing his eyes as if he was in another time and place. But day after day as the trial continued, Liam hearing the arguments by both the defense and prosecution, had given him hope and encouragement.

A week into the trial Liam had improve, and was able walking into the courtroom unassisted. This was such a relief to Darla Sue, she cried when she saw him walking into court room on his own. He looked over at her and winked, as if to say, "Everything is going to be alright."

Once the evidence by both sides had been given, and the jury sequestered to do their duty; all Liam could do was wait. The jury debated the case for two days before reaching a verdict. After the jury reached a unanimous decision, they were returned to the courtroom where the jury foreman announced to the judge, they had reached a unanimous agreement on all charges.

Judge Nicole Anderson was handed their verdict and read it to herself, then returned the sheet of paper to the bailiff who then handed it back to the jury foreman. Judge Anderson told the jury foreman, "Please read aloud the verdict."

"The jury finds the defendant guilty of all charges."

Silence followed the guilty announcement in the courtroom. Those who following the trial from the beginning were stunned beyond belief at the verdict.

Darla Sue was so over whelmed at the verdict; she broke down had to be helped out of the courtroom in a wheelchair. Liam looked on as they removed his wife, he tried to say something to her, but forcefully turned around and handcuffed. Not able saying anything to Darla Sue, he was immediately removed from the courtroom and taken back to his holding cell; he too was shocked at the verdict.

What could his attorney do to have this verdict overturned or reversed, was his next question?

The following day Liam's Attorney Fletcher O'Neal came by to see him, and tried to explain what his next move would be in getting a new hearing.

Several weeks later Attorney O'Neal was attempting in getting a new hearing, but every attempt at filing a new petition had been turned down. He had no recourse but to drop the matter, and return to his practice.

Liam was escorted to prison soon after being sentenced to life with no chance of parole. Darla Sue came as often as she could to visit him, but the separation put a major stumbling block in their relationship.
Several years later, Darla Sue finally sued Liam for divorce, and was eventually granted.

Meanwhile Liam, beside himself after learning of the divorce was once again mentally and physically exhausted. He was becoming unruly and causing trouble not only with the guards but several of the inmates. After all else failed he, was removed from his cell and placed in solitary confinement hopefully to teach him a lesson and break his spirit. But eventually released from solitary confinement and sent back to general population, where immediately he began his bad boy attitude once again.

It began by harassing his cell mate who he did not like Liam and had nothing in common. Finally, reaching his breaking point, took a shank he had been working on, stabbed his cell mate, killing him before guards were able in restraining him. This only added additional years to his life sentence which at this point had no hope of returning to the outside world anyway.

He was placed in a single cell, six feet by nine feet with only the bare necessities after the incident for twenty-three hours a day, with one hour a day outside his cubicle. He was escorted by two guards to a small wire cage alongside one of the many buildings located inside the compound, and not allowed to join other inmates using the yard for exercising and general relaxing.

He was not allowed to communicate to anyone and if caught lost his privilege of going outside for that hour each day. Several times he had been observed by guards trying to coach someone over to his wire cage, but to no avail.

Several years passed, he settled down and returned to general population, but still had not learned his lesson. His cell mate grew tired of his BS and one day, took his frustrations out on Liam and sent him to the infirmary for several days. After his return to the cell, learned he had a new cell mate.

This was a turning point in Liam's life. This time he decided not to cause any more trouble, but focused on one of the inmates in the next cell. After several months, one day while in the yard, Liam started an argument with the inmate in the cell next to him. It was not long until there was a free for all in the yard, and once again he was sent back to solitary confinement for an additional six weeks.

After serving his six weeks in solitary confinement, once again returned to general population. By now Liam was not aging gracefully, and starting to have many health issues keeping him from being this arrogant, self-assertive and self-confident individual.

He eventually slowed down and as time passed became a model inmate. But, in the back of his mind, he still sought justice, except now in a different venue. The more he thought of those less fortunate in prison, took it upon himself to help a few lost souls in turning their lives around, and become productive members of society. It was a major step for Liam, but the right path for he always believed helping those who could not help themselves, "The silent ones," as he called them.

Soon he began helping his cell mates tackle their problem of always being a follower never a leader. He had to instill in them not only take the initiative in accessing their lives independently, but take back their power, and take charge of their lives before allowing themselves to be used by those who already possessed that ability. He wanted to show them they too could become a leader and fight for their right and justice.

A few months of helping several inmates learn the art of speaking up no matter how uncomfortable or afraid they were. Say what you need to say was essential in changing one's behavior. Encouraging them to, "Take a stand."

The more silent inmates learned about Liam's tutoring and what he was accomplishing with other inmates, they too began asking for his guidance, and teach them to speak up and not be afraid. As the months and years passed, Liam had helped many inmates acquire the ability to stand on their own two feet and meet their daily challenges head on, face to face, and not shying away from their responsibility of speaking their mind in any given situation.

He became a mentor to many inmates who needed guidance and purpose. It was nearing his 20th year in prison when he became involved in a minor fracas and was stabbed by a shank of an old acquaintance from the past, Jacopo Gallo. Jacopo, better known as Jonesy had provided key evidence against several associates who were named in an indictment (due to Liam's articles of corruption in Hoboken) and promised full immunity if he testified against them. Which he did, but later was picked up for grand theft of a semi-trailer out of New York loaded with material for a new construction project in Hoboken. This time he was tried and found guilty and sentenced to thirty years, the maximum sentence for grand theft charge. He never forgot it was Liam who helped police in arresting him along with several others for destroying property and causing bodily harm to several construction workers.

Chapter 43

Meanwhile Detective Paulson and Callahan continued working on Liam's case, always believing Liam had been railroaded when found guilty of murder. Detective Paulson and Callahan knew Liam all too well to have gone to meet this Luther Weatherman with the thought of killing him. Liam had testified; "I had gone to meet this Luke Weatherman with intentions of discussing how to settle the problem between the two of us which I believed was not unsurmountable, but attainable."

Liam testified, "It was agreed we would come alone, but when I arrived, discovered a second car containing two occupants and immediately assumed they were there to run interference. Even though I had brought my firearm to the meeting, it was to be used only for protection in case things went awry."

So, wondered Detectives Paulson and Callahan; how did the justice system find him guilty of premeditated murder? Liam, found himself in a catch 22 and had to defend himself or be the one murdered. Which when he was found guilty and sentenced to life in prison for protecting himself. The Detectives needed to find the driver and occupant of that second car parked under the George Washington Bridge that evening and get their statement as to how the meeting went down. It was Liam's only chance to prove his actions at the time he shot Luke Weatherman.

But how were they ever going to find the two individuals after all these years?

Detective Paulson and Callahan in their spare time, searched every nook and cranny for leads to the two unknown assassins present the evening Luke Weatherman had been shot to death. As time passed and they were reaching the end of their rope and ideas, luck as it sometimes happens, happened.

While on a routine call, the two detectives ran upon a truck loaded with electronics parked in the back of an electronics store. Two men had cut the lock from the rear doors and were removing as many items from the trailer as they could cram into a smaller cargo vehicle they were driving. After being arrested and their arrival downtown at police headquarters, the two were questioned for several hours separately. During their questioning, detectives learning who the two were and who they worked for in the past, and by putting two and two together figured out these two were the same two individuals present the evening Liam shot Luke Weatherman. To help their situation out the two agreed to sign a sworn statement to the fact and then released.

Next day their statement was turned over to the prosecutor's office and after reviewing the case against Liam Johnson requested a hearing to reverse the charges against him. The process took several months, but Liam was finally exonerated and absolved of all wrong doing in the murder of Luke Weatherman. But still accountable for the murder charge against him while in prison. Liam was released from prison and returned to Hoboken.

He moved into a small one room apartment the same day and walked down to The Jersey Journal to see about getting his old job back. After a meeting with the editor-in- chief was told, "I wished I had an opening, but at this time I just don't need another journalist."

After meeting with the new editor-in-chief, Liam thanked him and walked back through the newspaper office, back outside where he decided to go back to his apartment. Returning to the apartment he thought about the choices he had, and qualifications for obtaining a job. He realized he was not qualified doing anything, but that of a journalist.

As he sat on the side of his bed, decided no one wanted to hire an ex-prisoner, it was not something respectable businesses did, even though he served time in prison and exonerated of the charge.

His back against the wall, decided to call Darla Sue, see if she could give him guidance. Leaving his apartment, walked outside and down the street where he used a pay phone on the corner. He phoned Darla Sue at the law office where she previously worked. A voice he was not familiar answered, "Dunn and Walker Law Group.?"

"Yes, may I speak with Darla Sue Johnson?"

"I'm sorry she no longer works here."

"Could you tell me if she left a forwarding address or phone number?"

"No, she moved out of state, and did not leave a number or forwarding address."

"Thank you," and hung up.

With Darla Sue gone, and no way of contacting her, he had no one other choice but to pound the payment looking for a job. He had very little money so it was imperative he find a job and quickly. He walked the streets the remainder of the day asking several businesses if they were hiring. All told him not at this time, "Business was not great and did not need extra help."

But just as things could not look more dismal, he happened to venture into a retail outlet store selling army surplus. Approached the counter and asked, "Is the manager available?"

"Yes, wait here, while I get him."

Soon a tall rather scruffy gentleman appeared from the back of the building, and as he approached Liam, he said, "I'm Lenard Jolliff, store manager, what can I do for you?"

"Yes, my name is Liam Johnson, I was wondering if you had time to talk, I'm looking for a job? I've been away from the workforce several years and need a job badly."

Liam asked the store manager, "Are you hiring?"

The store manager looked at Liam and replied, "As a matter of fact

I'm in need of a sales clerk, do you have any experience?"

"None, but I'm willing to learn."

"Okay, let me find an application, I'll be right back."

Returning shortly from his office, Lenard handed Liam a work application. Told Liam, "You can use the chair at the end of the counter to fill out the application form. When you finish let me know, and I'll go over it. Once I've read the application, I'll talk to you more about what the job entails."

Finished with the form, Liam handed it back to Lenard who read over his qualifications. "Looks like you have had a colorful career."

After discussing his prison sentence, Lenard told him he too had been falsely accused of a crime and served time in the big house, but had been totally exonerated. He told Liam, "I understood sometimes life is not fair, but everyone has to live with the cards they are delt. If I had not been absolved of the crime, I would not have been able in pursuing my passion, which is weapons of war."

Lenard explained the job description, going over each detail, the dos and don'ts of the business. After his spiel to Liam, Lenard asked, "Are still interested? If so, I will explain the hours you'll be working and starting pay."

"Oh yeah, I'm definitely interested."

"Okay. The job requires working long hours, we open at eight, close at six, six days a week. Holidays and Sundays are your only days off. If you are a no show or late, you will be immediately terminated. You are allowed an hour lunch break from 11:30 to 12:30. Two fifteen breaks during the day, one at 9:30 and the other at 2:30.

Lenard looked over at Liam and said, "If you are still interested in the position, it's yours."

"Yes, I'm definitely interested."

"Okay, you'll start at eight in the morning, see you then."

Liam left the surplus store, feeling upbeat for the first time in years. He headed straight to his one room apartment and made sure he had clean clothes to wear to work and even took the time to spit shine his shoes.

The following morning Liam showered, shaved, brushed his teeth and snacked on some pastries he purchased on his way home from the surplus store. By 7:30 he was ready to head out to the surplus store to begin his new job. But, in the back of his mind, he could not stop thinking of where he had seen or met this, Lenard Jolliff. Somewhere in his distant past, they had crossed paths, but when and where?

Arriving at work at 7:55, Liam was met at the door by Lenard who let him in. After exchanging greetings, Lenard called the other employee Harold Young over, introduced him to Liam and told him, "I want you to show Liam around and get him familiar with the stores set up and help him get settle in.

It was not long before the first customer arrived. Harold told Liam, "Stay where you are, and walked down the long counter to where the gentleman was looking through the glass case at one of the large knives on display. Harold stopped in front of the gentleman, and asked, "Can I show you something?"

"Yes, I'm interested in your Fairbairn-Sykes knife. I've heard my uncle talk about that knife all my life. He said it was the best knife ever made for close combat. He was in WWII and had been given one by one of the special forces groups from England he became friends with prior to the invasion of Iwo Jima."

Harold unlocked the sliding metal door, behind the glass case, removed the Fairbairn-Sykes knife, then laid it on top of the glass counter. When the gentleman picked up the knife, he handled it superbly. Seemed to know a lot about hand-to-hand combat by the way he twisted and swung the knife around, stopping in different positions with the knife's point pointing at an imaginary figure in front of him. After finishing his demonstration and use of the knife, told Harold, "Wrap it up, it's just what I was looking for."

Harold asked, "Will you be paying cash or putting it on a charge card?"

"Cash, don't believe in plastic."

Harold carefully picked up the knife from the counter touching the blade and found it razor sharp, he then carefully slid it back into its sheath. Wrapped the knife in heavy duty brown paper and placed the knife in a heavy-duty plastic bag.

The gentleman reached in his back pocket pulling out his billfold and counted out the exact amount of money for the knife, and handed the cash to Harold. After Harold received the money, he rang it up and handed the gentleman his receipt. The gentleman picked up his package, turned toward the door and left the store. Never looked back or uttered another word.

Liam, was curious as to why the gentleman had wanted such a lethal weapon in the first place, he was not taking it home to display that's for sure.

Chapter 44

Several weeks later as Liam left the surplus store, and heading home, felt as if someone was following him, but at a distance. The closer to the apartment he got, the nearer the person was following him. As he hastened his pace so did the invisible individual following him.

When he was ready to open the door to the apartment building, he was suddenly grabbed from behind and immediately felt pain in his belly. It did not stop there, two more thrust from a knife was felt in his side and back. At which time he was released, and as he turned, he saw his attacker, it was the same individual who came to the surplus store the first day he worked and purchased the Fairbairn-Sykes knife.

He leaned up against the building holding his stomach, when the clerk on duty at the apartment came running out the front door, reach out and helped Liam inside the lobby where he was quickly laid on the couch. The clerk immediately ran back to the counter and used the phone to call 911.

By the time the clerk returned to where Liam lay, he had blacked out. The following morning, Liam awoke in one of the local hospitals. He looked around and was amazed at all the lines hooked up to the numerous monitors and IV drip lines. A short time later was approached by the surgeon on call who informed him, "You are in the ICU after being brough in with several stab wounds last evening. We've performed three separate operations for the three separate knife wounds. You are one luck individual to come through this traumatic trauma as well as you have. I thought we lost you several time while in surgery, but we were able using the paddles to get your heart started. Looks like you should recover. Your very fortunate that no vital organs were damaged during the assault on you. You need bed rest at the moment and as soon as you've recovered enough, we'll take you out ICU, and put you into a regular hospital room."

"Thank you for all you've done, don't think I would have survived if not for your concern, thanks again."

Once Liam was released from ICU and taken to a semi private room; two new detectives came to talk to him about the stabbing incident.

"Good morning Mr. Johnson, I'm Detective Sienkiewicz and this is Detective Lowman. We would like to ask you a few questions if you're up to it about the event outside your apartment last evening."

"Yes, I feel I'm up to it."

"Great. First off, did you know or recognize your attacker?"

"I had seen him one time before. He came into the surplus store where I worked and purchased a knife called a Fairbairn-Sykes. It was a knife highly prized by commando troops during WWII as I understand. Used primarily in hand-to-hand combat and highly lethal if used properly, as I've learned later."

"So, you are sure this was the same person who purchased the knife earlier at the surplus store?"

"I'm positive. I could not forget those profoundly evil looking eyes."

"I see. Can you give us a description of the individual, like the color of his hair, was it light or dark, what color complexion did he have, did you notice any tattoos, what type of clothing was he wearing, or any other distinguishing features you can remember?"

"Let's see. I recall he was around 5'8" to 5'10" tall, medium build, somewhere between 165 to 175 pounds, his hair was black, with slightly receding hair line. Oh yes, I did notice a small tattoo below his right jaw bone on the right side of his neck, a name. I remember the tattoo because I thought it might have been a girlfriend or his mother's name. He also appeared to have a slight limp as he walked. That's all I can recall right now, but if I think of anything else I'll let you know."

"We appreciate your help. We're going to leave now and see what we can come up with. I will personally get back to you as soon as I have something concrete on the individual."

The two detectives turned and left the hospital room and drove back to police headquarters where they began their grueling job of putting a name and face to Liam's attacker.

Meanwhile Liam was told he had to spent the next few days in the hospital so the nurses and doctors could keep a close eye on his condition. His recovery was short of miraculous. The doctors and nurses had never seen anyone come in with such life threating wounds like Liam and mend so quickly.

He was released in four days and given a good bill of health. The doctor told him, "He was the first patient with such severe wounds leave the hospital in record time. He was their miracle patient."

Returning to his apartment, found it had been ransacked and in total disarray. Wondered to himself, *[Who could have done this? Why are they so intent on destroying me? I need to find out so I can get on with my life, at least what life I have left.]*

The next week he was able in returning to work, and as he went about working that day, he kept thinking about Lenard Jolliff the owner of the surplus store, but how did he know this, Lenard? Suddenly a light went off. He had seen him in prison during his incarceration. Now it's coming back to him. I remember Lenard had been friendly with the ex-mayor of Jersey City, Arthur Wiseman who was serving time because of his persistence in exposing the criminal element going on in city hall through his editorials. Putting one and one together, figured the ex-mayor after Liam's release, contacted Lenard and put out a contract out on him.

Liam, who by chance was hired by Lenard Jolliff who apparently recognized Liam immediately from prison. And later that day Lenard Jolliff was somehow able in contacting the former Mayor, Arthur Wiseman (who was still incarcerated) and told Lenard to hire someone to get rid of Liam. Once Lenard had been advised as what to do by the grapevine, immediately called a hired gun to take out Liam. It was all coming together, it now made sense.

That evening after work Liam walked to the local police station and found the two detectives who had previously visited him while in the hospital at police headquarters hard at work.

While they were talking, Detective Lowman told Liam, "We've ran into a few roadblocks in our investigation, and yet have no real evidence as why (a person of interest, a Nikki Labasa) who we believe was the individual that stabbed you."

After hearing what they've learned about the case, it was time Liam to explained to them his idea as to who was behind or responsible for the attempted on his life. After explaining the connection to the two detectives, they decided to bring Lenard Jolliff in for questioning.

Before leaving police headquarters that evening, Liam was told by Detective Sienkiewicz, "We want you to continue working at the surplus store, but keep your eyes and ears open, and act as if you are not aware of the situation surrounding the attempt on your life by this Nikki Labasa. He is somehow associated with this Lenard Jolliff, and we are still trying to figure out the connection. If you hear anything of interest or that might help us in connecting the two, call us immediately.

A couple of days later Lenard Jolliff was called by Detective Loman and asked to come to police headquarters, to answer a few questions concerning a fire arm which had been recovered from a crime scene a couple of months back and curious who it was that purchased that particular weapon at his store.

Lenard Jolliff told them he would be down after he opened the surplus store, and made sure his employees were there. After opening the store, the following morning, he drove to the local police station and met by the desk sergeant then quickly escorted back to one of the interview rooms.

When Detectives Sienkiewicz and Lowman entered the cubicle, introduced themselves, sat down across form Lenard. Without hesitation, not giving Lenard time to think, began asking him pertinent questions about an old case he had been involved earlier. And as they questioned Lenard, not giving him time to think or regroup, a name popped up out of the blue from one of Lenard's responses.

The name immediately rang a bell. Lenard had divulged without realizing it the name of the mystery hit man, it was none other than Nikko Labasa. Recognizing the name immediately from information they ran across while researching Liam Johnson's case. After the interview the detectives told Lenard, "We may need to ask you a few more questions at a later date and don't leave town."

The two detectives returned to their office to follow up on their new lead. Looking up Nikko Labasa's file, they quickly found his last known address was outside Jersey City in Greenwich Village, NY. Detective Lowman put in a call to New York City Police Department – 6th Precinct located in Greenwich Village and ask their assistance in locating a Nikko Labasa whose last known address was in Greenwich Village.

A couple of days later the New York Police Department called Detective Lowman back informing him Nikko Labasa had been arrested recently on a grand larceny charge and was in custody at the 6th Precinct location.

Detective Lowman asked Officer McDuffie, "If Detective Sienkiewicz and I come over in the next day or two could you arrange us some time to see and question this Nikko Labasa about an ongoing investigation concerning an attempted murder charge. We have reason to believe he's connected somehow in the attempted murder? So far, he's our only suspect we've come across and that was by chance. We also talked to the owner of a surplus store and by the slip of the tongue the owner mentioned Nikko's name. If we could talk to him, he could possibly lead us to the source and why the contract on Mr. Johnson was issued in the first place."

"Sure, I'm willing to help you guys out any way possible. Anytime, just call ahead and I'll have him sweating it out in one of our interview rooms."

"Thanks, either my partner Detective Sienkiewicz or myself will contact you as soon as we get permission to come over."

Detective Lowman hung up the phone and immediately went to his immediate supervisor's office down the hallway. Gently rapping on the closed door, he heard Captain McClain's scruffy voice say, "Yes, come in."

Detective Lowman opened the door and walked over to where Captain McClain sat behind his desk working on a new directive for the station's evidence room.

Excuse me Captain McClain, "Do you have a moment to talk about a situation which has been brought to Detective Sienkiewicz and my attention concerning Mr. Liam Johnson and the attempt on his life."

"Yes, sit down Detective Lowman and tell me about this new information you have on the case."

Well Sir, "Detective Sienkiewicz and I have been busy with Mr. Johnson's case and as we were interviewing Mr. Johnson's employer, a Mr. Lenard Jolliff, he slipped and gave us the name of a possible suspect. Both Detective Sienkiewicz and I recognized the name immediately, and after the interview we looked up this Nikko Labasa's file, and found he has a long rap sheet and two of the charges were for attempted murder. This is not his first rodeo at murder. We also found his last known address was in Greenwich Village over the bridge in New York."

I called the 6th precinct and informed by Officer McDuffie that Nikko Labasa had been arrested, and was being detained at this very moment. I asked Officer McDuffie, "If Detective Sienkiewicz and I came over in the next day or two would it be possible to interview this Mr. Nikko Labasa?" I've come to ask permission for Detective Sienkiewicz and be granted permission to drive over to the 6th precinct in Greenwich Village and interview this Nikko Labasa?"

"I think that's a splendid idea, and yes anytime you want to go, fill out the paper work and I'll sign it."

Thanks Captain McClain, "I tell Detective Sienkiewicz and we'll head over there as soon as maybe tomorrow."

Detective Lowman left the captains office and headed off to find Detective Sienkiewicz and give him a heads up on their upcoming visit to the 6th Precinct in Greenwich Village, where they will be able in interviewing their one and only suspect in the attempt on Liam Johnson's life.

The following day Captain McClain signed the trip voucher. After picking up the voucher it was time Detective Lowman call the 6th precinct to tell Officer McDuffie, they had been authorized to drive to Greenwich Village for their meeting with this Nikki Labasa. After confirming meeting with Nikki Labasa, it was time to headed over the George Washington Bridge to Greenwich Village, and the 6th Precinct for an interview with Nikko Labasa.

Chapter 45

Arriving later that morning at the 6th precinct headquarters, parked their car in one of the visitor's spaces on the south side of the building. Got out and together walked around to the front entrance of the building and entered.

As they approached the Desk Sargent on duty near the front entrance, they stopped to explained to the desk sergeant who they were and the reason for being there. The Desk Sargent having been briefed prior to their arrival, told the two detectives, "Hold on just a second, let me get hold of Officer McDuffie to inform him of your arrival. He will accompany you back to the interview room where your Mr. Nikko Labasa has been waiting since your call earlier."

It was not long until Officer McDuffie came out of one of the doors down the hallway heading in the direction of the Desk Sargent's domain. As Officer McDuffie approached the two detectives, stuck out his hand, and shook both their hands, and told the two detectives, "Glad you were able to come over. Your man is sitting in room #314 in the back of the building, completely oblivious as to why he's there. The only thing he was told was, two detectives had driven over from Jersey City and wanted to talk to him about an incident he may have been involved. I'm sure he has been racking his brain trying to think why he was being questioned by two detectives from across the river."

"We certainly appreciate your help in this matter. Hopefully this will be the break we have been waiting for."

Officer McDuffie told the two detectives, "Now if you will follow me while I explain to you about interviewing Nikko Labasa. We will be tapping the entire interview. Do either of you have a problem with that?"

"No, we do a lot of tapping of interviews back in Jersey City, seems to be the norm lately. Plus, it helps if we have a problem later down the road, and need to refresh our recollection of what a suspect said while being interviewed."

Officer McDuffie responded by saying, "It does save a lot of time and hassle not having to interview a suspect again." Both Detective from Jersey City agreed.

Soon Officer McDuffie stopped and pointed to room #314 and told the two detectives, "Well, here we are. It's time to get the show on the road." I'm going to our monitoring room and watch the interview. Good luck.

Entering the interrogation room, the two detectives introduced themselves to Nikko, as they pulled out the two chairs on the opposite side of the table from the shackled prisoner and sat down. "We would like to ask you a few questions about your whereabouts on or around 14th of August of this year. Could you tell us where you were on that date?"

"Well, let me see if I can recall. I'm sure I was here in Greenwich Village, working. I drive a truck around Greenwich Village picking up and dropping off supplies."

"What kind of supplies and what company do you work for?" "The company's called, Roth's Restaurant Equipment and Supplies. It's basically a delivery service for all types of restaurant equipment and supplies. Mainly the business includes the area around Manhattan, but on occasions, I deliver and pick up in New Jersey too."

"Do you recall if you had a delivery or pick up in Jersey City or Hoboken on the day in question?"

"I would have to check with the delivery schedule. Since I work odd hours and have a large territory to cover, I would not know if I was in that particular area on that day or not. You would have to check the work order at the company to find out that information."

Well, let me ask you, "Does the name Liam Johnson ring a bell? Have you met or know a Mr. Liam Johnson during your travels?"

"No, the name doesn't sound familiar."

Well, how about, "Lenard Jolliff who runs an Army surplus store over in Jersey City?"

"Don't recall the name, but I may have stopped in from time to time to look at some of the army surplus equipment. I've always been interested in combat related items used in the first and second world wars. My father was part of a special forces group during the second world war and was killed in Okinawa. It's always been of interest to me, the mindset of soldiers willing to fight hand-to-hand combat and sacrifice their lives without question. And for some reason I began collecting certain weapons used by special forces groups."

"What type of weapons are we talking about you are interested in and collect?"

"Mainly bayonets, knives, and rare Japanese swords."

So, mainly its knives you collect?"

"Yes."

Let me ask you, "Do you remember buying a Fairbairn-Sykes knife at Mr. Jolliff's surplus store in Jersey City say within the last several months?"

"Yes, as a matter of fact I heard about that particular weapon, and made it a point to stop in the next time I had a delivery in Jersey City. A few days later while delivering supplies in Jersey City, I found the store and purchased that particular knife?"

"Why, did you purchase a Fairbairn-Sykes knife? Any particular reason other than you liked it?"

"Because of its rarity. Not many were made and I've always wanted one. After seeing the knife, the price seemed reasonable, so I purchased it for my small collection.

"We have reason to believe that knife or one like it was used in an attempted murder back in August of this year. You do know it leaves a distinctive pattern when used, and there's no doubt that was the type weapon used in the attempted murder of a Mr. Liam Johnson because of the tell-tell signs left behind."

The detectives were muddling the issue by telling Nikko about the stab wounds left behind by the Fairbairn-Sykes. The pattern around the wound caused by the puncture mark were easily traceable to a FairbairnSykes. It's the only knife which carries its own signature, similar to a gun which has been fired. There are tell-tell signs on the projectile and or where the firing mechanism strikes the shell casing, it's like a fingerprint. Each spent shell or projectile leaves its own imprint, same as a FairbairnSykes knife.

They now had Nikko sweating bullets. Nikko had no idea they were bluffing, having never giving the matter a second thought.

He thought to himself, *[If the knife was traceable by the evidence left behind, and located, it would tie him to the crime scene.]* This came as a startling surprise. He thought he carried out his task with the skill of a professional and mastery of a soldier fighting hand-to-hand combat like those brave men during World War One and Two.

He was caught between a rock and hard place. He thought, *[If the two detectives obtained a search warrant and searched his apartment; they would find the knife displayed along with several others in a glass case in his apartment.]* And if they removed the knives and sent them off to a lab to be tested for traces of blood, that would spell disaster. It now caused him great concern, his life as he knew it would be over. Those knives held a treasure trove of DNA from former victims he knew existed on the handles and blades of each knife locked in the display case. He never wiped the blades off the knives he used removing evidence of DNA of his victims. He wanted to display the evidence as a reminder of his heinous crimes. This was his way of preserving his conquests and reprehensible legacy.

Nikki held his ground during questioning and refused to collaborate or cooperate with the detectives. He responded from that point only with answers of yes, or no, or when it was beneficial and he showed few emotions, you could tell he a seasoned pro. After an hour or so questioning Nikki Labasa without success, the two detectives decided to end the interview since it was getting them nowhere and leave.

But, before leaving Precinct 6, Detectives Sienkiewicz and Lowman ask if they could speak once again with Office McDuffie to thank him for his cooperation and assistance in providing Nikki Labasa. Also wanted to ask him, "If we are able obtaining more information relating to this particular case, would it possible to return later and question Nikki further?"

"Sure," Officer McDuffie said.

"If he is still here and has not bonded out. Don't know when he will face the judge or be given a chance to bond out. I'm not all that familiar with his case, but I think with this latest charge of grand larceny the bond, if granted, will be significant. If he's not able to bond out you are welcome back anytime to see him."

Arriving back in Jersey City, Detective Sienkiewicz found a note on his desk concerning Nikki Labasa. It was from an anonymous source, no name but an address to meet at 6:00 a.m. the following morning. If Detective Sienkiewicz was interested, he should arrive no later than 6:00

a.m., if not he would not be notified again.

Chapter 46

The following morning Detective Sienkiewicz arrived along with his partner Detective Loman at the restaurant to meet this mysterious informant. As the two detectives entered the establishment, they were met and quickly whisk away by the mystery man who had been sitting at the counter, to a table in the very back of the building. As they sat down a waitress immediately came along and asked the three of them, "Would you gentlemen like a cup of coffee this morning?"

"Yes, thank you," Detective Sienkiewicz answered.

Sitting looking at each other, Detective Lowman turned to and ask, "What is it you wish to discuss with us about an individual by the name of Nikki Labasa?"

About that time the waitress returned with a hot pot of coffee along with three cups. Poured each a cup of coffee and asked, "Would there be anything else?"

"No, that's all for right now," said Detective Loman.

After the waitress left, Detective Loman asked, "What is this all about?"

"My name is Harold Young. I work at the surplus store where Liam Johnson and I work together. I have worked at the surplus store for over a year and know pretty much what is going on most of the time. Just this last week I heard my boss and someone by the name of Sammy talking about another attempt on Liam's life. I decided I wanted to try and stop it if possible. Liam and I have become friends since he started to work at the surplus store and I don't want to see him hurt anymore."

"And what is it you heard?" Asked Detective Sienkiewicz.

"I overheard the owner Lenard Jolliff talking to an individual I've seen in the store from time to time at the far end of the counter. They kept the conversation among themselves, but overheard some of their conversation when things became a little heated and raised their voices trying to make a point.

Detective Loman looked over at Harold and said, "Tell us what you heard."

"I heard Lenard tell this Sammy he wanted to hire him to make a score."

Detective Sienkiewicz looking rather puzzled and asked Lenard, "What do you think he meant by make a score?"

"I think it meant he wanted Sammy to do away with Liam once and for all."

"Did you hear or know when this score as you called it, is to be carried out?"

"Only, soon. That's what I heard Lenard say, soon"

"Do you know where we can find this Sammy?"

"All I can tell you he stays down town Jersey City near Journal Square at the Plaza Apartments."

"Are you sure that is where this Sammy lives? And how did you know that's where he lives?"

"He came into the store recently and purchased a 45 automatic. As you know every firearm purchased in any store including a surplus store, the buyer has to fill out a questionnaire prior to purchase and then there's a waiting period, to make sure the individual is not a criminal but lawabiding with no priors.

I noticed after he filled out the form and handed it back to me, his address. For some reason it stuck in my mind because he seemed to be hesitant to hand it back when he finished. After returning the completed application to me, Lenard happened to come out of his office and I handed him Sammy application. Lenard took one look at it, reached under the counter and pulled out another application, and told Sammy to stay put. He took the second application along with Sammy's completed application back to his office, where I'm sure he typed out a second application altering it. Lenard then returned a short time later and had Sammy sign the second application, and proceeded tearing up Sammy's original application and threw it into the trash container under the counter. Then looked at this Sammy and told him, "Come back in a couple of weeks your application should be here."

"Okay, Mr. Young is there anything else you would like to tell us?" Asked Detective Lowman.

"No, that's about it. I must get up and get back to work, If I'm late Mr. Jolliff a stickler for promptness, he does not like anyone to be late. If I'm late he may decide to fire me."

"Thank you for the information and if you hear anything more, here is my card, call me," Detective Loman said as the three of them got up to leave.

Harold walked out and Detectives looked at each other, then Loman told Sienkiewicz, "Guess we need to talk to Lenard Jolliff again."

"Yes, let's get back to police headquarters and do some research on this Sammy Romano's application for not only the purchase of that fire arm, and what Lenard Jolliff did to enhance the application in order to sell him a weapon and getting a concealed weapons permit."

Back at police headquarters Detective Lowman looked up the sale of the fire arm and application submitted by Lenard's surplus store only a day or two before. As the detectives looked over both the application and permit saw major flaws in both. Immediately they informed the Concealed Weapons Permit agency of the purchase of the gun and application red flagged.

A couple of weeks later, Sammy Romano came back into the surplus store where he met once again with Lenard. Lenard told Sammy that both the permit and sale of the weapon had not been approved. This set back involved both men now. With pressure from Arthur Wiseman the former mayor and ex-inmate of Lenard Jolliff plus Sammy Romano's known activities around Jersey City and

Hoboken, were now on the line. No matter what happened now, all three were in Detective's Loman and Sienkiewicz's sights. One wrong step and the ex- mayor Arthur Wiseman, Lenard Jolliff and Sammy Romano, all three would become history.

Lenard with a small stash of unregistered guns and similar weaponry stored in the basement was able to supply Sammy with a 45 automatic hand gun, but if caught would be the end of the road for him. It would be his third conviction, and carrying a concealed weapon and a felon in possession of an unregistered firearm meant life behind bars. Sammy accepted the weapon and walked out the door.

Once again Liam's life was in danger, but had no idea until he was approached by Harold who warned him what was about to happen. Liam could not believe that he has stepped into a hornet's nest working for Lenard who took his orders from Arthur Wiseman and who had a vendetta against Liam. It was Liam who fingered him as a corrupt politician in his daily editorial and the mayor had held Liam responsible for his incarceration.

Detective's Lowman and Sienkiewicz came into the surplus store and asked Harold, "Is Lenard was available, if so, they would like to speak with him."

Harold said, "Let me check." He walked back to the office and knocked on the door and Lenard said, "Yes, who is it?"

"It's Harold."

"What is it you want?"

"There are a couple of detectives out front who would like a word with you."

"Tell them I will be out in a minute to see them."

Harold walked back to where the two detectives stood patiently looking down at the gun case. "Mr. Jolliff will see you shortly."

When Lenard finally appeared he looked upbeat as he approached the two detectives, asking, "What do I owe this pleasure detectives?"

"We would like to talk to you about an application your store sent to the fire arms department for sale of a Mossberg 45 automatic recently. A Mr. Sammy Romano who supposedly made the application and was red flagged because the application appeared to be altered.

"Do you have a copy of the original application for us to look at?"

"Let me go to the office and get my copy of the sale."

"A few minutes later Lenard returned with the copy of the application (ATF Form 4473) and handed it to Detective Sienkiewicz."

Both detectives examined the application and noticed where it asked, "Have you ever been arrested for felony, or convicted in a court of law of a misdemeanor crime?"

Detective Sienkiewicz asked Lenard if he knew this Mr. Sammy Romano?"

"I only met him the one time when he came into the store and purchase a hand gun."

"Well, he is a known criminal and has been red flagged and rejected from purchasing the weapon. You call us if and when he shows up to pick up his weapon, we would like to talk to him."

"Yes, when he comes back to pick up his gun, I'll call."

Chapter 47

Several weeks pass since the detectives had visited the surplus store, but had not heard from Lenard whether or not Sammy Romano had come by the store to pick up his weapon, so they decided to give Lenard another visit.

When the two detectives walked into the store, they saw Liam and Harold working the counter, and both had customers they were working with. So, they milled around the store and eventually Liam asked, "Can
I help you?"

"Yes, we would like to speak with Mr. Lenard Jolliff if he's available?"

"Hold on a minute and I'll check if he is in the office."

Liam walked back to the office and knocked on the door and was told, "Doors open come in."

Liam opened the door and said, "There are a couple of gentlemen at the counter who would like to speak to you."

"Tell them I'm on my way."

Liam closed the door and walked back to the counter where the two detectives waited patiently. Liam told the two detectives, "Mr. Jolliff is on his way," then returned to helping his customer with a civil war tin type photograph believed to be found near Hoboken's civil war training camp, Camp Hoboken. The photo was found buried near the water's edge inside an old rusted metal container alongside other relics of the period.

This particular item Liam was showing, had been traced back to a family who lived near the camp during the civil war period. It even came with a letter of authentication which is rare in these occurrences.

Soon Lenard appeared and asked, "What can I do for you?"

That's when Detective Sienkiewicz looked Lenard Jolliff straight in the eye and said, "You are under arrest."

"For what?"

"Falsifying a legal document. Rewriting an application of a known criminal for purchase of a fire arm."

"But…. But who told you, and how can you prove it?"

"We picked up Sammy Romano a couple of days ago and presented him with the falsified application that was submitted to the ATF by you. He took one look at the application and told me that was not the application he originally submitted. After further questioning of Mr. Romano, he eventually told me, "It must have been you who made the changes on his application. Since he did it in longhand and the one you submitted was typed written. We can easily verify what typewriter it was written on. All we have to do is check it against the one in your office, that will be all the proof we need."

"So, let me read you your rights."

Detective Sienkiewicz proceeded to read Lenard his rights and asked when finished, "Do you understand your rights?"

"Yes, but think your making a big mistake."

"We'll see about that when we get you downtown and book you for tampering with and altering a legal document, whether we made a mistake or not."

As they were leaving, Lenard reached over the counter handing Harold the keys to the building and told him, "I want you to lock up and both you and Liam go home and wait on my call.

That's when the two detectives grabbed hold of Lenard and handcuffed him. One on each side holding an arm walked him through the store and out to their car parked in front. Placed him in the backseat, then strapped him in and headed downtown for booking.

After being booked, Lenard was put in a jail cell along with several other inmates, all curious as to why he had been arrested. Lenard told them, "I had one of my customers rats on me after being arrested, and told he was in trouble because of a falsified application that was submitted to the ATF for purchase of a 45 automatic."

"Yeah, I bet you are the one who rewrote the application after he left so you could sell him the gun."

Another inmate spoke up and said, "I know you shysters in those type of businesses will do anything to make a buck. I've had that happen to me on more than one occasion."

Not long after he had been confined to the cell, one of the officers came down the hallway and was yelling his name, "Lenard Jolliff, step forward so I can see where you are. I need you to come with me."

Lenard stepped forward and grabbed hold of the bars and told the officer, "I'm Lenard Jolliff."

Okay Jolliff, "Turn around and stick your left arm outside between the bars.

After the left wrist was handcuffed, was told, "Now the right arm."

Once secured by the handcuffs, was told, "Step away from the bars and go stand in front of the cell door."

Opening the jail cell, the officer reached in and pulled Lenard out while locking the cell door in one fluid motion.

Lenard once again found himself in one of the small interrogation rooms shackled to a chain fastened to the concrete floor. As time passed, and the longer he sat squirming trying to get comfortable on the hard metal chair, in walked Detective Lowman and Sienkiewicz, both carrying briefcases and a cup of coffee. Ask him, "Would like something to drink before we got started?"

"Yeah, I'll have a coke."

Detective Loman returned to the door, opened it and told the officer standing guard outside, "The prisoner wants a coke." Yes Sir.

Soon the police officer returned, knocked lightly on the door, opening it and stepped inside. Quickly walked over to the inmate handing him the can of coke. Turned and left the room, closing the door behind him.

After the two detectives were seated, opening their briefcases and removed several documents. The two detectives made some headway that afternoon, but still had a long way to go before they could wrap this case up.

Lenard was not giving up any information that was damaging to the charges against him. He had faced this type of harassment and annoyances several times in the past and had a good track record of not giving up pertinent or damaging information relevant to the violations he had been charged with.

Late in the afternoon, not able in breaking Lenard's silence, called it a day. Detective Sienkiewicz had the officer outside the door remove the inmate and return him to his cell.

The following day armed with a search warrant for the surplus store. Detectives Lowman and Sienkiewicz returned to the surplus store with Harold, and began searching Lenard's office for fraudulent records or anything tying his store to duplicitous activity. After looking around, and rummaging through his files, found several deceptive files on sales considered bogus. Detective Lowman stuffed those files into manilla envelopes, and marked evidence on the outside of the envelope then sealed.

Next, the detectives after finding the key to the basement, decided to check out what was in the basement that could be used in their case against Lenard Jolliff. They proceeded over to the basement door and Detective Sienkiewicz inserted the basement key opening the basement door. Once the door was open, took the stairs into the basement to check if there were any type of banned contraband or illegal paraphernalia hidden in the underground storage area

Reaching the basement, found several illegal fire arms and restricted military merchandise forbidden by the armed services for a surplus store to be in possession of, let alone sell on the black market. Most of the items the detectives assumed had been stolen in the past by soldiers needing money or disgruntled with the military.

After searching the basement and taking pictures of illegal items found, and notated. Back upstairs they continued their investigation of the rest of the merchandise. After spending several hours in the surplus store collecting evidence, finally called it a day and drove back to police headquarters. Wrote their reports and when finished left for the evening.

It had been a long day for the detectives, but they had gathered enough evidence they could submit to the prosecutor's office, and hopefully with the all that evidence collected would be enough for the prosecutor's office to get a judge to hear the case against Lenard Jolliff in the near future. Now it became a waiting game.

A couple of months later, Liam, despondent, out of a job and no hope of a future, decided to find Dewayne Sours who had recently been paroled and was living on the boat previously belonging to his old boss Doc Nelson. Dewayne Sours was the person in the beginning, who kidnapped him and Darla Sue as they left the restaurant. This kidnapping was the beginning of a long and disastrous period in Liam's life. It eventually cost him his career at the newspaper, his wife, Darla Sue and his life as a reporter. Down and out with no hope for a future. Decided to confront this Dewayne Sours who started this whole mess leading to his eventual downfall.

Acquiring the nerve to confront this individual who he blamed was responsible for the trials and tribulations in his life. His need for revenge had festered long enough and was time for someone to pay. After several drinks at a local pub on the water front, Liam walked to the boat, climbed aboard and opened the hatch that led to the cabin where he found Dewayne laying on the bed watching TV.

When Dewayne saw Liam, immediately raised up and went for his gun on the end of the bed. By that time Liam was at the foot of the V berth bed and had already picked up the gun. Dewayne asked, "What the hell do you want?"

"I've come to settle a score."

"What? A score, what score?"

"It was you along with a driver by the name of Sammy (the man) Romano who kidnapped my date and I as we were leaving Phebe Reborn
Night Club over on Newark Ave. Do you remember?"

"Yes, but that was a long time ago, why don't you just drop it?"

"Easier said than done. You have caused me nothing but grief since that night. I have lived through hell because of you and tonight, it's payback time."

"What do you mean, payback time."

"I've come to even the score. I'm going to make you suffer like I've suffer over the years."

Liam slowly raised the gun, pointed it at Dewayne's right foot and pulled the trigger. As the sound of the discharge from the gun decreased gradually Liam saw Dewayne holding his right foot as he cried out in pain.

"Well, looks like you don't like pain any more than the next person. I'm happy to see you are not immune to pain. Let see if we can cause you to suffer a bit more."

Liam once again raised the gun pointing it at his left leg squarely on the knee cap and pulled the trigger. After the sound of the shot lessened, again Liam heard Dewayne screaming from the excruciating pain he was now suffering.

Liam waited until he settled down and told him, "I wish I had time to punish you more but I want to get this over, that way we both will be freed."

With that Liam leaned over Dewayne smiling and placed the gun against Dewayne's forehead, without further ado pulled the trigger. Liam threw the weapon back on the V-Berth and turned and headed back upon deck where he opened the hatch covering the engine compartment. He then removed a small knife from his pocket and cut one the rubber fuel lines. As he watched the gas drain from the severed line into the bottom of the boat, he reached in and pulled a book of matches from his shirt pocket, struck a match, lit it and then set the whole book of matches on fire and quickly threw the burning match book into the hatch.

His last thought before the explosion was,
[I've tried my best, and hope I made a difference.]

A Brief of Synopsis
Chilltown:
A Community Overwhelmed with Violence

The communities of Jersey City and Hoboken, New Jersey are plagued by continuous unrelenting city officials and those in power, as they play hardball with construction groups and subcontractors demanding they pay payments of money or some form of inducement if they wish to continue to working within the two cities.

From the mayor, taking bribes, down to city inspectors, council members and all in-between are working their own angles of corruption causing continuous violence, murder, and general mayhem in order to collect weekly payments.

This is the story of one man's attempt at exposing the illegal activity that's caused so much stress and suffering in the metro areas.

Liam Johnson a local reporter, continuously fights back the only way he knows how, by exposing those individuals through his daily editorials. Liam Johnson has taken on the dauting task of fighting crime plaguing two metro areas by his words.

The story is filled with many twists and turns, and just when you think he's succeeding in his fight for justice, another situation arises, and once again the status quo returns to square one.

The story is jam-packed with suspense, anger, love, and travel. In the end nothing's changed, corruption still rules.

Author's Page

Mr. Wilson begin writing after retiring and has published four different genres of fiction to date. This being his latest. He debated as to the subject matter, but once again settled on writing another suspense thriller. He likes combining the feeling of surprise, anticipation of success, vagueness and uncertainty, including the readers expectation of what comes next. So many areas are open to him giving his readers that array of variety, range of moods, and diversity which he includes in all his works.

Books by William E. Wilson

- The Ravenous Undertaker

- Nap-Town's Dirty Little Secrets

- Chat-Town TEN-A-KEY

- Chi-Town Dregs of Society

- CHILLTOWN: A community Overwhelmed With Violence